'Davidson was a fine, fine writer

'Avram Davidson, to me, combines many talents and attributes including imagination, style, and perhaps above all, wit'
Ray Bradbury

'An erudite and splendidly written novel, full of adventure and mythical lore' *Publishers Weekly*

Also by Avram Davidson

Novels

Mutiny in Space (1964)
Rork! (1965)
Masters of the Maze (1965)
Clash of Star-Kings (1966)
The Enemy of My Enemy (1966)
The Phoenix and the Mirror (1966)
The Ka-Chee Reign (1966)
Rogue Dragon (1966)
The Island Under the Earth (1969)
Peregrine: Primus (1971)
Ursus of Ultima Thule (1973)
Peregrine: Secundus (1981)
Vergil in Averno (1987)
Marco Polo and the Sleeping Beauty
(with Grania Davis) (1988)
The Boss in the Wall: A Treatise on the House Devil
(with Grania Davis) (1998)
The Scarlet Fig; or, Slowly Through a Land of Stone (2005)

Short Story Collections

Or All the Seas with Oysters (1962)
What Strange Stars and Skies (1965)
Strange Seas and Shores (1971)
The Redward Edward Papers (1978)
The Avram Davidson Treasury (1990)
The Adventures of Doctor Eszterhazy (1991)
The Other Nineteenth Century (2001)
Limekiller! (2003)

THE PHOENIX
AND THE MIRROR

AVRAM DAVIDSON

Text copyright © Avram Davidson 1969
Text copyright © Ultimate Productions, Inc. 1966
Introduction copyright © Adam Roberts 2013
All rights reserved

The two lines of Ovid's *Metamorphoses* quoted in the text are from
the Loeb Classics edition, edited and translated by Frank Justus Miller.
Copyright © Harvard University Press 1916, 1921

The right of Avram Davidson to be identified as the author of this
work, and the right of Adam Roberts to be identified as the author
of the introduction, has been asserted by them in accordance with
the Copyright, Designs and Patents Act 1988.

This edition first published in Great Britain in 2013
by Gollancz
An imprint of the Orion Publishing Group
Orion House, 5 Upper St Martin's Lane,
London WC2H 9EA
An Hachette UK Company

1 3 5 7 9 10 8 6 4 2

A CIP catalogue record for this book
is available from the British Library

ISBN 978 0 575 13038 8

Typeset by Deltatype Ltd, Birkenhead, Merseyside

Printed and bound by CPI Group (UK) Ltd,
Croydon, CR0 4YY

The Orion Publishing Group's policy is to use papers that are
natural, renewable and recyclable products and made from wood
grown in sustainable forests. The logging and manufacturing
processes are expected to conform to the environmental
regulations of the country of origin.

www.orionbooks.co.uk
www.gollancz.co.uk

The Author wishes to express his thanks and appreciation to James Blish, for early encouraging this novel, to Damon Knight and the late Richard McKenna for major suggestions concerning it, to L. Sprague de Camp, Karen Anderson, Walter Breen, the late Hannes Bok and the late Professor Willy Ley for valuable information included in it, Sayre Hamilton for help in preparing the manuscript, to Robert Silverberg and Virginia Kidd and Lawrence P. Ashmead for help in arranging its publication; to Don Denny, for information precognitive of this book; particularly to Grania K. D. Davis for assisting in its construction, and to that magical spirit of prophecy which – far more than corporal hand or conscious mind – actually wrote it.

Author's Note

During the Middle Ages a copious and curious group of legends became associated with the name of Vergil, attributing to the author of *The Aeneid* and *The Georgics* all manner of heroic, scientific, and magical powers – to such an extent, indeed, that most of the world forgot that Vergil had been a poet, and looked upon him as a necromancer, or sorcerer. From the Dark Ages to the Renaissance the popular view of the ancient world as reflected in the Vergilean Legends was far from the historical and actual one in more than the acceptance of legend and magic and myth. It is a world of never-never, and yet it is a world true to its own curious lights – a backward projection of medievalism, an awed and confused transmogrification of quasi-forgotten ancient science, a world which slumbered much – but whose dreams were far from dull. Such is the setting of the novel *The Phoenix and the Mirror*. It is projected as part of a series, the entire corpus to be known as *Vergil Magus*; and, though inspired by the medieval tales about him, it is not – though future parts may be – based on any of them.

Introduction

Magic charms must be thrice repeated to be most effective. This novel, charming in the strong sense of the word and dyed to its heart in magic, comes most beautifully alive on repeated readings. Accordingly I commend you to return to it three times.

On a first reading you will discover why this novel is regarded as one of the masterpieces of contemporary Fantasy writing. Its alternative early Renaissance Europe, a place and elegance and magic, is skilfully and vividly rendered; and through it moves Davidson's protagonist, the Roman poet Virgil. Now, the actual Virgil loomed large in the *actual*-historical medieval mind-set. The *Aeneid*, his epic poem of the founding of Rome, was so revered that millions believed the poem had supernatural powers to advise and predict. You can join them, easily enough: hold a copy in your hands, ask it your question and let it fall open at random. The line your finger lights upon will answer your anxiety. Try it: many people did, for centuries. Rumours about Virgil's magic abilities circulated, growing in splendour as they did. People traded supposed fragments of bone and other Virgilian relics in much the way they did those of saints and gospel characters. It seemed not to matter to anybody that the historical Virgil was not in the least a mage or wizard – he was, on the contrary, a retiring Roman gentleman who worked with obsessive perfectionism at his poetry (often he would spend a whole day composing a single line, only to scrub it out at sunset). Yet during the Middle Ages, as Davidson notes, 'a copious and curious group of legends became associated with the name of Virgil' to the point that 'most of the world forgot that Virgil had been a poet, and looked upon him as a nigromancer, or sorcerer.' This happened for reasons too complex to go into here – to do with the cultural dominance of Rome, Virgil's deserved reputation as Rome's greatest poet, and a perceived consonance between the pagan Virgil (he died a few years before the birth of Christ) and Christian theology according to which one of the poet's *Eclogues* was thought to have predicted the coming of Jesus. In *The Phoenix and the Mirror* (and the half-dozen 'Virgil Magus' novels that followed it) Davidson treats this legend as if true. He brings this impossible, beguiling late medieval world brilliantly to life; Virgil his hero, magic and wonder his idiom.

The result is powerful and idiosyncratic. Davidson tells the story of Virgil's seduction by the beautiful sorceress Cornelia; of her theft from him of that portion of his soul (embodied as a little manikin) that rules his manhood, leaving him weak, tired and unsexed. She assures him she will return it to him if he make her a mirror of virgin bronze – an almost impossible task. Compelled to obey, Virgil sources his materials, assembles his team, and performs feats of alchemical heroism.

Compared to many other Fantasy titles, *The Phoenix and the Mirror* may strike you on a first reading as both more literary than most and also *gentler*. There are monsters here that threaten life, pirates and bandits, but Davidson is uninterested in the torturous ingenuities of Grimdark pseudo-medievalism. Rather wonderfully, he is more interested in love and beauty than in war, violence and torture. He is more interested in things being made than things being destroyed.

A single reading of the novel brings all this out. But this is a novel you will want to re-read, and a second reading brings out a deeper sense of Davidson's craft. His research is wide-ranging and impeccable; his feel for his world is note-perfect. Stylistically too, this is a novel that rewards closer attention, its prose rich without ever being purple or overwritten. Re-reading it you may be struck, as I was, by how often Davidson's prose falls with unforced ease, and with enough metrical variety not to become merely monotonous, into iambic pentameters, for example: 'The bird prow lifted oars and dipped its nose/into the sea ...'

> The nigh shore was dim green, and the off-shore—
> Far, far across the white wave seas – lay dun
> And gaunt. Clouds paced across the Heavens
> Like giant's sheep, new-washed and fleeces combed ...
> Here and there from time to time a flash
> Of lime-white houses and thin plumes or clouds
> Of smoke marked (the) settlements of mortal men.

It's not *all* like this (over-extended, this trick would become wearisome indeed); but at moments of lyric intensity, or symbolic importance, the prose distils into poetic pentameters. This, I think, is not a tricksy, or even necessarily a conscious, game being played by Davidson. Rather it speaks to his writerly immersion in his world. Fantasy of this kind is by nature archaic; the challenge facing the writer is creating a living archaism, steering a course between (on the one hand) the ashes of rendering a dead world with merely academic precision and (on the other) the tinsel of dressing patently modern characters in fancy dress. Davidson plots that path very cannily indeed. His novel glows with its own life, but everything in it is grounded in a carefully thought-through and knowledgeable sense of medieval culture and beliefs.

So, the second reading makes clear that Virgil's 'magical' powers are not of the sort of that passes for magic in much contemporary Fantasy – the ability to shoot wands like pistols, say, or to throw great gouts or light or fire from your wizard-staff. The magic in *The Phoenix and the Mirror* is a matter of craft, wisdom and labour. The creation of the novel's key magical artefact takes many months of study and work. In this novel magic is alchemical; and reading this novel a second time makes clear that Davidson regards 'alchemy' not as a technological or pseudo-scientific process so much as the material manifestation of the underlying and universal principle of change. Not for nothing does this novel include quotations from Ovid's *Metamorphoses*; the mage's prime task is to work metamorphoses upon the materials of the world. To turn lead to gold; to alloy copper and tin into something radically, and magically, different from either.

With a second reading, then, *The Phoenix and the Mirror* starts to change in the reader's imagination. She begins to grasp (for instance) that all the detail Davidson provides about the manufacture of the brazen mirror is not merely local colour, or a patina of alchemical verisimilitude. It is a carefully worked-through integral layer to the work. It's not necessary for the reader to grasp this to enjoy the novel; but paying attention to it enhances and deepens the reading experience.

So what does the third reading reveal? I think it unveils the true nature of the book's alchemical conceit. The central figure of this novel – the magic mirror, within which can be seen wonders otherwise invisible to sight – is, of course, the novel itself. A properly magical novel takes a long time – perhaps a year – to make. Its components must be of the very rarest quality if it is to work its charm. Only a master of the craft can fashion it. And once it has been cast, what do we see in its reflective surface? Wonders, marvels and one great truth. The truth is love; for love is what the alchemical process renders. The bringing together of copper – which in this novel can only be sourced from the island of the goddess of love Aphrodite – and tin, from the chilly, distant north represents the coming together of female and male principles. The novel ends with the 'marriage' of white matron and red man; red and white metal; martial and pacific principles; man and woman – here, a particular man and a particular woman – but most of all: the red blood of the reader and the white pages of the book. It is a marriage made of magic.

Adam Roberts

ONE

His first meeting with her was quite by accident.

He had long ago lost his way in this vast, vaulted laby-
rinth, and the manticores, seeming to sense this, began
to draw closer. He could smell the strong, bitter stink
of them; could hear the guttural, gobbling noises which
passed for speech among them. From high overhead, at
regular intervals, slotted shafts of light came through the
grates. The man looked back, without pausing, and saw
the manticores, as they came to the diffused well of sunlight, divide into two groups and sidle, single file, along
the walls ... whispering, slithering, scuttling noises ...
scrabble of claws ... click-click-click.

The manticores abhorred the light.

He pressed on.

To move faster might prove fatal. So far they had
not come to deciding on a rush. The awe of men (along
with the hate of men, one of their seemingly instinctive
characteristics) still held them from it. He walked along
as steadily as if he were passing through the streets of
Naples – and some of those streets were darker than this;
and some of them were not even as wide – and some of
them, though not many, were almost as unsafe.

Behind him, just as steadily, came the manticores. In
shape they were like great bloated weasels, hair a reddish-
yellow for the most part and shaggy as goats, eyes bulging
and glowing and rolling every way, showing an intelligence
that, for all it differed so incomprehensibly from that of
man, was far more than merely animal. Around each neck

was a mane like a ruff of clotted plumes, framing a face which might have come from a nightmare – like a human face reduced in size and stretched to distortion: nose shallow and wide, eyes narrow, mouth broad.

So as not to attract attention the man did not now raise his head, but lifted up his eyes. Whoever had built these great tunnels through which the rains of Naples were drained off into the Bay, whether the Titans or the Greeks, the Carthaginians or the Old People of the Land, the Etruscans or whoever (Clemens would know if anyone knew, but Clemens would say only that the tunnels were places to be avoided, which was why Clemens was not here) – they had provided shafts and stairways. If he could manage to find one, if his finding one did not precipitate an attack, if the upper exit was not closed off ...

Many such doorways were known to exist. Some would require weeks to open, so firmly had they been sealed with cement and masonry, with a gorgon's mask or the Sign of Methras Invictus or some other talisman or apotropos fixed into them. Others were guarded by heavy doors, locked; but keys existed and hinges were well-oiled, in case those who held the gates wanted a quick way out with no necessity of advertising their movements in the streets. And there were, there had to be, other openings of which no man knew ... or at least, which no man guarded, either personally or by proxy.

It must have been through one such passageway that the manticores had come, a century before, and stolen a human child. The raid had been witnessed by the child's mother, who told of it before dying of her tainted wounds, and the tale had passed into legend. So far, though dreadful, it was easy enough to understand. But why had the manticores, instead of killing the child, kept him alive for forty years? And why, then, released him? No one could say, and, seemingly, only one man ever conjectured.

And how few outside the secret-burdened family of the

'child' knew that the 'child' was still alive (though himself insisting he had died!) at far more over a hundred years than was believable by any who held by the purely natural law. How much longer would he, how much longer *could* he live? How much did he know? Would his knowledge die with him? Had there not to be another store or source of it? And where else, where better, where likelier, than down in these dim and dirty mazes?

Down the center of this arm of the maze, a trickle of water flowed, and it was wet, too, near the mossy walls, from seepage. But there was a dry enough path – in fact, two – one on either side. The man walked down the left-hand one. Somewhere, far above, a dog barked. The sounds behind him changed at once. For an instant the pad-pad ceased. So did the grunting. The dog barked again – then again and again, without stopping. Then it stopped, abruptly, as if someone had commanded it, or thrown a stone.

Another grating was up ahead; like all of them, impossible to climb to unless someone at the surface sent down fathoms and fathoms of knotted rope. Dust motes swam lazily in the bars of light, then began to dance in agitation as the manticores broke into a trot. A querulous whine that was almost a question was succeeded by a deep gobble that was almost an answer. The movement was toward his right – they were not going to rush him yet – the intention was evidently to pass him, to cut him off. Knowing what little he did of the manticores, guessing from that little knowledge, the man believed that they would not have chosen this plan unless something favorable to it lay up ahead – unless something unusual lay up ahead.

The dog barked again. Or was it another dog? No, there were two of them, one behind and one before, neither visible, but both in the tunnel.

The manticores halted. And the man broke into a run.

There it was. A huge projecting leaf of the original

rock thrust itself into the corridor, which turned aside to avoid it. The way was only half its usual width here; evidently the passage at this point was merely a fissure in the substratum. It would have been an ideal place for the manticores to hold him at bay. When they saw him run, the pack of them began to howl and gobble, but the dogs barked, a man's voice called out, then another, and another. Behind him he could hear his pursuers hesitate.

A dog began to bay in a half-frenzied, half-frightened fashion, which meant it had caught the bitter, pungent scent of the manticores. There was the grating of metal on metal, a loud creaking, a flood of light from high up on one side. A voice called out. The man fled up the damp and shallow steps.

Behind him, as the door was shoved to, locked, bolted, barred, he heard the devilish things below shrieking their frustration and fury.

The gray-bearded man who had let him out demanded, 'The other men? And the dogs?'

'There is only me. There were no dogs.' The place was some sort of grotto. Benches had been hewn out of the rock.

'But I heard,' the graybeard insisted. He had a sharp, watchful face. Two dogs barked, one after the other. Men's voices called. The graybeard's eyes swung up to the half arch of the ceiling, where the voices had seemed to be; swung over to the man he had just admitted.

'Was that what you heard?' the man asked. He looked at the door. It bore the image of an obscure god, one he had never seen before, an equestrian very much like that other godling, the Thracian Rider; but this was instead a woman in a strange headdress. More to the immediate point, perhaps, the door was sturdy and the huge bolts had slid smoothly into the living rock.

'Filthy creatures,' muttered the older man. 'Why

4

doesn't the Doge send men, thousands of them – armed – with torches – and clean out the conduits once and for all? Is it because the manticores have so many burrows that the ground is riddled with them like an old cheese? They told me that's why.'

'They told you rightly,' the newcomer said, turning to go.

But his rescuer was ahead of him now, blocking the way. 'Is it true no man can follow? That hundreds would be lost – never find their way back?'

The younger man moved past him. 'It's true, and I thank you.'

A hand was laid on his shoulder, tightened. 'Then why were you in the conduits?'

'Because I was a fool.' Their eyes locked. The hand took a firmer grip, then relaxed.

'No ... you're not a fool. And neither am I. So ...' A curious sound came from not far off, like a bird call, but of no bird known. The graybeard removed his hand, placed it flat against the newcomer's back and pushed him firmly ahead. 'We'll go and see her now,' he said. Two half flights of stairs brought them to the surface. They were in a garden, far too large to be located anywhere within the city. A huge oak wreathed in vines stood not far away, and a row of cypresses marked a path. There was a white froth of almond blossoms on the trees to his right, and the air was sweet with the scent of them. The curious call sounded again, nearer.

'I am coming, ma'am,' the graybeard said. '*We* are coming. "In the name of Poseidon Horse-breaker," I asked him, "why were you down in those daemon runs?" "I'm a fool, is why," he said. And—'

A woman's voice said, sharply, 'Tullio, be still!'

Tullio's face broke into a broad smile as if he had been complimented, and he nodded vigorously to the newcomer as if inviting him to share his pleasure. He composed himself as they rounded the great oak, and he bowed. The woman who sat deep in the shade of the tree was probably handsomer now than in the first, fresh days of her nubility; that was clear. If she had been merely *beautiful* at another period was uncertain. It was sure that she had never been merely pretty. Behind her, on a slight rise of ground, was a large villa. Servants were behind her chair, crouching at her feet, and on either side; yet she had the air of being quite alone. A golden whistle lay in her lap, as lovely as her golden hair.

'Are you hurt?' she asked – concerned, yet more bemused than aware. 'What happened? Who are you?'

The man bowed. 'I am not hurt, ma'am,' he said. 'I was lost – pursued – attacked – then saved, thanks to your servant. My name is Vergil.' He felt the breeze touch the back of his neck and was prepared when the white deerhound, who had been nuzzling the lady's hands, leapt howling to its feet. A deep sound rose from Vergil's throat, and the dog stood back, subsiding, but with its hair still bristling.

'I think that I will stand over here, if I may, ma'am,' Vergil said. 'The wind brings him the smell of those creatures.'

She nodded, abstractedly. 'Yes, we have it sometimes when the air is still and heavy. Earthquake days, or when Vesuvio is about to be angry. A bitter smell, deep and bitter. Foul things, and yet ... yet they must have some awareness of beauty, don't you think? They dig up rubies and emeralds and all such precious stones, and make piles of them only to look at them. Or so one hears.'

Tullio chuckled. His lips smiled, but not his eyes. 'And so Master Vergil hears, too, ma'am, I dare say – which is perhaps why and how he happened to get lost. Eh, sir?'

Vergil said nothing. The lady said, 'Tullio.' Reproof was implicit in her tone. Then: 'Give him refreshment – no, *you*, Tullio.' The cheeks above the sharp gray beard were slightly flushed as Tullio, with the slightest of shrugs, the

6

slightest of smiles, took the tray from a silent servant's hand and gave it to Vergil, as a servant girl, who had started to move, sat down again. There was wine, bread, a dish of oil, a dish of honey, soft cheese, a sliced lamprey. Vergil bowed his thanks, poured a libation, began to eat.

'But ... weren't there others?' the mistress of villa and garden asked. 'We heard ... it seemed ...'

He swallowed a mouthful, took a sip of wine. The air was cool in the shade of the great oak. There were many questions in his mind, but he could wait for the answers. He lifted his head slightly. A man's voice spoke from the top of one of the almond trees. All eyes turned to look. There was no one there, but the voice went on speaking. And then, from the very summit of the oak, a dog barked.

'I see,' the lady said. 'And I know little about such matters. This is no mere mountebank's trick.' She nodded. Her fingers played on the golden whistle. 'I understand, now. You are *that* Vergil.'

Vergil bowed.

Her deep-set violet eyes gazed at him intently. Her long, white, blue-veined fingers clenched, so that the single ring on them thrust forward its crested signet. 'Magnus,' she said, 'can you make a speculum for me?'

'No, madam,' he replied after a moment.

She beat her hands together. 'Do you understand me? I mean a speculum of virgin bronze, prepared according to the Great Science which is your art.'

The wind had stopped, the air was still. Crouching on the ground behind her lady's seat, holding in one small hand an embroidery ring with a long needle thrust through the unfinished design – a bird of strange sort *sejant* upon a heap – a servant girl looked up at him aslant with red-brown eyes. 'I understand you, madam. In theory I can make a virgin speculum. In fact, however, at the present state of things, it is impossible.'

The lady gave a gasp of despair. She threw out her

hands, opening, somewhat, with the force of the gesture, the carefully arranged folds of her robe. An inch or two of bordering showed, and – a sudden stroke of light illuminating a corner previously obscured – Vergil now had the key to the puzzle. But it did not increase his pleasure. There can be too much gold.

'I should hope, ma'am,' he said, calmly, 'that you understand that no simple willfulness prevents my agreeing.'

The despair ebbed from her face, and was succeeded by the slightest of flushes. 'No,' she murmured. 'No, no … after all, you have eaten my bread. *You* have drunk my wine.'

Something stirred in his mind. 'And not only here,' he said.

'What …?'

He came close, spoke so low that only the two of them could hear. '"*I, perishing with thirst, was given to drink of the waters of memory. I drank from the cymbal, I ate from the basket.*"'

Memory was in her eyes, enlightenment upon her face. ' "*You have seen the sun rise at midnight,*" then, too,' she said. 'You have seen the Eleusinian mysteries. We are brother and sister, but we …' She looked about her, held out her slender hand, and he helped her rise.

'Not here.'

They left the oak and the almond tree and passed along the lane of cypress trees to the villa. She still held his hand, did not let it go until they were in a room of darkly gleaming wooden walls, faint and musky with the scent of the beeswax polish. Arranged upon the walls were tapestries of Draco and the Gryphons, rich in crimson and scarlet and purple and gold. She sat upon a couch and he, upon her gesture, knelt beside it on the soft, dyed fleece.

'Now we're alone,' she said, placing her cool fingers against his cheek. 'I'm not going to speak to you from one

8

rank to another, but as mystagogue to mystagogue. I'd like to speak to you without speech ... "*by the unspoken secrets of the mystic chests, the winged chariots of the dragon-ministers, the bridal descent of Proserpine, the torch-lit wanderings to find the daughter, and all the other mysteries that the shrine of Attic Eleusis shrouds in secret.*"'

'Yes ...'

So low was her voice now that she seemed almost to speak without speech. 'I am a mother, too,' she said. 'I, too, have a daughter, and, like Ceres, I don't know now where my daughter is. Ceres learned from Helios, the bright, undying, unconquered sun. I would learn from the mirror, round as the sun. And even if I, too, must search the dark halls of Hell, torch-lit or in utter blackness for my daughter then let Hell itself be harrowed.'

'You don't know the problems involved,' he said. 'If the speculum can be made at all, it might well take a year to make it. And I have not the year to spare. The task which brought me here today is one which must engage me tomorrow, and for many tomorrows after tomorrow, and there are other works of labor, too, which have been too long delayed. They call to me insistently. I cannot, ma'am, I cannot, I cannot, not even for the sake of the common and holy bond between us. ... Not even for the Mystery.'

He said, 'Though much I wish I could.'

There was no trace now of the confusion and despair that had come with his previous refusal. The violet eyes were calm, and then they seemed to glow in the dim light with another and deeper emotion. She said, almost in a whisper, 'There are other Mysteries besides that one. Have you been at ...' She spoke a name, and she spoke another, and then she spoke a third.

'Yes,' he said, his own voice now but a whisper. 'Yes ... yes.' He was aware, and aware that she was aware, that his answer was assent as well as affirmation. He put his arms around her, and his lips on her lips.

9

After a moment she said, her words now not even a whisper, but a breath, 'Then come, my bridegroom, and let us celebrate the wedding.'

Dim as the room was, it seemed to grow suffused with light, light which turned to color: the pink of a dawn which never was on land, the rose of a sunset which never was on sea. The colors began to ripple slowly ... slowly ... in measured, steady change, around and around, in a circle of change and a cycle of constancy. Cornelia lay beside him, he knew that with a joyous knowledge so much greater than anything he had ever known before. Cornelia lay in his arms. Yet, and he was aware of no confusion, no discrepancy, Cornelia sat somewhat before and above him on a sort of throne, naked and in profile, grave, sweet, serene, solemn and beautiful. Her nipples and breasts were like those of a woman who had never borne a child. Light rose-colored waves broke slowly and softly into spray and beat upon the base of her throne and the globes of the Two Earths revolved beneath her bare and outstretched arm. He saw her and he knew her as the Queen of all the World. All remained the same, everything simultaneously changed. He saw her as a maiden of the green north forests, with her hair in plaits, and with the archaic smile upon her lips. She played high strange entrancing music for him on curious instruments. He saw her young and he saw her old, he saw her as a woman and he saw her as a man. And he loved her as all of them. In every speech and language he read the words, *Everything is Cornelia and forever*, and, *Always more ... Always more ... Always more ...* Every touch and every motion was joy, was joy, joy, joy, everything was joy ...

As a great wind shakes the fruit upon the tree, ripe and rich and sweet; as the wind seizes hold of the field of grain, making the full ears tremble and await the harvest; as the wind, strong and tumultuous, drives the ship ahead of it straight as an arrow toward the harbor ...

And then, even as the fire blazed up fiercely upon the hearth, it vanished. And there was nothing but the cold and the darkness.

Vergil cried out in shock and pain and anguish.

'Where is it?' he cried. 'Witch! Sorceress! Give it back to me!'

Cornelia said nothing. He could not move. He watched her as she briefly opened the palms of her hands, and instantly closed them again, with an almost involuntary smile of triumph. The swift glimpse showed him the tiniest naked simulacrum of himself, pale as new ivory, passive as pallid; then, even in that short shaveling of a second, even that ghost of color faded from it. Tiny, translucent, a mere shape, a shadow, a fraction ...

'*Give it back to me!*' He lunged forward. He fell back, as she pressed her palms together, fell back with a scream of anguish, lay, sprawled inertly, upon her naked flesh; and she moved from him, contemptuously, unseeingly, with her naked legs, and he fell from the couch onto the floor. She cast one long and level and totally impassive look upon him. Then she was gone. And Tullio was there.

'Get up,' he said. 'Get up, Vergil Magus, and dress. And then go from here and into your house and begin the work of making the magic mirror, the virgin speculum. You are still as much magus as ever—'

'You are wrong,' he said, dully. 'And it wasn't necessary ...'

'Even though you are no longer as much man as ever – If I am wrong, if you are not as much magus as ever, being no longer a full man, then this is your problem and none of ours. If there are things of science and of sorcery now beyond you, then let this be a goad to your flesh not to slacken in the task we have set for you. Do not think, though, to persuade me, that *this* task is one of them. I know better.'

'What do you call this which she took and which now I

have and hold? Not the *ka*, and not the *ba* and not the – it does not matter. I have the thing and so I do not need the name. It is one of your souls, that is enough. Without it you are only part of a man. You will never be complete without it. You will never know the flesh of women more without it. Do my work, and I return it to you. Refuse – fail – I destroy it. Tarry – I punish it. Dally –

'But,' he said, regarding him without passion and with utter certitude, 'I do not think that you will dally.

'No, no, my Magus. I do not think that you will dally.'

TWO

The street of the Horse-Jewelers lay in the older quarter of Naples, but was wider than many of the streets there. This may have been the reason it harbored the trade it was named after – those wanting the ornaments of which no horse or mule or ass in Naples was ever seen entirely devoid: necklaces of great blue beads to ward off Evil Eye; emblematics of brass polished to a high shine (crescents, stars, hands-of-the-Fay, horns-of-Asmodeus, sunbursts, and scores of others); woolen and even silken pompoms and tassels in a dozen dazzling colors; and those curious objects set to ride like tiny castles or attenuated towers between the animals shoulders; to say nothing of bells in all sizes and shapes and tones, and even drops of amber for the mounts of the moneyed – those having business in the street called The Horse-Jewelers required space for their mounts, their teams and wagons when they had any.

There was no place wide enough to turn more than a single horse, not even in the broad place by the Fountain of Cleo, but the street retained enough width all the way through to drive into Kings Way. A lorimer named Appolonio had his business a half flight up from the Piazza of the Fountain; and on the street side of the same building, in the basement, was the wineshop officially entitled The Phoebus and Chariot, but generally called The Sun and Wagon. When Vergil as a younger man had passed through Naples from his native Brindisi, en route to study at the Academy of Illiriodorus in Athens, the three upper stories had been let each to single sublessors who filled the rooms with what tenants they liked – journeymen, whores, astrologers, waggoners, unsuccessful fences and even less successful thieves, poor travelers (such as students), menders of old clothes. So it had been in those days, so it still was; save that now, on the roof, in a hut of rubble and rushes, a madwoman dwelt quite alone save for fifteen or twenty cats.

Up the steps of the house adjacent came the same man (older now, beard still black as tar, dark of skin, gray-green of eye, and greyhound-thin) at sunset this day. Of all the houses on the street, by this one alone no one loitered, no one rested, no one begged, or ate supper out of a handkerchief or nuzzled a street wench or crouched fanning a charcoal brazier on which cheap victuals cooked for sale. No little boys paused to piddle or scrawl things on the temptingly smooth and clean pale yellow plaster of the walls. In a niche in the wall on the left-hand side, three steps from the bottom, was a brazen head; and, as the man in his slow and painful ascent trod upon the step level with it, the eyes opened, the mouth opened, the head turned, the mouth spoke.

'Who goes?' it demanded. *'Who goes? Who goes?'*

'He who made you goes,' the man said. 'And will enter.'

'Enter, master,' said the brazen head. The door at the top began to open.

'Guard me well,' said the man, not pausing (but a grimace twisted his face); 'as ever.'

'Thus I hear and thus I tell and I will always guard you well.'

'As ever,' the brazen head replied. The heavy voice seemed to echo somewhere: *ever ... ever ... ever ...* The eyes rolled – right – left – up – down – the mouth muttered a moment more. The mouth closed. The eyes shut. For a pace or two, the man staggered.

The man walked slowly down the hall. 'My bath,'

he directed; adding, after a moment, 'My dinner.' Bells sounded ... once ... twice ... the soft chimes died away. He pressed his palm upon a door showing, in a relief, Tubal-Cain working in metals and handing something to an awed Hephaestus. The door opened. Somewhere, water had begun to splash. The room was lit by a glowing globe of light upon a pilaster of marble of so dark a green as to be almost black – 'dragon green,' the Phrygians called it.

He moved to the first of the other pilasters which ringed around the room and lifted a helm of black enameled work which fell back on golden hinges, disclosing another glowing globe. A voice from one side; 'I found that too many lights were diffusing the reflections of my inward eye, the one which lies behind my navel, so I covered them.'

After a second, the voice said, in a tone of mild surprise, 'Greeting, Vergil.'

'Greeting, Clemens,' Vergil said, continuing his slow round until every light shone unhampered. He made an effort. 'I know that very sensitive eye which lies behind your navel. It is not light per se which inflames it, but light which shines through the goblets in which you have captured the fifth essence of wine ... before imprisoning it, for greater safety, also behind your navel.' He sighed, stepped out of his clothes and into his bath.

The alchemist shrugged, scratched his vast and tangled beard, made rude and visceral noises. 'The *quint' essentia* of wine, taken judiciously by a man of superior physique and intelligence, such as myself, can only aid reflection. I must show you some notes pertinent to this point in the commentary which I'm making on the works of Galen. Also – fascinating! – my invaluable discoveries anent his prescription of flute-playing as a cure for the gout – the Mixo-Lydian *mode*, tonally ...'

Vergil continued to bathe, all absence of his usual zest in this seeming to escape the alchemist, who, having demolished to his own satisfaction all recent galenical research (particularly that of the Arab Algibronius), suddenly bethought himself of something else; smote the conical felt cap atop his mass of curly hair.

'Vergil! Have you ever heard of a metal with a melting point lower than lead?'

Vergil, pausing briefly in his ablutions, said, 'No.'

'Oh ...' Clemens seemed disappointed. He said, 'Then it must be an exceptionally pure form of lead, sophically treated to remove the dross. I've seen only a few beads of it, but it melts in the heat of a lamp wick, and if a drop falls on the skin it doesn't burn ... remarkable ...'

He fell into deep thought. Vergil emerged from his bath, wrapped himself in a huge square of soft white linen, and (quickly suppressing a shudder) crossed over to a table and seated himself. The top rolled back, the inside rose slowly, lifting a covered tray. Vergil made a start at eating, but his hands began suddenly to tremble and he clenched them upon a quaff of strong, sweet, black beer, and bent his head to sip from it.

Clemens gazed at him for a while, a slight frown passing over his face. 'I take it, then, that you met the manticores ... and escaped from them.'

'No thanks to you.' Yes, he had escaped them ... the brief and bitter thought came to him, *Perhaps it would have been better if he had not!* He muttered again, *'No thanks to you ...'*

Clemens thrust out his lower lip. 'You wanted information about the manticores. I gave you the best information available, namely, that they are best left alone. Anything else would only embroil you more deeply, more dangerously.'

Vergil pondered. The time was passing as if this were any ordinary night succeeding any ordinary day. Yet, what else was there to do? Reveal all to Clemens, entreat his immediate aid? He shrank, with all his nature, from the

16

former; the latter could be, for many reasons, productive of nothing. He recalled his own words to Cornelia; *You do not know the problems involved ... it might well take a year ...* And, echoing louder and louder in his mind: *I have not the year to spare!*

A year. A *Year!* – And yet, God knows, if the year were to have been spent with her – !

'Well, never mind for now,' he said. 'Someday you'll want something from *me*. I'll go back down below and get what I know is there. It has to be there. And I have to have it, for the Great Science. But I'll wait, if I have to.' And he did have to! 'Meanwhile, Clemens, here's a conundrum for you.'

'Who is it that has a villa in the suburbs, speaks our tongue like a Neapolitan, dresses like a foreigner – but with a strip of purple on the border of the robe?'

Again, Clemens snorted. 'Is that your idea of a conundrum? Cornelia, of course, the daughter of the old Doge, Amadeo. She married Vindelician of Carsus – good-looking boy, not very much else, who was making the rounds of the minor courts, playing the exiled claimant and all that.

'Doge Amadeo didn't think much of him, but Cornelia did, so they were married and the old man gave him a villa in the suburbs, plus a few Oscan and Umbrian villages to lord it over. Then the actual King of Carsus died of a hunting accident – "accident," huh! – and his twin sons soon had a nice little civil war going for the succession. Mind if I just taste one of these squabs? You don't seem to care for them.'

Vergil left the table to consult his map of the Econ-omium. Clemens continued the story and the squab. The claimants so ravaged the country that the Great Council of Carsus met in secret and appealed to the Emperor, who, suddenly reminded of Vindelician, supplied him with three cohorts, and a councillor called Tullio and sent them off to *'restore peace and commerce, suppress brigandry, and allow the smoke from the altars to rise unvexed.'*

The twins met under a truce to discuss joint efforts to put down the invaders; but Tullio, in the name of Cornelia (according to Clemens), sent each of them a confidential message urging him to slay his brother – after which Cornelia would betray Vindelician, marry 'the rightful king,' and, presenting the Emperor with an accomplished fact, obtain his support and favor. The scheme worked out perfectly. The twins fell upon one another, inflicted fatal wounds, and their leaderless armies capitulated to Vindelician, who had reigned without opposition, Tullio doing the actual ruling, for the rest of his life.

Vergil turned from his map. A dull tale of a dull country, and one which told more of Tullio than Cornelia. Carsus was a landlocked and mountainous country of no great extent, no great resources, and no great interest to him.

It mattered little, after all, where she had learned the cunning of the evil art practiced by her upon him. That she had learned it, used it, was all-sufficient. He did his best to throw off a painful weariness which no sleep could assuage while he stayed in his present, deprived condition. He had heard of men continuing to feel pain in an amputated limb; now he knew how it must be. And yet, what had passed just before had been so glorious, so indescribably beautiful … So indescribably false. *Everything is Cornelia, and forever. Always more, always more.…*

'Why,' he asked, 'is she back at her villa here?'

Clemens, having finished his story and the squabs, belched, wiped his fingers on his tunic. 'She's a widow, that's why. And by the law of Carsus, no royal widow, unless she's a queen regnant – which Cornelia, of course, isn't – can remain in the country for fear of her engaging in intrigue. Damned sensible of the Carsians, say I. Tullio, of course, was retired on pension. Bides his time, I have no doubt.'

18

Vergil listened without comment, gray-green eyes expressionless in dark, dark-bearded face. His hands wandered, as if independently, to the case of books set into his great table. The table was circular and revolved at the touch of a hand, from right to left. At its center, three tiers high, was a cabinet which revolved with equal facility from left to right. Thus the immediate necessities of several current projects, as well as standard needs such as the map, were always at his fingers' ends.

The case of books formed part of the inset cabinet. There were scrolls of one staff, scrolls of two staves, scrolls made of a single long sheet of parchment and requiring no staff at all; there were codices – books made up of single sheets of papyrus and bound in covers – books written in curious tongues of the Nether Orient and upon a curious material unknown to the Economium, pressed together between ornately inscribed boards; and 'books' which were so only for lack of any better name to call them: scratched upon dried leaves, incised on split twigs, painted upon bark and carved into thin slabs of wood … and, of course, the notebooks of ivory and ebony and beech, insides inlaid with wax for the scratchings of his stylus, in haste or with deliberate slowness.

His hands rested on the bottom shelf of the bookcase, and lay inert.

Vergil said, 'No … it isn't here. I shall have to go to my library.' But he did not move. A numbness so cold and deep that it almost stilled the insistent pain of loss (of Cornelia – of manhood – of Cornelia) came upon him as he realized how nigh to impossible was the task he was bound to perform. He repeated, mechanically, 'I shall have to go to my library.'

Clemens raised a quizzical eyebrow. 'Why bother? I am here.'

The faintest of faint smiles touched his host's lips. The numbness began to fade. 'I suffer your boundless arrogance,'

Vergil said, 'only because it is so often justified. Yes, my Clemens. I see that you are here. The question is, why?'

On its pedestal a smaller replica of the brazen head in the niche in the outer stairway now opened its lips. A sound, repetitive, and hollow as a drumbeat, came from somewhere inside it. Dull, insistent, it would eventually force itself upon Vergil even in his deepest revery; and it was designed to do so.

'Speak,' he said now. 'What?' As though he cared.

'Master, a woman great with child. She would have a nostrum for a good delivery.'

Ignoring a snort from Clemens, Vergil said, wearily, 'I have none. Tell her if she wants a nostrum to go to Antonina the Wise-Woman. Tell her, too, that if she wants a good delivery she should go neither to Antonina nor any other wise-woman. Have you heard?'

'*I have heard and I will tell and I will ever guard you well ...*' The voice died away.

Clemens said, scornfully, 'Now *that* instead of being recognized as a piece of minor common sense of which any properly educated child should be capable – will be spoken of in every house and hovel in the Dogery as if it were a paradox as heavy with wisdom as that imbecile slut is with child.'

'For one who is in so little practice among women as you are, you have a remarkably poor opinion of them.'

The alchemist picked up a stylus and thrust it into his poseidon-heavy poll of curls. 'That is why I am in so little practice among them, perhaps,' he suggested, scratching. 'However ... as to why I am here. I came thinking you might know something of antimony. I remained to medi-tate. I remain, still, because I am full of food – as well as knowledge – and hence, for now, inert.'

Vergil stood up abruptly, dropped the toga-long piece of linen and walked over to his dressing table. Into a basin of water he poured out of habit a very few drops of a preparation of balm, nard, and seed of quince; bathed his hands in it. He paused in the act of drying and said, 'What was that word? Anti ...'

'Antimony. The supposed metal softer than lead.' He yawned, picked up a lyre, touched the chords with a tortoise-shell plectrum. 'But I am tired of philosophy. ... Shall I play you something from my *Elegy on the Death of Socrates?* Oh, very well!'

He put down the lyre. 'I will say what I know you want me to say. I came also because I was somewhat concerned about you. And now tell *me* – what does Cornelia want of you?'

Vergil paused, immobile. Then he tucked his long shirt into his tights and adjusted the codpiece. He fastened his tunic and sat down to pull on the soft, form-fitting, calf-length boots. 'Not very much,' he said. 'She wants me to make a major speculum.'

The alchemist pursed his lips and cocked his head. 'I see ... nothing simple, such as going to the Mountains of the Moon to gather moonstones, or bringing one or two of the Golden Apples of the Hesperides for her supper. No mere piece of easily obtained trivia such as a unicorn's horn, or the Peacock in the Vase of Hermes. Oh, no – the Dowager Queen of Carsus only wants a virgin speculum, such as Mary of Egypt herself made but one of in her entire life. By Nox and by Numa! *Why?*'

'She has a daughter on the Great High Road, coming here from Carsus, and is concerned for the girl's safety ... wants to know where she is ... The girl is late.'

Clemens rolled up his eyes and blew out his lips. 'Oh, for some of that essence of wine, distilled five times in my alembic! Only therein, more spirit than solid, could I find refuge from this woman's incredible ... incredible ... I lack the word. What next? Will she burn Naples to warm the soles of her feet? Oh well. A filly, a fool. And I daresay you told her as much.'

The magus held up his hand. In the silence of the room there was only the ringing in their ears to hear, at first. Then there was a soft, steady hissing sound. And then the tiny drip ... drip ... drip of falling water. Vergil pointed his hand to the right. Clemens followed the gesture. There stood a statue of Niobe, surrounded by several of her children. As they watched a single drop of water welled up slowly in one of Niobe's eyes, then in the other. First one tear and then a second welled, swelled, strained at the meniscus, broke, and fell into the pool at her feet.

As the last ripple died away the pool became agitated. Bubbles arose and broke at the surface ... one ... two ... three ... five ... seven of them. The pool emptied. And one of the children sank from sight into the pedestal.

It seemed that they could hear a faint cry, as if from grief.

Vergil's hand moved slowly in the air, pointed to the left. A tall column, enchased with figures emblematic of the hours, stood where his finger indicated. A mask of Boreas was set into the top; above and facing it, one of Zephyr. And, as they gazed, a puff of steam emerged from the mouth of the face below, grew into a spume. A metal ball shot up in the steam, struck the face above and rang out like the silvery note of a small gong, and did so again and again and – 'What is all this miming and mumming?' Clemens demanded, staring. 'Either the water clock is faster than the steam horlogue, or the other way around. Easy enough to determine which is correct when the sun's at high meridian. Why the posturing and posing?'

Vergil's countenance remained grave and set, his hand with its outstretched finger stayed still; then once again described its arc and came to rest pointing at Clemens. The alchemist made rude noises, originating around that eye said to lie behind his navel; tutted and tittered, then grew uneasy, fidgeting in his chair of Mauretanian leather; finally started convulsively and twisted to look behind him.

Where there was nothing.

Vergil burst out into a laugh of pure good humor which ended almost at once. Sheepishly, his friend settled back again, smiling. Then his laugh followed Vergil's, he not noticing how abruptly the latter's humor had ceased.

'Come, now,' the magus said, a twisted smile trembling slightly on his lips. 'Am I not, with you and with one other, all that remains of wisdom in this brute and bawdy age when decadence and barbarism contend for bay leaves, staff, fasces, crown and curile stool?'

Clemens considered, a short moment. '"One other ..." Appolonus of Tyana, that would be. ... True, sir. True. Then ...'

'Then allow me my tiny joke. If I dared take my position seriously the whole day long, I would go mad ... or agree to make Cornelia her speculum.'

The other got lazily to his feet, half-heartedly tugged at his robe to straighten it. 'What did she say when you refused?'

Said Vergil, 'I didn't refuse.'

'Ingots ... I mean, without even any regard to the question of *making* the speculum – which is a labor only somewhat less slight than making an aqueduct – there is the question of getting the materials. Very well ... ingots of tin, to start with. To start our discussion with, that is. Of course you can't start the work of the speculum with ingots.'

Book after book lay open on the long library table at which they were seated, one on each side. Clemens held his finger in the codex of the *Manual* of Mary of Egypt, in which the woman, the greatest alchemist of the period, had put down the observations of a long life devoted not merely to theorizing but to actual research and work. Alongside were commentaries made by her scholars. Vergil gazed into the scroll that contained the fifth book of the learned Syrian, Theopompus BinHaddad, *On the*

Affinities and the Sympathies, a treatise devoted to the philosophy of the psyche and its multiple counterparts. His chin rested in one hand so that his index finger pushed up his lower lip.

No, one could not start the work of the speculum with ingots. Not a major speculum. The entire foundation of the work lay in the principle of creating a *virgin* article; the ordinary, or minor, speculum was merely a bronze mirror, fitted with a cover that opened on hinges, rather like a large locket. There were rumors, legends, that somewhere there existed – or had at one time existed – mirrors made, somehow, of glass. But in no work on the subject did anyone claim to have seen a mirror of this sort, let alone give directions for making one.

But directions of the artificing of the sort which they now sought, though not copious, were explicit enough. Mary recorded having fashioned one for the Imperial Advocate in Alexandria. The anonymous genius who was known only as the Craftsman of Cos described how he had made no fewer than three, of which two had been successful. There were further accounts in the *Chalcheoticon* of Theodorus and in the *Text-Book* of Rufo.

'We might conjecture a theory,' said Vergil – breaking his silence and announcing his descent from the clouds of thought by a slight humming sound – 'to this effect. The atoms which comprise the viewing surface of a speculum are not merely passive, reflecting without receiving. To assume that is to assume that a look is completely intangible, and this we cannot assume, for we have all seen a person obliged to turn around because he has become somehow aware that he is being looked at.'

Clemens judiciously, said, 'Granted.'

'If any surface,' Vergil continued, formulating his thoughts aloud, in an academic drone which numbed his emotions but left part of his mind untouched, 'received an impression which was tangible, some imprint of this

24

impression had to be left upon the surface. Hence,' he said, 'a speculum which has been in use, however briefly, has become as it were clouded, however imperceptibly, with the accumulated impressions it has received. Nor will it suffice simply to fashion a new speculum. It is essential that the very atoms of the metals involved have received as little disturbance as possible. The ordinary craftsman works with scraps of old bronze. A somewhat superior craftsman uses bronze which has not been worked before – as bronze.'

But bronze itself was not a pure metal, it was a fusion of copper and tin. The smith who made bronze made it out of ingots of tin and – usually – ingots of copper; although copper was sometimes available in sheets formed in the shape of an oxhide. The smith, therefore, could not forge a virgin bronze because he was not working up virgin tin and virgin copper. Only the pure ores themselves, which had never been shaped by the hand of man, could be used to form the virgin bronze for a virgin speculum. And then …

'You annoy me with your tedious recapitulation of details known to every apprentice, let alone an adept,' Clemens interrupted testily. 'Somewhere on your shelves are works on the music of the Upper Orient, by masters who arranged the compositions played at the courts of the kings Chandraguptas and Asokas – you know that I would dearly love to see them. But every time I come here – every time that I am not myself engaged in other research, that is – you distract my attention, you occupy me with matters not to my tastes, and so the time goes, and it is always later than you think. Enough.' He rose to go.

Vergil raised his hand. 'Stay a moment,' he said.

Clemens paused, fretting and muttering, while his friend returned to his thoughts. Then Vergil smiled – a rather painful and weary smile.

'Help me with this concern,' he said, 'and you will be

able to consult the works of the music masters of Chandra-guptas and Asokas as often and as long as you like. I will give them to you.'

Clemens drew in his breath. His vast figure seemed to swell. He cast his eyes around the book-crowded room as though looking for the words just mentioned. His face grew red, and he rested his clenched fist upon a curious globe whose surface was covered with a painted map according to the theories of that Aristarchus who taught that the world was round.

'Listen,' he said. 'You have had these books as long as I have known you. We have long been friends. You knew of my desire for them. What is this Cornelia to you, that now and only now you offer me this gift to gain my help? Did she threaten you? And with what threat? Did she bribe you, cozen you, slip the gold and ivory key to her chamber into the palm of your hand? The time and the toil it will take to gratify her whim – *if it can be gratified at all! – why ...*'

His voice died away, growled in his chest.

Vergil's face twitched, and he pushed away the scrolls. 'Time and toil ... I worked two years for the Soldan of Babylone, that wise and great man,' he said, 'casting two hundred and twenty-one nativities in order to find one man whose elevation alone could prevent rebellion and bloodshed, after which I devised a system of gates and sluices for the Soldan's canals whereby one province could be saved from flood and two others from drought. At the end of those two years he took me by the hand and led me through his treasury, gold and silver and ivory and emeralds and purple, he led me in by the nearer door and let me out by the farther one. And then he said to me, "*It is not enough.*" And he gave me as my wages those two books of the music of the Eastern Kings. ...

'Do you think he did not value them, or value my time and my toil? Do you imagine that I do not value them, merely because I do not understand them? When it is time for the chick to crack the shell, no heralds are needed to blow trumpets. Time and toil. … On my way back from Babylone I traveled through Dacia and stayed one night at the same rude inn with the magnate Lupescus, who farms the revenues from the Imperial mines in that rich land. I heard him tell of the tedious and wasteful process which they used in having slaves pick over the buckets of rubble brought up from the earth. Then and there, remembering what I had done for the Soldan, I sketched for Lupescus with a piece of charcoal on a piece of board a plan whereby the same work could be done with sluices of water – cheaper, quicker, better.

'He gave me into my own hands a thousand ducats of gold, and horses to carry them, and every year he sends me a thousand more. It is useful to have, but I do not particularly value it, for I know he does not either – he must make by that process alone easily a hundred thousand a year – and besides, I earned it in a few minutes. … From time to time I ask myself, Did I really toil two years' time for the Soldan of Babylone, or for Lupescus? And, if for Lupescus, was it not rather for five hundred of his slaves whom my discovery freed from labor which drew blood from their fingers when they worked fast and blood from their backs when they did not?'

Clemens cleared his throat. He pursued his lips. 'You've become quite a philosopher,' he said at last. 'Well, well. Very well. You shall have my help and we shall see what chick hatches from this egg. And now, Master Vergil, allow me to point out to you that there are two requirements which must be fulfilled before anything at all can be done toward making a major speculum – and both requirements are impossible of fulfillment!'

He lifted one wing of his moustache with his stylus and leered on that one side. Then, replacing the stylus in the writing case fastened to his belt, he held up two huge and hairy fingers. He pressed down one. 'You cannot get ore of tin.' He pressed down the other. 'You cannot get ore of copper,' he said.

With a slight sigh Vergil leaned across and pulled the casque down over the globe on the table. He got up and stretched, his shadow gesturing grotesquely in the now dimmer light. 'I know we cannot,' he said, yawning. 'Nevertheless, we will.'

THREE

Westward into the the sea the last rose strokes of sunset painted the sky. Smoke of wood and charcoal drifted up to Vergil leaning over the parapet on his roof. Fish and squid, lentil and turnip, bread and oil and garlic, and a little meat – Naples was having its supper before retiring for the night; though few in Naples would have all of these for supper. A few horses still thumped their way down the street below, and a single heavy cart rumbled. Horses and cart were probably heading for the great stable at the foot of the hill. Women spoke in tired voices, filling their amphoras at the Fountain of Cleo. A baby cried somewhere, the sounds of its wailing thin upon the cool air. The lights of tiny oil lamps flickered like fireflies, and here and there the mouth of a brazier glowed, redly and briefly, as someone fanned the embers or blew upon them through a wooden tube. From the Bay came the faint *thump-thump* of a galley bailiff beating out the rhythm for the rowers as the ship put into port.

'Abana! Bacchus! Camellia! Dido! Ernest! Fortunata! Gammelgrendel! Halcyon! ... Halcyon?'

The voice called nearby. Someone clapped hands, summoning. 'Halcyon? Ah ... my pretty! Come along, come along ... India! Jacynto! Leo! Leo! Leo ...?'

The old madwoman was crying her cats home. Vergil walked to the side of the parapet, plucking a sprig of basil from one of the flower pots and bruising it between his fingers. He held the fragrant leaf to his nose and leaned over.

'Dame Allegra, where is Kingdom?' he asked. She fed her covey of cats on the innards of fish and whatever other offals she could gather up, poking about the streets and wharves and alleys in her stained and tattered gown. Sometimes a choicer scrap of victual fell her way, from someone who pitied her or – more likely – feared her for the Evil Eye; this she ate herself. Not because she was better or more deserving than the cats, she would explain. Because her taste had been corrupted and theirs was still natural.

'Kingdom?' Her voice came clearer now, as though she had lifted her head and was peering up through the darkness. 'Kingdom, my lord, hath gone back to Egypt. Often did he tell me he would, an the season were aright for't. To fare upon the sea, my lord, in these crank craft – nay, it were not befitting my handsome goddikin – in one of these common and stinking galleys? Nay, sir. But yestere'en, when the moon were all o' gold, saith he to me, Cat Kingdom saith – Allegra, nursling mine, th' imperial galleon goeth a-post tomorrow to Alexandria with my lord the proconsul aboard of her. And I'm half of a mind, sith, to gang along of him.'

And so, while the deep blue deepened into purple and thence to black, she crooned her madwoman's tale of how Kingdom (a lean and rangy tom with scarred flanks) had been welcomed aboard as befit his demidivinity, provided with silver dishes and golden drinking bowls, and had sailed for home, promising to speak good words for her to Sphinx and to sacred Bull Apis and to all the hieratic hawks and crocodiles. … The truth of the matter, Vergil reflected, was that he – Cat Kingdom – had probably been knocked on the head by some starveling slum-dweller and was even now stewing with an illicit onion and a clove of stolen garlic and a borrowed bay leaf. Naples was known to relish a dish of 'roof rabbit' when the chance and an empty belly occurred together.

Of course, it was not altogether impossible that some

pious Egyptian actually *had* picked up the cat and taken it back to be cuddled and cosseted and reverenced in a village by the Nile for the rest of its life; and to be embalmed and entombed and worshiped after it died. What was fact and what was fancy? With old Allegra, it was often hard to know – and not with her alone.

Clemens had gone home, shaking his massy head and muttering, but had promised to return the next day to discuss the making of a major speculum. Vergil, alone, found study impossible. And so, he reflected, here he was, instead, discussing cats with an ancient madwoman. It was a diversion of a sort, and required less effort than most. And her withered womanhood could not taunt his missing manhood.

'How fortunate for Kingdom,' he said. 'But you will miss him, Dame Allegra.'

She crooned, wordlessly, while her cats scrabbled on the roof and clawed the walls of her hovel of a hut. So she lived, so she desired to live.

'My lady fears for the fire,' she said, breaking off her keening.

The door of the Sun and Wagon burst open with a splash of yellow light and a stink of sour wine and the noise of teamsters and drovers and tavern wenches and tapsters; then it swung shut again, and in the faint echo Vergil asked, 'What lady?'

Somehow he knew the answer without knowing how he knew it.

'It's the Empire that's wanted, my lord,' the madwoman mumbled, scuffling about for another handful of fish tripes to fling to her horde of pets. The bitter, nasty smell of their staling and spraying brought the basil leaves to his nose again, but not before he was reminded of creatures more noisome – and more dangerous – than a pack of cats.

'Cornelia,' he said, half aloud … though his conscious thoughts had been elsewhere … Cornelia … musk and roses ... but for the present and indefinite future, more dangerous than any, more dangerous than all. *If I must search the dark halls of Hell, then let Hell itself be harrowed ...*

'Cornelia,' he repeated.

'The Empire is what's wanted. Leo! Myra! Nettlecomb! Orpheus! Hither to me, my conies. Dame Allegra will feed ye. *She's* not for the fire, nay ...'

The old woman's voice died away. Was it the Samaritans who claimed that after the destruction of their temple by Pompey the gift of prophecy had passed to children, fools, and madmen? There was no use calling to this one, now. In her hut, on her sack of straw, warm and verminous and covered with cats as with a blanket, Dame Allegra had bid the day good-bye. It was time, Vergil considered, that he do the same.

Below and later, in his bedchamber, he considered his own day, and some of the questions it posed. Why did the manticores, who shunned light, collect lamps? How long would he have to postpone his attempt at their habitations? Would it not have been better had he never gone there? What did the proconsul hope to find in Egypt – rest? Plunder? Wisdom? How did Allegra know that he had been with the Queen of Carsus? What was 'the fire?' How long would it take to make the speculum? How long would Cornelia wait? How could he still love her? How could he not?

He cleared his mind of all these questions by constructing in it a diagram of great potency and then concentrating on the center of this, in which lay absolute nothingness. Gradually, slowly at first, then more rapidly, the diagram faded away and simultaneously something else took shape in the center before the gaze of his inner eyes.

A door.

He saw himself get up, walk forward, open and step through it. He saw it close, saw it fade and vanish. Once again there was nothingness.

The humming was that of bees. He could not see them any more than he could see Mount Hymettus. He could smell the sweet scent of the violets growing on its slope, though, the rich carpet of flowers nourishing the bees. Illiriodorus sat upon his stool, and he at the old man's feet, happy in knowing that the old philosopher was alive; vaguely troubled at recalling he had dreamed he was long dead. 'A handful of wheat will do, my son,' Illiriodorus was saying. The other students weren't present; whether they were in the Agora or where they were, Vergil neither knew nor cared.

'A handful of wheat, the flight of a flock of birds, the liver of a victim, an oracle or a prophecy. The truth exists and the truth can be known. It exists in everything and you exist in everything and therefore it exists in you.'

'Yes,' said Vergil.

'Since the truth exists in you, as well as existing outside of you, it is only necessary to bring it – somehow – out from inside, up from below, down from above. For this the focus is necessary, the precipitator. A speculum of virgin bronze will do as well. In this particular instance, perhaps it will do better than those others I mentioned.'

'Yes,' said Vergil. There was a small table by the sage's side, and on the table was a bowl of honey, the fragrant and delicious honey of Mount Hymettus. Leisurely, he reached his hand toward it.

'No,' said Illiriodorus, warding off Vergil's hand with his own. The bowl fell, falling slowly, striking the floor with the noise of a bell. Illiriodorus smiled, raised his hand in farewell. The sound of the bell echoed infinitely and echoed forever.

There was a painted room and in it lay a figure with waving hair and full lips, a figure that was human-like, but as a great doll might be human-like. This figure, which was neither man nor woman, made an agonized face and turned the face away from him. But he was in front of it,

33

facing it; he was always facing it. The creature groaned, closed its eyes, opened them a moment later – hopefully, fearfully.

'Still there,' it said. 'Still there,' moaned the epicene voice.

He said nothing.

The room was brightly, almost garishly, painted, as it might have been by a somewhat talented child, with the figures of people whose faces – eyes round as circles rimmed all about with long lashes; red spheres for cheeks; double cupid's-bow mouths – whose faces were turned full frontward but whose bodies stood sideways underneath trees almost their own size and alongside flowers even taller; with the pictures of striped and dotted birds, blue dogs, red cats, green marmosets ... an almost insane panorama which, still, arrested rather than repelled.

'I have had this dream before,' whimpered the figure on the bed, sexless as a doll. 'I know I have, and I have caused it to be written down and I have referred it to the Wise Men and the Chaldeans and I have consulted learned Jews and even the Women Who Serve 'Ditissa ... no one has given me a good interpretation, not one.' It looked at him, consumed with woe and self-pity and a measure of genuine foreboding and horror.

It wept a little and it sniveled.

He said nothing.

'I would give you what you desire, if I knew what it was. You smell of Rome to me, and of all known things I fear of the Romans. They burn and they slay and they carry off captives. Go away!' it screamed. 'I will not have this dream! Go away! Go ...'

He was in a chamber hewn out of solid rock. A candelabrum of three lamps supplied thin light. The room was not large, and it was crowded. Matrons wrapped about the head with gauzy veils were there, and those whose dirt and ragged nakedness proclaimed them to be slaves

34

of the lowest sort. A patrician was there, next to him an apprentice boy, next to him a girl in a rustic robe. Vergil seemed to be up toward the front; others, whom he could not see, pressed close around him.

Up at the very front was a table bearing vessels, some of common use, others whose function and design were unknown to him. To one side stood an old man with a long gray beard, his countenance thin so that the bones showed.

'Yet a little while, my children,' he said, 'and all this shall pass away. Why do they persecute us, indeed? And why do they harry us? Have we swords? Do we plot rebellion? Are we bandits or brigands, pirates or thieves, to be treated thus? Ah, no, my children. We are weak, we are few, we are humble, we are peaceable. We are here to worship our Lord and Savior Daniel Christ, who gave His flesh to be eaten by lions and His blood to be licked by them, in order that we might be saved and have everlasting life.'

The congregation murmured a word, evidently in response, which Vergil did not know.

'And as for those lost in heresy,' the old man declared, his face becoming burning-fierce, 'worse than those who merely persecute our bodies – as for those who say that our Lord and Savior Daniel Christ did not die in the lion's den, let them be anathema!' The crowd responded with the same short word as before. 'And those who claim that The Christ is yet to come and that he will bear some other name or die some other death, let them be anathema!' Again, the response. 'Let them be harried, let them be persecuted, may their flesh be torn and their blood spilt! May they be hanged and nailed upon the limbs of trees! For the Lord Daniel suffered pain and agony for them, and they refuse His sacrifice! Woe! Woe! Woe!'

He took a deep breath and opened his mouth again, but before he could speak a girl screamed. The room was suddenly full of soldiers, seizing and binding all who were there. For just an instant the old man shrank back, his tongue running in and out of his mouth like a snake's tongue. Then he thrust himself forward, his face almost truculent, and offered his wrists to the cords.

Heart numb and swollen and cold with fear, Vergil waited, but no one touched him. No one noticed him. All were silent, all went dim, all vanished from his sight.

The lulling noise, as of waves lapping against a hull, died away. Light, with reticulations of darkness, shone upon his eyelids, and Vergil awoke. The morning had come, brightening through the thin plates of horn in the window lattice. He was in his own room once again.

FOUR

The front part of the elaboratory and workshop of Vergil occupied all of one floor of the house in the Street of the Horse-Jewelers; the rear part of it rose upwards the height of two more stories. There, in the measured darkness interspersed with broad shafts of light slanting down from the upper windows (there were none on the lowest level), he addressed his few assistants.

'We want to make a speculum majorum,' he said, standing with one foot on a workbench. 'You have all heard of such a thing, doubtless some of you at least have read of it as well.' Behind him rose tall engines, their wheels and hafts casting odd and baroque shadows on the floors freshly sanded – as they were at least twice a day – to prevent both slipping and the chance of fire. As he spoke, one of the men, turning his head occasionally and nodding to show he was both hearing and listening, added bits of charcoal to a fire under a closed vessel. He weighed each bit in a scale, and checked the time of adding it to the fire by an hourglass. The fire had been going, maintained with the most scrupulous care by day and night in order to ensure as even a temperature as possible, for four years without cessation. It still had two years to go, after which it would be allowed to die down over the course of a year, and then for six months to cool.

The master recapitulated the matter. 'Such a mirror is made of virgin bronze, made carefully and diligently according to the arcane science of such a work, and without anyone's looking into it during its manufacture. If this is done properly, then whoever is the first to look into it will see whatever he or she desires most to see. But the speculum majorum cannot see into the past, neither can it look into the future.

'Nor is it permitted to attempt to peek into the private realm of Immortal God. The sighting must be of something actually and presently existing on the earth and in the world of mortal man, "*Who must*," – says Hesiod – "*till the earth, for bread, or perish ...*"'

The attentive silence was emphasized, rather than broken, by a slow clicking of a rachet wheel turning somewhere in the shadows of the great room. One of the men, white-haired and white-bearded old Tynus, made a reflective noise in his throat. 'It will be necessary to seek a favorable hour with unusual precision and care,' he observed. 'This is a matter of philosophy as well as artisanship.'

Iohan, a squat, long-armed man with a chest like a tun of wine, his voice rumbling and echoing, said, 'But it is also a matter of artisanry as well as philosophy. I leave observations of nodes and cusps and houses and hours to others – for my part, I say, let the clay be of the finest quality, the wax of the purest, the ore of the soundest – and let the cooling not be hurried, no, nor the polishing, either.'

But Perrin, an open-faced young man with a smudge of soot across his face where he had wiped it with his hand, said, 'Master, I don't understand. The disciplines involved are rigorous, but beside the point. Such a project is impossible, practically. Iohan says the ore should be of the soundest. I agree. We all agree. But I have to ask, What ore? There has no ore of tin or copper come onto the market in Naples in my life time. Except for small specimens, samples, such as you, sir, keep in your cabinet, I've never even seen what these ores look like. Of what use is it to observe the signs and mark the seasons, as Tynus says, this being so?'

Perrin had hit upon the crux of the matter. Copper came from Cyprus – the island of Aphrodite was so rich in it that it had given its name to the metal – but the route to and from Cyprus was cut off by the ships of the fierce Sea-Huns, and had been for well over a decade. The Sea-Huns allowed, by agreement and for tribute (euphemistically termed *guard money*), one great fleet a year in each direction – from the Empire to Cyprus, from Cyprus to the Empire. There were, to be sure, blockade runners of a sort: small, swift vessels plying between the eastern shore of the island and the nearer coast of Little Asia. But these risked only cargo light in weight and precious in every ounce – gold, perfume, pretty girls.

Copper was too bulky, and not nearly so valuable as to justify the risk. Three swift trips in a smuggling craft and the captain could retire for life. Load his ship with heavy ingots of copper and he might well wallow in the narrow seas – and retire onto an impaling stake, having first been flayed (slowly) of every inch of skin. Or as near as made no great matter – a man in such an acutely uncomfortable position was not likely to quibble over an inch or two here or there. One did not in any event quibble with the Sea-Huns.

Once a year, then, the great heavy galleys and galleons came and went in their convoys, laden down and lumbering slowly over the tideless sea as far as the eye could reach. Vast as was the supply thus obtained, it was not yet equal to the demand. The trade was in the hands of a guild of merchants who charged what the rich traffic would bear; orders had to be placed years in advance. There were warehouses in Naples piled from tile roofs to stone foundations with copper – but it was copper smelted down into ingots for the most part – a small part of it still came in bullock hide-shaped sheets for the old-fashioned, country trade – and, in either event, it was not copper *ore*.

It was copper changed by the acts of man. It was not *virgin* copper.

The agreement to 'guard' the convoy (i.e. to allow it through) had been wrested only with great difficulty from the three rulers of the Sea-Huns – or, at any rate, from two of them. Osmet was said to be the brains and cunning of the lot; Ottil, to be the fighting heart of the far-flung, restless, and water-borne hordes; Bayla, the third royal brother, was reputed a sot or an idiot – in any event, a cipher. The chances of getting them to make any change in an arrangement to which their greed and recklessness made them at best but luke-warm were nil. And the uncivilized crews of the black and blood-red boats of the water hordes would have no mercy on any independent craft at all.

'Copper is our second problem,' Vergil said. 'First is tin.'

Tin came, of course, from Tinland, a mysterious peninsular or – likelier – island realm, in this respect if in no other like Cyprus. But whereas Cyprus had once been and still was officially part of the Economium, Tinland had never been. It was located somewhere to the west and north in the Great Dark Sea, far beyond Tartis. Nothing more was known about Tinland (though legends thereof were not lacking); almost nothing about Tartis. No man of the Empire had ever seen it – at least, none had ever left any account. A rumor persisted that Tartis itself had long ago been conquered and destroyed. It might have been – but throughout the Empire there were small colonies of Tartismen, living under a sort of autonomy by ancient treaty right. Each ward, as their colonies were called, was ruled by its own captain-lord. They were reported to own immense wealth. But they continued to trade.

'Tin is our first concern,' Vergil said, 'because access to the suppliers is near at hand. However – leave the obtaining of the virgin ores to me. In the meantime, start the work of preparation. I do not know how long even the preliminaries will take – but begin to begin, *now*. I will have fair copies made of what is available in my books. Read them carefully, and read them again and again. Start laying in the supplies – the clay for the mold, the wax for the model, the crucibles, the fuel, the cutting and the grinding tools – even the rouge for the polishing. Check every item with the utmost care, and do not hesitate to discard anything which is not the best.

'Let the best vellum, pens, and ink for drawing up the plans be procured. And beware lest strife or impurity enter in upon you while this work is in progress.'

He paused. 'We will not be alone in this work,' he said. 'Dr Clemens has agreed to assist us.'

The men received this news with mixed thoughts. On the one hand, Clemens' hold on both the philosophical and practical aspects of alchemy had the men's absolute respect. On the other hand, his many eccentricities and outspoken ways of exercising them ('Onions!' he would snort. 'What in blazes do you mean by eating onions at a time when you're working with gold? Do you want to turn it into dross? Nox and Numa! *Onions!*'), as well as his short way with dissenters, prevented the news from being heard with utter joy. But they would soon adjust to the situation. The very prickliness of Vergil's friend would become a source of rueful pride among his men, and they would boast of it to their fellows.

After a few more words – the nature of the project was for the time being to remain confidential; the sponsor of it was paying well and they would share in the sum even if the scheme should fail – he left them to their work of preparation.

Tartis ward in Naples consisted chiefly of Tartis Port, a rather small harbor, and Tartis Castle, a hugh Cyclopean mass of stone. It was not in the least like any other castle in the whole dogedom. Passing from the Great Harbor into

Tartis Port, Vergil was struck immediately by the difference in tempo. Everything was slower, quieter. Everything was ... yes ... poorer. A hulk lay careened, but no one worked on it. Another one lay half sunken into the mud, and had lain there long enough for a good-sized young tree to have taken root on the quarter-deck. A pair of calkers worked at no great pace on the bulkhead of a small carrack. And a short caffle of slaves loaded supplies aboard a galley.

And that was all.

An old crone, her dirty skull naked save for an even dirtier rag pulled askew over her few witch locks, sat plucking a thin fowl on the doorstep of a cookshop. She muttered at her task, but did not look up as Virgil's thin shadow fell across her.

It was said that the Captain-lord was inaccessible, that he did not appear in public even at the coronation of a new doge, that he received the Imperial Legate on one day a year fixed for the purpose, and – after the brief ritual of passing a coin of gold over a tray bearing earth and water, corn and wine and oil – retired from the audience room and left the rest of the interview to a deputy.

There were no guards posted at the foot of the castle steps, which might indeed have been built by the gigantic four-armed Cyclopes in the Age of Dreams, so wide and deep and tall (and so irregular) was each vast shelf of stones. Vergil toiled his way upward, pausing from time to time to rest – and to examine the view. He had never before seen it from this particular angle or series of angles: Vesuvio and its almost invisible fume of smoke, Mount Somma hard by, the Deer Park beyond, the blue waters of the Bay, the Great Harbor (its clamor now barely a distant hum), parts of the city and its near and distant suburbs. Now and then as the steps curved and turned – its blocks and those of the walls to either side so irregular and often protruding that it seemed only the weight of the others piled on top kept them from slipping out of place and hurtling down like so many thunderstones – now and then the view was cut off as the steps sank or the walls rose; then, when he had for a moment forgotten everything but the task of mounting the stairs and placing his feet so that they did not slip in the deep hollows worn by endless ages of use and passage, an entire new panorama would flash open before his eyes again.

There was no guard at the top of the step, either; indeed, he had not at first realized that he was at the top, so gradually did the steps become shallower, so irregular did the footing yet remain. He did not at first notice the man in the scarlet cloak, either.

It was the legs he noticed first.

They stood upon a block of stone set by itself in the middle of a courtyard, by their look strong and healthy legs; and yet they trembled. Planted firmly on the stone, feet unmoving, tremors of nerve and muscle ran through them without ceasing. Vergil raised his eyes.

The man was dressed in the embroidered and pleated linen garment that was the traditional habit of the Tartismen, and over it he wore a short cloak, dyed in scarlet. All this Vergil saw in a second, and in another second he had said, 'Sir, I seek the Captain-lord'; but before he had finished saying it his voice had almost faltered, having seen the man's face.

This man is blind, this man is deaf, he is looking out to sea for a ship that will never come – so ran his rapid, startled, and successive thoughts. Then: *He has taken a vow to stand here, thus, for a certain length of time, and will stand here thus though the Heavens may fall* ... and the man turned his gaze on Vergil. ... *This man is mad. He would kill me, if he could.* The eyes were like dark green stones lain long under water, full of something duller than rage and sicker than pain. The lips were tremulous with a voiceless mutter and a drop of sweat – though the day was not at all hot – ran down his brow from his hairline to his nose.

In a low voice, Vergil said, 'Sir, my pardon for disturbing you.' And he passed on. Rounding a corner, he came upon two other men – both wearing Tartis clothes, but neither in a scarlet cloak – emerging from a door into the interior of the castle; and to them he repeated that he was looking for the Captain-lord.

Both showed surprise, as much at his presence as at his request. One of them nodded, the other looked over his shoulder as they continued on their way, and he followed them. They spoke together in what he assumed was their own language. Down a ramp the three of them went, into a roofless chamber, turned at a right angle and went down another ramp, crossed through a balcony overlooking a hall as high as his house in which other voices echoed thinly, came by and by to what appeared to be an office or an antechamber. The Tartismen gestured to Vergil to sit – and vanished through a narrow door that closed behind them. Vergil sat.

This was the first part of the castle he had seen that was furnished, and its furnishings were scanty and curious. There was a saddle rug, or blanket, of Parthian weave spread on a wooden trestle with carved ends, a desk on which lay a codex in an extreme state of disrepair, a silver dish with a stale piece of bread and a fish bone, and a leather screen. Feeling the muscles in his legs begin to ache from the climb, Vergil sighed. From behind the screen something stirred.

'I didn't know anyone was here,' a voice said, and the screen was pushed aside. The light from the embrasure fell full into Vergil's eyes and he squinted, shielding his eyes with his hand.

'I am waiting to see the Captain-lord,' he said.

'Ah ... please, then, come and wait here. It is more comfortable.' There was a long bench by the window niche. His eyes adjusting now, Vergil examined his host. The man's voice hinted of Punic or Syrian origins, his clothes were of good Neapolitan make. His manner, though tense, was controlled. He might have been of any age. His eyes were pale, pale blue-green. His complexion ...

'My name is An-thon Ebbed-Saphir, but they call me the Red Man. It's easy to see why. I'm a Phoenician. Our skins seem to take the sun, to retain it, but we do not tan. "Phoenician," of course, means just that – the Red People. But you know all this, of course.' He waved his hand a trifle wearily. His voice died away. He took his place at full length upon the bench. After a moment he said, 'The Captain-lord. I have never seen him, myself.' Giving over the effort of speech, he invited Vergil, with gestures, to admire the view. He did not look up or speak when a Tartisman with a woolly beard came bustling in and motioned Vergil with both arms and an expression of great importance to come along. Vergil tarried a moment.

In a low voice he said, quickly to the Red Man, Ebbed-Saphir, 'Who is the one in the scarlet cloak?'

A flicker of something disturbed the raptness of the Phoenician's gaze. 'Don't ask, do not interfere,' he said. And his look returned to the prospect of the suburban villas stretching along the Bay for miles.

'Well?' cried Woolly Beard. 'Well? Captain-lord? Why?'

And then he screamed – a scream of utterly unbelieving agony, such as tears unbidden and unchecked from a laboring woman by whom a child struggles to be born.

Scarlet ran before Vergil's eyes. Woolly Beard lay doubling on the floor. The Phoenician was not to be seen. The man who had been standing outside on the block of stone went rushing through the inner door, his cloak streaming and whipping. His voice cried terrible, inarticulate things. His short sword ran blood. And Vergil ran behind him.

The course he ran was a nightmare course down the endless Cyclopean corridors, echoing with the frenzied cries of the man ahead – a man who, every now and then, would turn and lunge at him. The face was no longer more than faintly human. Vergil fell and hit his head a sickening crack against the stones. The man in the scarlet cloak turned around and ran again. The cloak caught upon the protruding socket of a burnt-out torch, ripped, hung there. Vergil snatched it as he ran past, holding it in one hand as he groped desperately with the other, got hold of the writing case in his belt.

Suddenly they were in a suite of furnished chambers. A door burst open and a man stood there, frozen before he could show either astonishment or terror. The madman howled, leaped forward. Vergil leaped after him, bent, whipped forward the cloak with the writing case knotted into one end of it; stopped short, jerked back.

Tripped, felled by his own cloak, the attacker lay before him on the floor, motionless for an instant, which Vergil dared not let pass unused. He jumped, coming down with his knees and all his weight upon the place just below the ribs, turning his toes so he could move back on the balls of his feet; and pinioned the madman by the elbows.

Now men poured forth, it seemed, from everywhere. They beat the manslayer to the floor again, and one of them raised the sword.

'Good is the strong wine,' the Captain-lord said, in his guttural voice, 'and I have had put in it a medicine or two. But it is to be drunk, not held in the cup.'

Vergil drank. The wine was of a vintage strange to him, and tasted of herbs. It was somewhat bitter and despite himself he shuddered. Then, as if with the shudder, all the weakness left him. 'Why did he want to do it?' he asked.

The Captain-lord took in a hiss of breath, held it, shrugged. 'To explain it, fully, would take long – and then there would be explanations of the explanations. I will speak shortly. There was a matter of a woman, a punishment, a consent I could not give.' Seated, he looked

46

immense. Huge head, huge chest, broad shoulders. His legs were short, though, and he limped. The thought came to Vergil that in this, as much as anything, might lie the reason for the man's inaccessibility, his never appearing before the gaze of strangers. His hair was white; his face, seamed.

'Once there were guards all around,' he continued, 'to protect from a danger. I, thinking there was none, re-moved them. And so – look – danger ... and from within. Tell me, now, with truth, who you are and why you came.'

The room was elaborately, richly furnished, but every-thing seemed a little old, a little shabby; a little dirty, too.

'Speculum majorum, I have never heard of one. Magic. I have no concern in it. Queens, Carsus, copper – all things strange to me.' The Captain-lord shook his massy head. He raised his eyebrows, his great chest filled with air. 'But – *tin?* Ho! Tin! Yes! With this I have a concern. The Captain-lord does not sell you tin, but he can give all you want. So ... Vergil. Doctor. Magus. How much tin is enough?'

Slowly, carefully, as simply as he could, Vergil explained that he required only as much tin as would fit into the palms of his hands ... but that it must be virgin tin.

'I understand,' the old man said. 'You explain to me most carefully. I will explain – I will *try* to explain to you, also carefully. Look. You are in your house. You want something, you send your slave to the market. You say, Go. Buy this. So? Simple. But what you want now, it is not simple. Goods come down to us slowly, from the north, from the west, from ward to ward. Virgin tin, it comes not here. It is cast into ingots so far away that I, even the Captain-lord, I do not know where. I can try to obtain. But I am only Captain-lord *here*. In another ward I am only another name. Far enough away to find virgin tin, I am not even only a name.

'Here I have power of life, power of death. Elsewhere,

I have no power. My influence is strong at Rome, weak at Marsala. Ice – do you know ice, Doctor? Pass one piece from hand to hand. It melts. It melts away ...'

More than ice and personal influence melts away, Vergil thought. The whole Tartis system seemed to be melting away, seemed to be in decay, a shadow of its past. And so seemed he himself.

But so long as even a shadow of it remained, he had to make use of it.

'I will try,' said the Captain-lord. 'Why not? It is gratitude. Perhaps in three years time – virgin tin.'

Someone came and lit the lamps. No longer dim, the room seemed no longer shabby, old, worn. In the dancing shadow the old Captain-lord grew younger. A spark of light glittered on the boss of a round shield hanging on the wall by an auroch's horn.

'Sir,' said Vergil, 'three years time will not do. Three months may be even too long, too late.'

A faint, wry smile touched the old man's lips. 'Doctors of Magic and Science, even you are bound by time? And what, then, of me? Never mind. Bring here the horn.'

The lowing note sounded deeply. After a while a servant came. Torches were obtained, by their hissing flames they were lighted down the same vast, turning, Cyclopean steps; and into a courtyard filled with a strong, rank, sharp odor. A man with leather wristlets looked up from placing bits of meat in a bowl of water. He was obviously a falconer, thought Vergil. But where did the Tartismen hawk? And who had ever heard of their hawking? Furthermore, not all of the equipment to be seen was the familiar 'hawks' furniture' of falconry.

The two old men spoke together in their own language, then turned to enter a wooden outbuilding built against the castle's wall, the Captain-lord beckoning his guest to follow. The place smelt like a mews and there were subdued bird noises from the cages and roosts.

'This is the Master of the Air,' said the Captain-lord. Vergil bowed. The Master grunted, looking far from honored, far from pleased; and when his commandant went on to say 'He will arrange the sending,' the Master of the Air protested bitterly – so his tone and manner showed, though Vergil could understand no word. Still muttering, he reached into a cage and took out a bird the like of which Vergil had never seen before. It was gold in color and had a crest upon its head, and it bent forward and nibbled gently on the Master's index finger with what seemed like affection. The man's gaunt face softened, and he spoke to Vergil for the first time.

'She was sent me in an egg,' he said. 'One of a clutch of two, under a broody hen. The other hatched not. I raised, I taught. For only great danger was she to be sent—'

'The danger came today,' the Captain-lord interrupted. 'And he, this Vergil Magus, saved from danger. He has earned the sending, I say, enough.'

The Master of the Air seemed almost about to weep. Touched, Vergil would have liked to decline whatever it was – he was still not sure – what the order touched on. But he remembered his own need, and his own pain. And he stayed silent.

With a final mutter, the Master of the Air tucked the golden bird under one arm and went off into the shadowy corners of the mews. He came back with a small falcon-eagle on each wristlet, glaring fiercely from their yellow eyes. The Captain-lord took the bird of gold in his hands, gently, and the bird looked up at him. He spoke to it, and it seemed to follow. He spoke again – stopped – spoke again. The same words seemed to occur each time. It was as if he were instructing the bird.

'Am I to understand,' the thought occurring suddenly to Vergil, 'that this bird of gold will carry a message? You will teach it to speak the words – like a popinjay? And will it learn them quickly?'

'No. It cannot speak.'

'Then ...'

'It will carry your message as my message. And where it puts down, there it will write the *Word*.'

Write!

And the Captain-lord did not believe in magic!

'Enough, then. It has learned. The two others go with it for guardians. Master of the Air, let it be done.'

The Master of the Air caressed the birds, all three, lovingly, gently. He whispered in their ears, he kissed the fierce heads of the falcon-eagles. Then he loosed their leathern jesses. They fluttered their wings. The bird of gold was tossed up. The torchlight glittered on her golden pinions. She circled once. Twice. A third time. The falconets shot up like crossbow bolts. The three vanished into the night. One soft gray feather came floating down and landed at Vergil's feet. From far, very far and above, a faint scream sounded on the night wind, and the torches smoked and flared.

FIVE

Declining with thanks the offer of a torchman to light him home, Vergil took his leave of Tartis Castle. Scarcely noting the strong, familiar smells of the Main Port, he let his mind run freely. ... What a journey lay before the bird of gold and its pair of protectors! Seas and storms, crags and forests – how far? No one knew. Over farmland and marshland and woodland and barren moors, beyond the distant border marches of the Empire, past the remote boundaries of the Great Economium itself ... perhaps all the way to Ultima Thule, farthest land of rock and freezing seas. Who knew where Tinland was?

They would see sights, as they veered and circled, that no man ever saw: the sun rising from the sea beneath them, like a disc of burnished brass; beneath them, too, the icy alps; the Great Forest, stretching farther than the knowledge of man; and, at length, after many days and many perils, the storm-buffeted air and water of the cold, gray Northern Sea, where the shape shifters turned seal instead of wolf.

A blind beggar, alerted by the approaching footsteps, began his singsong chant, broke off in mid-note as he heard the coin clatter in his bowl, mumbled a thanks. Gobbets of meat sizzled and smoked, beans bubbled, spiced wine simmered in an open-front cookshop lit chiefly by its own cheerful fires. Porters and dockers squatted on the step, dipping chunks of bread into their suppers, reminding Vergil that he had not yet had his. A woman with a painted face and no bosom to her dress leaned over a lamp-lit window sill and called an invitation. A ragged child and a scabby dog slept belly to belly in an alley.

Presently the busier part of the port, busy even at night, began to give way to the warehouse district, busy only in the daytime. He walked through pools of black shadow. The lights were dim and few. Up ahead, past the archway where the street began to climb the hill, came the noise of a brawl. Vergil turned aside to avoid a heap of sand and gravel, which the builders had left when they stopped work for the day, and found himself in the middle of the fight.

Clubs thudded against each other, shouts of warning, obscenities. Men circling for position, crouching and darting. A broken jug lay in a splatter of cheap, sour wine – perhaps a result of the brawl, perhaps its cause. Vergil began to pass by, staggered as one of the men – there may have been five or six of them – fell heavily against him. A protest would be wasted breath. He caught his balance and had started on his way again when the man who had fallen against him whirled around and came after him. Shouting. Cudgel raised.

It was no time for explanations. His long knife was in his belt. He drew it. 'Keep off,' he warned. And began to move away.

The gesture did not bring him unopposed right of passage. The men dropped their private quarrels, began to close up, to move in toward him. 'Drew a knife on us,' one muttered, with the sullen rage of the bully who feels wronged when resisted. Another stopped, swung at an angle, his hand whipping up and out. Sensing rather than seeing the stone, Vergil ducked. It was the wrong thing to do.

He thought the arc of light he saw appear on the paving was from the sharp, sickening pain of the blow. In an instant, as the men stopped short, staring down, he knew it was not. The curving line expanded like a slow ripple, licked up into a circle of fire. His flesh prickled, he sensed a pressure which he did not feel. His knife hand still out-thrust, the blade pointing up, he turned his head. There was a man behind him whose hand also was thrust out, but it held no knife. The index finger indicated, almost negligently, the circle of fire. The finger rose. The level of the fire rose.

The attackers – dirty fellows in patched jerkins – breathed noisily through open mouths. The stranger moved to Vergil's side, made a sweeping and violent gesture. In an instant the circle was sucked into one flaming heap, which went roaring down upon the thugs, spreading out, fan-wise, as it did so. They fled, whooping in terror. Now the fire was a great serpent, undulating in pursuit, nipping at the heels of each of them. The shadows danced madly on the grimy bricks of the buildings. The fire moved more slowly, but the fleeing brutes did not slacken, nor look behind. And the fire sank down, drew in upon itself, its heat seeming to leave it, its color changing from yellow-orange-red to the blue-white of phosphorescence. At last there was but a spot, a speck, like the glow of a firefly. Vergil turned to see the Red Man beside him.

And then even the reflection vanished from Vergil's eyes.

'I should like to know how it is done,' Clemens said, speculatively. 'The proper control of fire – or, more exactly, of heat – is a perpetual problem in alchemical work. As I am sure that you, Captain An-thon, know. Hmm. Hmm. There is an account of a man named Eliah or Elio or something like that, who lived in Samaria or Philistia, and who could bring fire down from Heaven. It's said that he finally ascended in fire and was seen no more. ... Hmm.'

The Red Man said, 'Yes. Right. As to how it is done – everything is a pattern, a configuration, of the atoms, as Lucretius teaches. Some patterns are stable, some static, others are in flux. The figures of fire are always flux. They bend to the wind, they yield to the water. It is a matter of knowing how to begin. Once that is learned ...' He smiled, but the smile did little to dispel the waiting tautness of his face. The air of watching from within something distant.

Clemens leaned forward, nodding, his fists buried in his beard, his elbows on the table. He, too, waited. But the Red Man said nothing more. Clemens sighed, sat back. 'Someday, perhaps,' he murmured.

'Someday.' Vergil reclined at comparative ease, his dinner digesting leisurely, his muscles relaxing from the long climb of the afternoon, the dull ache and fear for the moment stilled. 'Someday I must learn not to become involved in altercations. Two in one day, well – although neither one turned out badly for me. Perhaps that is because you, sir' – he turned to the Phoenician – 'were near at hand on both occasions.'

Ebbed-Saphir looked up from a model of a new astrolabe (a project of Vergil's which had been put aside a while back), thrust out his lower lip doubtfully. The two cases were coincidental and dissimilar; he would accept no compliments. One was that of a single man gone mad from brooding on his wrongs. The other was most probably – almost certainly – a put-up job.

'You still think so? You really do?'

The Phoenician was not to be swayed. 'It was no brawl,' he said. 'It was an ambush. The biggest of the lot – and the worst – the one with the slashed chin, is in the pay of Thurnus Rufus.' Clemens snorted. Half Naples, and the worse half, was in the pay of Thurmus Rufus. But the Phoenician continued his argument. Throughout the day, he went on, the rumor had swept through maritime Naples that trade with Cyprus was going to be opened up completely. The copper factors were in dismay – their profitable monopoly would be destroyed; the stocks in their warehouses reduced to a fraction of present value. Who

54

was the chief of the merchants sharing in the monopoly? Thuraus Rufus. False though the rumor undoubtedly was, Thurnus must have believed it. It was not necessary that he be entirely convinced, it would be sufficient if he thought there might be even a grain of truth in it.

'If you are right,' Clemens said, 'there will be more trouble. Our friend Vergil has never learned to leave well enough alone.'

Their friend Vergil did not seem deeply concerned. He began to talk of his visit to Tartis Castle, and of the Tartismen themselves.

The Red Man took up the thread. 'I visit them whenever I am in a port that has a Tartis ward,' he said. 'I've carried cargo for them upon occasion, and I've always found them honest – though not always easy. Besides, I feel a certain affinity with them. I, too, am of a race of exiles. I have said that I am a Phoenician. This is true. But I am more specifically a Tyrean. You have heard of the Tyrean War?'

Vergil and Clemens encouraged him to tell them about it. Wine was poured, and some of the fifth essence of wine, distilled by Clemens, added to the goblets. A glow came over Ebbed-Saphir's wind-red face as he described the grandeur and the glories of seagirt Tyre. Her palaces. Her navies. Her great halls of scented cedarwood. The cloth of that imcomparable purple, the secret of which Tyre first learned, and the trade in which first made her rich.

'Oh, there was great wisdom among us,' he said, his eyes shining. 'Our astromancers studied the skies, learning from the heavenly configurations and profigurations how to sail out of sight of land by night, and what nights were auspicious and what ones were best spent at anchor or ashore. Our philosophers conned the secrets of man and matter and the tri-part psyche, our priests and prophets communed with the Supernal Figures. Wisest of all was Perez, son of P'er-Hiram, King of Tyre. But his wisdom was not without flaw...

'One day there came to him the Great Elim – Mikha-El, Gavri-El, Raphoy-El and Ori-El.

'These, Princes of the Four Quarters of Earth and Heaven, asked Perez to decide which among them was the wisest. And, in an ill-starred moment, he agreed to make the choice, and his choice fell upon Ori-El. Then he demanded his reward.

'He demanded the love of the most beautiful woman in the world – Eleana, the promised-in-marriage of Alexander Magnus, who, wroth at his loss, and with all the tribes of Greece for his allies, crossed into Asia and besieged Tyre for seven years.

'Every day his men sank huge stones into the water to build a causeway connecting Isle Tyre with the mainland. Every night our swimmers dived down and tied grapnels to them so they could be pulled up. Seven years the Greeks besieged us. Then we were betrayed. Well, Good Fortune upon your venture, Dr Vergil. If you need a boat—' He did not finish.

For a moment the two, not having yet grasped the abrupt termination of the narrative, gaped at him. Nodding curtly, the Red Man wrapped his cloak about him and departed.

'What do you suppose …?' Clemens, on his feet, was amazed. 'Emotional reaction at the memory of that old tribal legend?'

Vergil shook his head. 'There's more to the matter than that. Much more.'

'But …'

'This has been a tiring day for me. Will you spend the night? … No? Then I will excuse myself. There is much to do tomorrow.'

He had not realized that he was so tired. Almost numbed with fatigue, he climbed into his bed. Before the singing darkness overwhelmed him there came one thought – but it came not clearly. Wishing only to lose himself in the black, soft cloak of slumber, he yet strained for the thought. It came, at last, briefly but vividly. *The ring.* The Red Man's ring ... The picture faded, was succeeded by a faint, failing wonder as to why it had appeared in his thought at all. He had caught only a glimpse of it ... could not remember it ... could not collect it ... could not Cornelia ... rings. *Who goes?* he demanded, voicelessly. The brazen head moved brazen lips.

But all was silent.

SIX

The parchment of the invitation that arrived the next day was large enough to have represented the entire usable hide of a sausage bull, but although it could have contained the whole texts of the Sybil-line Books, the small amount of actual wordage occupied only a few widely separated lines. This was high courtesy indeed; Vergil had not realized he was held by the Dogical court to be worthy of such. Even Clemens, so fresh from the baths that drops of moisture still glistened here and there in the thickets of his curls, was impressed.

'The fact that they even invite *me* shows that they must really value *you*,' he said. 'My last and only audience with the Doge probably established a record for brevity.'

'How so?'

'Why, he said, "Will you make me gold?" and I said, "No," and he said, "Go," and so I went. ... It is fortunate that the Fates have made him Doge. He leaves the business of government to his intellectual superiors among his servants, whereas, were he a teamster, he would manage to tie up traffic at least daily, you may be sure. Well. Hmm ... hmm. A stag hunt. To what elaborate lengths the equestrian classes go in order to draw out the simple business of butchering venison. Ah well, it keeps their bowels open and their attentions occupied, and better King Log than King Stork. Anyway, we ought to have a good breakfast given us. I may even enjoy it.'

The hunt was being given by His Gracious Highness the Doge of Naples to honor the return of Dowager

Queen Cornelia and the visitation of His High Excellency, Andrianus Agrippa, Imperial Viceroy of the South. The Master of the Hunt, come hither expressly for the purpose, was none other than the famed Count Phoebus, son of King Modus, and called the First Captain of the Chase. Obviously, for such a distinguished occasion, no worthy mounts were likely to be found in the livery stable on the Street of the Horse-Jewelers. Vergil's perplexity on this point had evidently been anticipated, for, within an hour of the arrival of the invitation there was a great stir in the street and the brazen head announced the presence of 'the Servants of the Doge.'

The swart-faced man in the forest-green jupon and tights introduced himself as the Sergeant of the Hunt, and, 'This one's His Highness's chief groom, who we hope will help high Dr Vergil and this other high doctor – Duty, mesire' – he doffed his cap to Clemens – 'to pick out one of the horses here. But if so be none of 'em suits, he will be happy to bring along another twelve or twenty, won't he? Yes. And the compliments of Gracious high Doge. Likewise, also are saddles and other tackle and gear.' He kissed and smacked his lips to a passing wench.

Thus it was, quite early of a morning, that Vergil and Clemens found themselves at breakfast in a pavilion set up in the Deer Park near Mount Somma, on this side of Vesuvio. Lamps were still lit and charcoal braziers of the type called *scalde-rini* kept away the chill. Doge Tauro, that huge and hairy man, waved a vast paw at them, but his mouth and bristly black beard advertised not only the menu but his inability to talk. Cornelia smiled a dim, sweet smile, as at one not disliked, but only vaguely remembered, and sipped her hot wine. The gathered nobility and gentry looked at them with mingled respect and curiosity, but did not engage them in conversation. This was left to that suave and slender man, keen of eye and sharp of nose, Viceroy Andrianus, clever and competent link between the indifference of the Emperor and the incapacity of the Doge.

'Sages, your pleasure?' he inquired, '"Where there is no bread, there is no philosophy." I suggest this delightful hot bread baked with orangewood, for a start. It is better than cake. We have cake, too. A glass of hot wine, Dr Vergil? Or would you prefer the mulled ale with spices. Here is excellent honey. Try the toasted cheese, Dr Clemens. It is from the Imperial farms. Let us divide this great grilled sausage between us – veal and suckling pig, what could be more tender. Nor will we ignore this dish of roasted pears with thick cream. As for – dear me' – he broke off into a lower, very slightly lower, tone – 'I believe the Bull is about to bellow.'

The Doge was gesturing at them, his eyes wide with intent, his massy jaws masticating furiously, as he left his place at the table and stamped down to clap Vergil and Clemens upon the shoulders. By this time he had swallowed most of what was in his mouth. 'Mustn't waste time!' he directed, in a low roar. 'Important things like hunt, all right. 'Morrow – back to work. On' – he looked around, bent closer, said in a conspiratorial rumble – 'on you know what! Eh? Me cousin's daughter – the Lady Laura – three months ago – left Carsus – no sign of her. Mrrr ... look!' He rummaged in the hairy thicket of his bosom, pulled out a thick gold chain, opened the locket to display an ivory miniature. 'See what I mean? Haaa ...'

Proudly he showed the face of a young girl of the age of entering womanhood, his manner almost proprietorial as he said, 'Her grandfather was Doge, too.' When the miniature had been much admired, he snapped it shut and bellowed, 'So see you make it – you know what – eh? – quick! Find out where she is! Go there meself! And as for them that I find there ...' He made vast gestures of tearing apart, swaggered back to his seat to repeat the movements immediately over a plate of roasted pullets. And a curious, calm look passed between Cornelia and sly Agrippa.

Snatches of conversation reached Vergil's ears as he sipped the hot, honeyed wine.

'Gire falcons and a falcon gentle ... plump goats and sometimes good hens ... best thing ...'

'No hare?'

'Well ... perhaps once a week, a hare.'

'Doge keeps good game. Mamma mine, if I've ever seen less than two inches of fat on the flanks of the poorest buck pulled down here.'

'Our Lady Venus, well, when Doge isn't feeding or futtering, depend on it, he's hunting.'

He caught the Viceroy's eye. The official said, 'If one could only get them to show as much interest in sound fiscal policies or adequate water supply. ... There is another pavilion set up, Dr Vergil, part way along the course, and unless your passion for the hunt is much greater than mine, you may wish to pause there. If so, then, with your permission, I should like to elaborate on the matter the Doge mentioned. But not till then. Meanwhile, sir, before the servants reach us with water, geminors, and napkins, to what may I help you for a savory? The larks seem good, and so do the smelts. Allow me, sage. Allow me.'

Cornelia looked at them and sipped again at her wine. This time she did not smile. Grave, serene, baffling, beautiful, she seemed now not to see him at all.

There was still dew sparkling on the grass as they came out into the freshness of the morning, but if the birds were sounding their love songs it was impossible to say. Huntsmen and horses and grooms moved about, none silently, and there were the greyhounds and the hounds *de mota* – running dogs and lyme-hounds – voicing, it seemed, their determination to earn the obol a day allowed for each one's keep to the berners and fewterers. The Sergeant of the Hunt was there, the yeomen of horse and the yeomen of bow, the foresters and parkers, the chacechiens. The lyme-hounds strained their sleek black necks against the lymes or straps of horsehide, a fathom and a half long, but the white and brown brachets rested more patiently, confined by the berners in the couplets made of mare's tails, three couples per relay.

These hunted by scent and hunted in voice, melodious and deep. Not so the great gray and gray-white alaunts, ferocious beasts used in war as well as hunting: they quested by sight alone, and they ran mute.

The merry confusion and tumult died away as the noted Captain of the Chase, Count Phoebus, stroked his thin mustache, came forward and began to examine the dogs one by one, bending his comely head of golden hair as he picked up each foot. 'There may be someone here who knows less about all this than I do,' Clemens said, 'but I can't imagine who.'

This seemed to touch the Sergeant's sympathy. 'Now, perceive, mesires,' he said, 'the beasts of venery, or beasts of the forests, if you prefer, they be five – are called *silvestres tantum* – the hart, the hind, the hare, the boar, the wolf. But not the buck, no, mesires. Because why? Because he's entitled a beast of the field, is why. Now, the beasts of the forests, making their abode all the daytime in these great coverts, and have their secret places in the woods ... yes. And in the nighttime coming out into the meadows and pastures and all the pleasant feeding places ... a-hah. Mamma mine! And that's why we says about a park, "What's a park? Vert, venison, enclosure – that's a park." Forest, now, or chase, perhaps having venison and it perhaps has vert, or peradventure the two both, but enclosure, no, Lord, indeed. Only your park has all three.'

And now Count Phoebus had concluded his inspection of the dogs, and summoned the lymerers to him, one standing a bit forth of the others to answer for all the traditional questions.

'Lymerer, did you yestere'en make your ringwalks?'

'Yes, mesire.'

'Did you find slot, trace, voyes, pies, or foil?'

'Found slot and trace, mesire.'

'Fresh slot, good track, heels and cleeves and toes, clear of mark?'

'Yes, mesire.'

'You made scan-talon and you hold him to be warrantable? – a hart of right age, and no hind, buck, or brocket?'

'Yes, mesire ...'

Next the Count called the chief parker, and questioned him if he had checked and observed abatures where the stag had lain and pressed down the herbage, thus showing where it harbored and what size it was. The parker, answering in the casual and confident manner of an experienced and trusted servant, declared that he had. He had made blemishes to mark the spot, and blazoned the trees where the beast had frayed its horns. He had put the nets and blinks all in place to keep the stag from scaping the course when in full flight, and had seen to it, too, that sewels and sewings and other scarecerfs were hanged up to keep the stag from running down the hidey-lanes. And all the trystes and stablestands had been set up and yeomen of office stationed in them to blench the game if it turned.

Count Phoebus turned and addressed the lymers once more. 'Have you found fewmets?' The stag's clean stools were presented on leaves before him and he examined them, his face relaxing into a smile. 'It promises a large and healthy stag, wouldn't you say, lymerer?' ('I would, I would, mesire.') 'Then sound the stroke and divide the relays.'

The treble notes of the stroke sounded and quavered, the company began to mount, and the hounds were divided into the three relays – vauntchaseurs, middlers, and perfecters. And, to the sound of the horns, the company began to move unto the hunt.

Clad as were his mounted companions of the day in a loose green robe and a cap tied under the chin lest swift riding dislodge it, Vergil laid aside for the moment his curiosity concerning the Viceroy's words, and sank gladly into the rich and ceremonial activity. For the quest as such he had no particular taste or relish, but it was something new and therefore something to be considered with interest. And, most of all, the labor and concern of it made his incessant sense of loss and woe almost forgotten.

'Lymerers,' Count Phoebus called from his cream-colored horse, 'lay the dogs on the fue!'

'Ho may, ho may, hole, hole, hole!' cried lymerers and berners and fewterers. The dogs spread out, lymehounds and brachets straining and sniffing, alaunts peering – suddenly the hounds opened and cried challenge, belling and pulling. The chacechiens cheered.

A huntsman came running up, cried, 'Trace and slot!' and threw himself down on the ground and measured. Then jumped up with a look of chagrin, holding up two fingers. A groan, and shouts of 'Rascal!' and 'Folly!' – a hart below the age of warrant – and the company moved on. Almost at once, however, the eyes of the alaunts caught what the noses of the hounds had missed, again the huntsman flung himself down to measure the newfound tracks ... and this time scrambled to his feet, beaming, holding up four fingers.

'Four! Four! A warrant of four!'

The slot was four fingers breadth in width, one more than the three needed. 'Unharbor and imprime!' cried the Captain of the Chase. The dogs pressed forward on the trail, the footmen and horsemen followed – there was a shout, a crash, and 'the great, grass-fed stag,' his head crowned with wide-spread antlers, rose and reared from his harboring and bounded forward and away.

'There he goes! There he goes! Ecco, ecco!'

Two notes were sounded on the horn for the unharbor-
ing, three (by Doge, Count, and Sergeant, in turn) as the
first relay of hounds was uncoupled, and four – by the
Sergeant alone – as the hunt burst into full motion. First
the stag, flying effortlessly with his head well up, down
the velvet corridors of trees and turf, behind and well
behind him the first relay of hounds, the brachets and
alaunts; then the horsemen, Count Phoebus' long golden
hair whipped by the wind, Doge Tauro crouched upon
his black stallion with his knees and elbows out, the Lady
Cornelia as secure upon her side-saddle as if it were a seat
in her garden (and as grave, as lovely, as indifferent); then
lymerers, berners, hounds held, all others.

'*Cerf! See cerf!*'

'*See staggart! See stag! See cerf!*'

It had been observed that the stag was not sole, but was
accompanied by two younger harts – staggarts or brockets.
'*Rascal, folly, and herd!*' was the cry, and, '*Emprime the
esquires*' – the lesser, attendant deer – '*Make the rascals
void!*' The esquires were separated and sent away, the great
stag singled. The fewterers cried, '*Hark back, hark back,
so how, so how!*' and the chacechiens cracked their supple
charcions and began to whip at the few young hounds who
had parted to follow the folly; either this or the sounding
for this purpose of the *trururu, trururu, truru-truru* of the
recheat upon the horn drew them back in line.

'*Forward, sirs, forward!*'

'*Avaunt, avaunt!*'

'*Here how, friends, here how-suavely, my friends, suave,
suave!*'

'*Ecco, ecco, ec-co-o-o!*'

And again the *trururu, trururu, truru-truru* of the
recheat, the belling of hounds, the thudding of hooves,
wordless cries, the wind ...

Yet, still, the great red-brown stag ran with his crown
of horns up and back, ran so well and so well ahead that

he had time for a moment to pause and turn and look, standing at gaze. Then suddenly he bounded off again and was lost to sight as he harbored again in the covert.

And the horn blew the questioning notes of the seeke.

Seeing the pavilion at the stable-stand off to the left, Vergil left the quest and rode cross-park to the place – the stabling station, as it was called – which twice required keepers to undo nets and move blinks to let him pass. Sooner or later the stag must go by the 'station'; the course was so arranged. The hounds of the vaunt-relay waited there, and crossbowmen ready to be called if needed at the morte. Outside the sun was high by now, and hot; within the pavilion all was cool and dim and green herbs of fragrant scent were strewn upon the floor and the walls were green with fresh-cut boughs; there was fruit and cooling drinks and couches with silken cushions.

And there was Queen Cornelia and the Viceroy, too.

'Sensibly done, Lord Magus,' said he, breaking off some secret-seeming, sibilant discourse with the Queen and coming forward to greet him. 'For my own part, if I had followed the hounds much longer I believe I would have begun to bay. Enough of that. It amuses the idiot aristocracy and keeps them too busy for intrigue, conspiracy, sedition, treason – in short, art – if one may so term it – substituting for nature and to the benefit of everyone. Except, of course, the stag. *His* fate, if I may quote that irascible Israelite, Samuelides, "is predetermined and exact." Let him run wheresoe'er he will, however swift, however slow, he cannot escape.'

Cornelia looked at Vergil, and, for the first time, her look seemed timorous. He spoke first. 'It was not necessary,' he said. 'Not in any way. I would have helped you anyway. I thought you knew that. I thought that, however small a portion of your heart I had, you would have known that much.'

She shook her head swiftly, swiftly. And in a voice so low he barely heard, she said, 'My heart belongs to someone whom I dare not see ... As to the rest of it, I didn't know. I didn't understand, no, not at all. I'm sorry. But I can't undo it, things have to take their course now.'

'You saw me naked and afraid. How you must have despised me.'

Her eyes protested. Her lips denied. 'I cherish your friendship and respect,' she said. 'I hope I haven't lost them forever. But I was powerless to prevent what happened.' Her gaze, her thoughts, wandered, she seemed to look upon strange seas and shores. 'No man holds me long, save one. I would do anything for him ... anything ... except the one thing he wants ...' Vergil's mind asked, *Tullio?* And almost at once answered, *No;* asked, *Who?* but had no answer.

A dish clattered. Cornelia's head snapped up. She looked at him directly. 'I am sorry,' she said. 'But the mirror must be made.'

The Viceroy had moved to a table farther away and there busied himself. He heaped a basic with choice fruit, filled a goblet with snow-cooled drink, brought them to Vergil, and drew up a seat opposite the small table. From the golden case in the bosom of his robe he took a small, jeweled knife and began to peel and quarter a pear.

'The ignorance, the obduracy, sage, of the provincial ruling class of the present time, is hard for the truly sophisticated mind to grasp. I wince to reflect how many scores of thousands of ducats go into the annual maintenance by this Doge of his hunting preserves, his parks, his forests, his warrens and chases. And yet when it comes to paying the very moderate costs levied for his share of the upkeep of the Imperial roads as they pass through his own realms, why – Jove defend me! – if I've ever heard such bellowings and bleatings!'

Vergil said, cautiously, 'Roads, Your High Excellency,

are the very veins and arteries of the Empire.'

Something flashed in the Viceroy's eyes, and his face seemed about to open. Then it settled back into its accustomed lines again. And his voice, when he answered, was equally and noncommittably cautious. 'Indeed, this is so. You can easily understand, then, Ser Doctor, how important it is to the peace and prosperity of the Empire and its allies and confederates – we can say of the whole Economium, the western civilized world – that our roads remain open.

'Of these the Great High Road is certainly not the least in importance. If so important a traveler as the Lady Laura, the sister of the confederate King of Carsus, cannot travel this road in safety, then who can? Brigandage cannot be tolerated. Somewhere on that road is a place which spells danger to all of us. The Emperor – yes, *himself, the August Caesar* – wants to know *where*. And he desires to know soon. Now, sir. We depend upon you, on your art and science, to find this out for us. We would not incite your just contempt with talk of bags of ducats, or the like. It is by no means certain that you lack anything which Caesar can supply. Still …'

He paused. He smiled. He shrugged. 'It is by no means certain that you do not.' He passed him the plate of peeled fruit. Vergil took it, put one of the pieces in his mouth. It was cool and sweet and full of juice. The noises of the hunt, of the horn, came dimly to his ear, muted.

Presently he said, 'Well, Viceroy, I should be a fool if I did not keep in mind what you say.'

The Viceroy, with a quick, short, expressive breath, dismissed the matter. 'Let us see how goes the chase, then,' he said.

Below them and a long way away, they saw the stag break covert. The horns blew the two long notes, two short, two long and one long, of the forlange as the stag – through the long grass and through the short, beneath the great trees and down the shady glens – trajoined as he crossed and recrossed to confuse the hounds; proffering at the reedy covert of the fens, refusing, then making for the open water, and there descending. The horn sounded the veline. The stag foiled downstream, vanished, doubled back upon the land again and menaced a man on foot. The horn sounded the jeopard, the stag bounded off and away, with the hounds now babbling, now bawling after him, and the grim, gray alaunts still pressing on in silence.

Behind him now the stag left 'racks and entries' in the form of bruised branches he no longer took time to avoid, and of *imbosh* (flecks of foam). More, when now and then his slot was seen in softer soil, it was observed that it was wider spread, a sure sign of fatigue; and by and by, even in hard earth, the print of the oses, the dewclaws, showed that he was grown sarboted or footsore. Now the hounds picked up a good scent and were in full cry and good order, justifying the long, long horn call of the perfect. The stag at last came lurching by the pavilion, his coat now black with sweat, and then swerved aside from the hounds of the vauntlay, now at last loosed upon him.

'He embosses! See how he lurks and tapishes!' The horn sounded the tromp. The stag ran stiff and high. *'How, how, ho there, ho!'* And then at length the beast 'burnished and cast his chaule' – head hung down, mouth blackened and dry, he set his back to a hedgeside and turned to face the dogs, sometimes striking out with feet, sometimes with antlers, sometimes just staring. The horn sounded the weep. *'Bay, bay, he burnishes, at bay!'* The Sergeant came from behind and cut the stag's throat. *'Ware haunch!'* – the chacechiens whipped back the dogs, the horn blew the prise, the deer fell down and rose and fell and kicked and the berners dipped bread in his blood and tossed it to the younger dogs. The stag kicked once more and kicked no more. And the horn sounded the mort.

Somehow, Cornelia was on one side of Vergil and the Viceroy was on the other. 'What I did,' she said, urgently, intently, 'to you, I did because I was desperate. I never meant to hurt you, I was powerless to prevent doing what I did. But I swear it now, may I die as that deer died if I do not return what I took the instant I see the child's face in the mirror.' Her eyes beseeched him.

The Doge seized the beast by its great crown of horns and turned it over onto its back. 'Say, say!' he cried, grinning widely, 'who's to hold the forelegs and who's to hold the pizzle and who's to draw the knife to take say?'

As someone's younger son carefully 'took say' by opening the belly to see how deep the fat was, Vergil took a last look at the stag. He saw in it a symbol of himself and his own predicament. He could run. But he could not escape.

SEVEN

They rode along together, Vergil mounted on a white hackney, and Clemens on a sturdy, dun-colored mule which now and then rolled one wicked-looking eye back at him and snapped a mouthful of yellow teeth. Cypresses lined the road. Here and there was a tomb. They slackened the pace, read the epitaph on one.

Ave Julia Conjux Carissimma
Salve Ad Eternitam

'I would be moved by that,' the Alchemist said, 'if such things moved me. In all probability they fought like cats and dogs and he smiled all the way here. ... Did you get the letters of state?'

Vergil nodded. Out of sight, a shepherd whistled to his dog. There was an answering bark, a chorus of bleats, and the dull *bonk-bonk* of the lead-wether's bell.

The Viceroy's secretary had been incredulous and far from encouraging. 'Really, my sir,' he said, 'unless you go with the great convoy these documents are useless. The Sea-Huns will attack first and read letters later ... if they bother to read them at all. If they have anyone along who can read. Why *not* wait till next year's convoy?'

'There isn't time,' he had answered.

The Secretary's worried look had dissolved in a sudden relief. 'Of course!' he exclaimed. 'Doubtless with my sir's arts magical he will interpose something between his ship and theirs, and make it invisible. Or take the wind from

71

their sails – or make their oars heavy – or – or something like that.'

'If necessary … something like that.' And the secretary had handed over the documents of vellum and parchment, lettered in glossy black, vermilion, and purple; here, with seals affixed to the page, and there, with seals dangling upon ribbons tied through slits – all very impressive.

If the Sea-Huns paused long enough to be impressed.

Clemens' mule made another snap at him, and he gave it a slap on the muzzle which echoed, and which caused the beast to shake its head, and to subside, convinced, into relative good manners. Then he pointed, with the same very large hand. 'That, I believe, is the gate of the villa – but what, may I ask, is that arrangement in gray?'

Tullio, clad in gray silk, his iron-gray beard cut sharp, was waiting for them at the gate, mounted upon a gray charger. He was accompanied by two squires in gray linen on dappled gray ponies, and a pack of the small grey-hounds that were (outside of the Italies) called 'Italian' capered about them.

'It is her seneschal. You know of him. His name is Tullio – he's the one who opened the door to the conduits when I was here before, and let me out.' He said nothing as to what other door Tullio had helped to open. And to close.

'I don't know what you find to laugh at. The closer I get, the more impressive it looks.'

Vergil did not begin to explain that his laugh was an affected one; there would not have been time to finish. The company rode forward to meet them.

'Magus, I bid you welcome in the name of Her Majesty Queen Cornelia, Dowager Queen of Carsus.' He bowed from his saddle.

The bow was returned. 'Sir Tullio, my thanks. This is my companion, Dr Clemens, a savant learned in the lore of metallurgy, and a leading alchemist, as well as master

72

of music and many other subjects. He will help us in our present task.'

Various expressions moved slowly over Tullio's face. He was impressed with Clemens' title and attainments. He was *not* impressed with his mule. The contrast between Vergil's neat and fashionable cut garments and his companion's – which were neither – seemed to confuse him. He approved of Clemens' considerable size. After a moment be nodded, as if having digested all and come to a conclusion. Then, with a courteous word and gesture to the alchemist, he and Vergil fell behind.

Cornelia met them in a chamber floored and walled and roofed in marble of many colors. The lucent stone seemed to give as well as receive the soft flood of light in which her chair (it was almost a throne) swam in the center of the room. She had taken some pains with her toilet. The high collar of her robe, around which was bound a rope of gold, became her more than the lowcut garment she was wearing when Vergil had first seen her, under the great oak-tree. It was more feminine then the severe hunting costume she had worn at their second meeting, and – perhaps more than a hint of the native garb of Carsus being present – there was a certain vigor and splendor to the ensemble which was at the same time barbaric and sophisticated. Certainly there was nothing of the softness of current Neapolitan fashion to it, and this absence complimented her own decisive personality very well. There was a glow in her cheeks that did not seem altogether the result of cosmetics.

'I'm not Queen this afternoon,' she said, having greeted them, 'only Lady Cornelia. Please sit in my presence. Wine.' The wine appeared, as if conjured, was poured, served. 'Have you made progress, Magus? How near are we to beginning the work of the speculum?'

Vergil suppressed a sigh. 'Lady Cornelia, we are one day nearer than we were yesterday. I hope tomorrow to arrange for passage to Cyprus on one of the Imperial ships.'

A spasm shook her face for an instant, was quickly controlled. 'Another day and another day. My daughter is in danger, Magus – a danger no less terrible for being unknown. Why is it necessary to risk your person and to spend your time in making this trip to Cyprus? Why can you not, with your art magical, simply *bring* the ore of copper to Naples? I knew a nigromancer—'

'Madam, I am not a nigromancer.'

The serene and lovely face lost its composure, dissolved. 'Please do not vex me with these subtle distinctions, Magus,' she cried. 'I am in agony over the necessity of this matter. Each moment's delay may bring death so much nearer.'

Vergil bowed, slightly. 'The work will be carried on as rapidly as I am able to do it,' he said. 'But it is I who am doing it, and no one else – not even the Lady Cornelia is capable of judging or of correcting me in it. She may, however, if dissatisfied, dismiss me, and seek other assistance.'

She looked at him, her mouth open, her eyes lost. Her hands worked convulsively upon the carved lions' heads that formed the ends of the arms of her chair. Tullio placed his hand upon his sword. Clemens picked up, as if negligently, a marble-topped end table, and held it in one hand.

Vergil did not move from his place. His head slightly to one side, he appeared to be listening. The room went from sunlight into shadow, and, in the shadows, dim figures, which had not been there before, moved indistinctly. Voices murmured. The shadows grew darker, thicker; the obscure figures more numerous.

The Lady Cornelia's eyes moved from side to side. She opened her mouth, shuddered. Vergil, turning to that side of the room where the ghostly company seemed thickest, shook his head. Gradually the shadows dissolved, the voices fell away, the strange and umbrose crowd vanished entirely, and the sunlight was bright and warm once more upon the marble.

In a low, distressed voice, wherein there were now quavers and tremors, she said. 'You ought not to have vexed me with these subtle distinctions.' She threw back her head, gestured with both hands. 'I'm only a woman, I don't understand matters of science and witchery. There, Magus, on these tables, as you have asked, are all of my daughter's jewels and tiring-gear – except for what she has with her on her journey – for you to choose among. Shall I have them brought to you?'

He nodded, took a seat at a long board facing her. She snapped her fingers. Instantly, from right and left, servants came, bringing boxes and coffers and cases, set them down before him with their lids turned back.

'We can't use pearls and gems,' he said. 'Only things of metal can be of virtue in this work.' He waved aside the necklaces of coral, ropes of carnelians, beryl rings and bracelets; pushed away from him the heaps of rubies and emeralds, set and unset. Gold rings and armills which had no stones he kept, also plain brooches and ear baubles of silver filigree. 'Any of these will do, I suppose,' he said. But he seemed hesitant. His fingers moved among the gold and silver articles, moved uncertainly. Nothing ... nothing seemed to *feel* right.

Or, at least, not right enough.

'The Lady Laura has, as I suppose, so many, many things to wear—'

'She is the daughter of a king,' said Cornelia, 'and the sister of a king. Her grandfather was Doge of Naples, and her grandmother's grandfather was an emperor.' The lady's face grew prouder as she recited this lineage, and her eyes sparkled. 'Of course she has many jewels. What of that? Why should it be otherwise?'

Slowly, carefully, choosing his words, Vergil explained

to her exactly what it was that he wanted – something which the Lady Laura had had very often upon her person. With such a rich supply to draw upon, it was likely that her ornaments were constantly varied, none of them being worn very frequently. It was natural for her to prefer variety when she had it. But, was there not, perhaps, *one* single and particular item, an item which was not among those spread out on the board, but was nonetheless available; a favorite pin, perhaps? Or anything at all, as long as the missing young woman had worn it very often?

Cornelia listened intently, little gleams of gold glistening and sparkling about her, then she spoke words which Vergil did not recognize. Instantly, a maidservant left the room. Vergil, glancing after her almost automatically, noticed the marble-topped table which Clemens had hefted as easily as though it were made of willow withes. Clemens, Where was Clemens? Nowhere to be seen.

The maid returned, and with her was an old woman – an old, old woman, barefooted, shawled, some sort of ornament on one of her ankles tinkling as she walked. Vergil noted, with a start of surprise, that the crone actually had a ring in her nose: something he had heard and read of, but never before seen. She moved forward confidently, speaking without ceremony in a foreign language, and holding out a little box. Cornelia took it, opened it, wrinkled her face, gave it to another servant to give to Vergil.

'This is my daughter's old nurse,' she said. 'Her name is Desfiyashtsha – barbaric, is it not? – but she's a dear and faithful old thing. I'd let you talk to her, but she knows only the language of Carsus. She assures me that my daughter wore this almost every day. I'd forgotten she even had it, but now that I see it, I remember. *Tsan foa, Desfiyashtsha'n, Laura't?*'

'*Anah, anah, Passilissa'n,*' the crone said, vigorously, nodding her head, and gazing at Vergil out of tiny, dark, deep-set eyes, bright as a bird's.

'Yes, it is hers. Will it do?'

It was a small, worn, copper fibula in the form of a brooch, very crudely depicting a lion trying to shove his tail into his mouth with both paws. It was the sort of thing that might be used to fasten an under tunic. He picked it out from the box. For a moment he stayed quite motionless. Then he smiled, very faintly. There seemed a faint tinge of bewilderment in the smile.

'It will do, Lady Cornelia.'

'And you would really rather not have gold or silver or electrum?'

'It would not make much difference, really ... but, of course, copper will go into the flux very well when we are preparing to cast the speculum. It is not virgin copper, but so small an amount will make no difference. The addition of this article – which was worn very often and very closely by the Lady Laura – will physically connect her person with the speculum, which is to reveal where that person is at the moment of revelation. That is its only function. Its intrinsic value makes no difference, you see.'

It seemed as though she wanted to speak, almost strained to speak. Then an expression of absolute helplessness crossed her face. She slumped in her chair, made a helpless gesture. 'I see only danger, agony, death. I tell you that I know nothing of science or witchery. Please make the speculum quickly so that we can discover where – where my daughter is.' She got to her feet in one swift motion. 'Magus, I wish you well upon your voyage, and I will offer victims for your safe passage and return.' The formal words of farewell. Again she hesitated. 'I know you won't dally. Farewell.' With a final nod to Vergil, and another to Tullio, she swept from the room. He caught one glimpse of her eye, face half turned. Then she was gone.

Most of the servants followed her. Last to leave was old Desfiyashtsha, Laura's nurse. She examined him with curiosity, spoke to him in her own language, smiled in wonder that he really did not understand, and at length hobbled away, tinkling as she walked.

'Yes, but what is your *real* reason for having agreed to make the speculum majorum?' Clemens asked, insistently. The afternoon was sinking away as they rode back along the road to Naples. They would make home before night-fall, but not much before.

'Perhaps my real reason is simply that I have never made one before,' said Vergil.

His companion gave a gusty sigh. 'I'm glad,' he said. 'I hope it's really that, and only that.'

'Why?'

The sight of a fire some distance from the road revealed that what might have passed for a small hillock was really the mud and brushwood hut of some shepherd or farm laborer; and the smell of aubergines having their purple skins singed off disclosed the menu for supper. The few notes of a song which came on the wind were too faint for the words to be distinguished.

'Because,' said Clemens, 'I'm afraid the whole thing may be a wild goose chase – an elaborate, though mystifying, hoax. I'll tell you why.'

When Vergil had first begun to examine the missing girl's jewels and ornaments, Clemens, he said, suddenly became aware of that necessitious summons to which even kings are subject, and left the room to find a closet of ease. He asked his way of several servants, but they either spoke no Latin or had but a few words (' – and most barbarously butchered, too—'). He blundered into several wrong places before he finally found the right one.

'Do you remember that miniature which Doge Tauro has, and was showing all around at the stag hunt?'

Vergil frowned. Once again he felt the same pricklings of his flesh which he had felt when the Doge had snapped open the picture case. 'Of Laura as a younger girl? Yes. What about it?'

'That's how I knew who she was, you see.'

'Knew?'

Clemens said, quite calmly, 'Laura. The missing girl. She isn't missing at all. She's right there, at the villa. Don't tell me "impossible" – I saw her. She was five years older than the picture, of course, but it was she all right. Her hair was red, with glints of brown. And her eyes were brown, with glints of red. Very white skin, nice ears, nice mouth. Not my particular taste, you know – I prefer them either younger or older. Like cheese. However ... what's the matter?'

Matter enough for his companion to strike his thigh with the flat of his hand, causing the white hackney to break pace, in alarm. 'Upon my life!' he exclaimed. 'And by my father's ashes! I saw her too! How could I have forgotten? When I first saw Cornelia ... it was just a fleeting glimpse ... but no wonder I felt that odd stir when the Doge showed the miniature ... *yes!* She was dressed as a servant, sitting there at Cornelia's feet, holding the embroidery.

'And ...' He frowned, trying to concentrate. Shadows grew long, grew blue. What was it? The embroidery? Clemens' next words shattered the image slowly taking form.

'Dressed as a servant. Correct. Well, there you are, O Vergil, doctor mirabilis – are they trying to trick the Doge, or perhaps even the Emperor (may he live forever; though it's not likely – better King Log who does nothing than King Stork who'd devour us), perhaps even Caesar himself, into accepting a servant girl as a princess? If so, then this whole affair of the mirror of virgin bronze is so much flummery, a device to gain time while the girl perfects her role. And then Cornelia will pretend to have her sighting in the mirror, and – lo and behold! – everyone will trot off and "find" the semi-promised or twice-promised spouse at some prepared hideaway. ... Do you think that's it?'

Vergil shook his head. No. No, he didn't, couldn't, think that was it. The young dowager's intense interest in having the speculum prepared was too genuine, her concern too obvious and sincere, for him to accept Clemens' notion. But if that wasn't the real explanation, what was?

The alchemist had another question. 'Have you made any philosophical preparations for your work and journey? You surely don't intend to go stumbly, blind, do you?'

The Magus assured him that he had no such intention. 'I have gone through the Door,' he added.

Clemens nodded vigorously. 'Good!' he exclaimed. 'Good! Good!'

Going through the Door ... the metaphysical exercise of placing the mind or psyche on another level of awareness or experience, in order to find out what lies ahead, was often done through the medium of a dream. It demanded a state of intense concentration and projection, of which few were capable – and those few, not without long study.

'But of all the things I "saw,"' Vergil said, slowly, 'the only thing that made sense was what my old teacher, Illiriodorous, said.' And he told him of that.

Clemens listened, combing his vast and flowing beard with his fingers. At length he said, as they approached the Pompeii Gate of the Naples city wall, 'As to what you "saw" making sense, you ought to know that often enough these sights make no sense at all until one experiences them in the flesh. Sometimes, not even then ... not until later, looking back. And as for what Illiriodorous told you, certainly that makes sense, excellent sense. The act of looking into the virgin speculum is an act of catalysis. Whatever is done – anywhere, everywhere – is at once imprinted on the universal and omnipresent ether, which is present in each and every of us, as each and every of us is present in it. The rays of the sun are present everywhere, although it is true that one can see the sun only by its own light, as the wise Jews of Alexandria have reminded us – but one needs the lens of a burning-glass to concentrate the rays. The speculum majorum *is* such a concentrating agent, such a focus.

'But what Illiriodorous told to you is not in any way so important as what Illiriodorous did for you. It would have been a fatal act for you to have tasted his honey. That would have brought the metaphysical into too direct a contact with the physical. In the instant that you tasted it – had you done so – your psyche, soul, spirit, *anima* – call it what you will – that part of you which was *there* would have been trapped there, forever incapable of returning *here*. Your body might have lingered alive awhile, but it would have been a mindless, idiot thing.

'It would not have been the Vergil we know ...'

And the Vergil he knew reflected, half-wryly and half-bitterly, that the Vergil Clemens knew was hardly the Vergil Clemens thought he knew. How many Vergils or parts of Vergil were there? this particular part of this particular one wondered.

Dusk was upon them. Torches flared, were set in sockets by the Pompeii Gate. Slowly, ponderously, the great portals began to swing shut. They spurred their mounts, cantered forward. A soldier shook his head, gestured at them, lowered his spear as they still came on. Then he flinched, darted back, speaking over his shoulder. They heard the words, *'Vergil Magus! Hold! Hold!'*

The massy doors halted. The soldier brought his spear to the salute, half grinned, apologetically, as they trotted through. The men twisted their heads to look, then once again put their shoulders to, pressed on. The gates shut with a clash of iron. The bolts were dropped. They were safe in Naples for the night – where 'safe' was, would always be, a relative term.

'Let us be thankful, at least,' Clemens remarked, as they

urged their mounts toward the livery stable at the foot of the Street of the Horse-Jewelers, 'that the Vergil we know is still so well-known.'

Vergil did not voice his bitter and bewildered thoughts.

EIGHT

The admiralty office had informed Vergil's courier that Sergius Amadeus, Lord-of-the-Sea, commanding the Fleet of the South, would receive him and his request provided he arrived before noon.

Accordingly, well before that hour, the day after the puzzling interview with Queen Cornelia, he set out in state to pay his visit. No formality had been neglected. He wore his doctoral robes, and the golden chain signifying his rank as honorary member of the Senate; in one hand he carried the bag of purple silk, embroidered with the Imperial monogram, in which were his letters of state; and in the other was the bacculum, or wand, of hazel-wood, symbolic of his association with the Order. The Imperial Navy was not what it was, but ritual things were yet important.

He neither went afoot nor on horseback, but rode in a litter carried by six bearers, with two footmen preceding and two following; these four with staves in their hands. The whole team of ten had been selected and trained by a famous and luxury-loving old proconsul, Lentonius, when Governor of Lesser Nubia. Freed by virtue of a testamentary manumission, of old Lentonius, who also left them perpetual stipends, they hired out their services for special occasions.

They moved smoothly enough in the hilly, narrow streets, but on entering the broad and level range of Kings Way, they slipped immediately into their intricate and ritual pace, said to have been derived from that in use at the courts of the Candaces, the Queens of Cush, whose territory was adjacent to that of Lesser Nubia. They took a step forward, halted, drew the other foot slowly up to an exact parallel; paused; stepped forward on the other foot.

So they made their slow, almost hieratic way through the crowded morning streets. The people responded in their individual ways – some by ignoring the sight; some with awe; some with fear; some with shouted comments (not always respectful), and with quips, taking advantage of that tradition of Naples which held that Fate and Fortune – having bestowed wealth or power – compensated those who received neither with the right to be free of tongue about either.

So they passed by fishmongers with baskets full of squirming sardines; processions of schoolboys off to take lessons in archery, swordsmanship, or harp-playing; porters bowed beneath loads of charcoal; peripatetic vendors of woven stuffs, displaying lengths of yellow broadcloth and striped cotton; a squad of gentlemen cross-bowmen marching out to a target shoot; swarms of children with dirty arms, dirty legs, and dirty noses, who had never seen the inside of a school and never would.

It was one of those – or so he thought – who came running up and jumped and darted to attract his attention, crying, 'Lord! Lord!' A grubby boy who might have been ten, or perhaps a stunted twelve.

Placing his wand in his lap, the Magus began to grope automatically for a small coin, when the boy leaped up, seized the frame of the litter, and pulled himself in. The footmen broke pace and came to drag him out, but the boy eluded them.

'Lord!' he exclaimed. 'Your house is on fire!'

'What!'

'For true, lord – it burns, it burns!' Vergil called to the bearers to let him down, to fetch him a horse; instead, at a word in their own language, they wheeled about in an instant – the fore footmen clearing a way with shouts and gestures – and set off, back the way they came, at an effortless run. Old Lentonius had trained them well.

Soon enough Vergil saw the plume of smoke; he could not have told exactly that it was his house, but it was in the right direction. *Fire!* He thought of his books, collected with infinite pains and expense from all the known world. Of his machinery and engines, constructed with loving labor over the course of the years – there were not three men alive who could reconstruct them; perhaps there were not even two. He ran over, in his mind, the experiments and works in progress – that of the speculum majorum had barely begun, was only one of many: there were some of such long duration and great delicacy that to interrupt them even briefly was to destroy them. He thought of his cunningly wrought water system, his globes of light, his automatons, homunculi, horlogues, his mandrakes, his instruments, equipment ... his furniture and personal gear, his objects of art. ... And he thought of his three master workmen: Tynus, Iohan, and Perrin, any one of whom was worth an Imperial ransom.

And all of whom were flesh and blood – friends – had families .... .

News of the fire had spread, crowds were thicker, the footmen cried out their coming in unison, voices rising higher than the noise of the crowds, cleared a path for the bearers – who, saving their breath, spoke not a word, but loped along.

The Street of the Horse-Jewelers was a contrast between plan and panic. Some there were whose houses lay at the extremities, safe of fire for hours, probably – who had procured carts and wagons and were carrying their movable property to places of safety. There were others, such as Appolonio the lorimer, and the tavernkeeper of the Sun and Wagon, a notorious old rogue named Prosenna – whose places lay adjacent to Vergil's house, and these had formed a bucket brigade from the Fountain of Cleo. The leathern vessels, brimming, splashing, passed rapidly along the line of men, which vanished from sight through the open door of the House of the Brazen Head.

Shouts and cries, not all of alarm and fear, filled the smoky air.

From her roof, old Dame Allegra caught sight of Vergil, coming up from below as fast as the Nubians could part the crowd ('*Abrech!*' the fore footmen shouted, a cry as ancient as the Crown of Egypt; '*Abrech! Abrech!*').

'My lord!' she screamed. 'My lord! Greek fire! A charm! A spell! A tetragrammaton! Greek fire! My lord! Greek fire!'

The bearers forged steadily through the swarm till they reached the foot of the steps. A word – they brought down the poles from shoulder-height to the length of their lowered arms; before he could get out, at another word, they knelt. Vergil raced up the steps. They placed the litter down against the wall, stood in front of it with folded arms. Their dedication was perfect, but it did not include fighting fires.

The men at the door of the balcony of the great hall, from which smoke came billowing, saw Vergil appear in the midst. Before they could say a word to him or to each other, he had vanished into the obscurity where blackness was from time to time shot through with a red and orange tongue of flame. Sweaty, sooty, coughing, they continued to receive the leather buckets of water, to dash them forward over the balcony, to return them down the line.

At length he reappeared. 'Enough,' he said. 'Stop!' They had fallen into a rhythm from which his words could not remove them. He seized the wrists of the man in front. 'The fire is out!' he cried. 'It's out!'

They gaped at him. Then the man whose wrists he held said, 'Sir ... the smoke ...'

'The smoke will be a long time in going away. But the

fire is out.' He raised his voice. 'The fire is out! Men – friends, neighbors, strangers – I thank you for your work of saving my house. Let Prosenna bring out his best wine and I will pay for it, and for an ox—'

'There are embers enough to roast him, for sure,' someone said. A burst of laughter followed; died away, uncertainly, as they gazed at the buckets in their hands, suddenly become an encumbrance. After a moment the brigade took up its work again, now returning them as full as they got them.

From out in the haze, in rustic accents, perhaps those of a wagoner, a comment – 'You may thank us, sir, it be your courtesy to do so ... but we all knows it weren't our work as put the fire out. You'd only to return and douse it with a spell. All's we did was keep it in check till then.' A murmur of agreement followed. A familiar figure approached through the murk – Iohan.

'Master, it was Greek fire,' he said. 'A projectile—'

'Ah,' the countryman agreed. 'A sallymandros, it were. Bain't that a Greek word? I see un and I heard un, a-flyin' and a-flamin' through the air. I tell 'ee—'

'I haven't time, I must get back at once – the Admiral—' Even as he spoke, Vergil was moving. He glanced at an horlogue. It showed close to noon. He broke into a run. The floor was slippery with water, but he held his footing until he reached the stairs. And there he lost it ...

Sergius Amadeus, Lord-of-the-Sea, commanding the Fleet of the South, stood on the quarter-deck of his flagship and squinted shoreward suspiciously. Everything he wore was white and freshly starched. At length he pointed a hairy, freckled hand.

'What's that cockleshell craft approaching us so fast from astern?' he demanded.

Bonifavio, the ship's navigator, followed the gesture.

'An it please Your Lordship, looks to me like a Punic ship's boat,' he said.

The Admiral continued to look suspicious. He never fully trusted anything on shore, near shore, or coming from shore. 'She wouldn't be overhauling us if this damned wind hadn't dropped so damned low,' he said. 'Who's that aboard of her, clutching that gear in his hand and dressed in all that flummery?'

'An it please Your Lordship,' Bonifavio said, 'I do b'lieve it's that famous mage, as they call him. Vergil, he is by name. Them would be his doctor's uniform, what he's got on, me lord.'

'Damned chap broke an appointment with me this morning,' growled the Admiral. 'Don't like that. Shan't let him aboard. A woman, a white horse, and a witch doctor – bad luck, all three, on shipboard. ... Damn that wind! Where's it gone to?'

Bonifavio looked up at the drooping sails, looked aft to where the craft steadily gained on them, its four oars flashing in the sun. 'And it please your Lordship,' he said, 'the thought what's occuring to me is, maybe the mage has taken the winds outen our sails so's he could ketch up to us, in a manner of speaking, me lord.'

Sergius Amadeus swore, stamped his foot, but made no objection to a line being thrown to the swift, slender little shell when she overhauled his flagship. Then, suddenly deciding to make the most of a bad matter, he invoked protocol. Two trumpeters wound their horns and a company of spearmen presented arms as Vergil, not indicating by anything in his manner that his doctoral robes were filthy with soot and water or that the blood on his bruised forehead was scarcely dry, came aboard.

Vergil saluted the quarter-deck with his wand, extended the pouch of purple silk to the Admiral, who touched it, did not take it. 'Neptune's navel!' he exclaimed, throwing protocol to the winds. 'What in Hades has happened to

Your Sapience? Flood, fire, and civil commotion, it looks like. … I trust the Emperor's enemies were not involved?' he added, suddenly grim, seemingly prepared to put his ship about to grapple and board anything reachable on a heavy dew.

'You'd better come below, sir,' he said, pretending not to notice that Bonifavio had surreptitiously spat three times to ward off the malign influences, then dipped his right great toe in the water still dripping from Vergil's robes to attract the benign ones.

Briefly, in the Admiral's cabin, the Magus explained his errand.

The Lord-of-the-Sea was interested. 'Speculum majorum, heard something about 'em here and there,' he said. 'Be useful to have one on board to see where enemy forces are located. Sea-Huns, filthy swine. They stay out of *my* sea, I can tell you, else I'd hang 'em up on high, directly I catch them – only, of course, sometimes one *can't* catch them, skittering away like water bugs. Cyprus … Paphos port … Temple of Aphrodite … ah-ah, Doctor!' – here he dug Vergil in the ribs, guffawed – '*there's* the kernel in the nut, eh? No? Hmm, well, I'm sure Your Sapience won't take an old sea dog's little joke amiss. Surely you'll at least *see* the Temple? Respect all religions, is my motto, believe in none. Sensible principle. Still, you know, must say, after all, two thousand beautiful priestesses! All ready, willing, able – and I must say – dextrous! – to do their best to inspire male worshipers with love for their goddess, hah-hah!'

The Admiral's wind-burned face took on an added glow of recollection, which was, despite his disclaimer, almost pious. Then he sighed. 'Use of Imperial ships to get to Cyprus, quite impossible, sir, sorry, like to be of assistance. Impossible.'

'Why so, Lord-of-the-Sea?' asked Vergil.

Use of an Imperial ship, the Admiral explained to him

(looking up at the drooping sails with dismay, regret, and semiconcealed impatience), was impossible without Imperial consent. The Viceroy could no more give such consent than he could coin money or issue patents of nobility. Letters of state were one thing – pieces of parchment with pretty words on them. But to risk one of the Emperor's ships? Only the Emperor could permit it.

Vergil beat one fist into the other palm. 'So we must send to Rome,' he said, vexed. 'A delay of—'

Sergius Amadeus interrupted him. 'Sorry, sir, Rome's no good. Wasting your time, Rome. No official business been done for weeks by the August House, and everyone knows why … don't *you?* No? Surprised at Your Sapience. Well, sir, the Crown and Staff – that is to say, the Emperor – has a new girl, the Empress is wild, so himself has gone to Avignon with his doxy. He likes 'em young, always has, no secret. And herself is not only long in the tooth, but bad-tempered about it. That's a fault I could never abide in women, so why should the Emperor? Of course, this is just a bit of fun and games, this latest girl, it won't last – but the scuttlebutt has it that the Imperial marriage won't, either, don't you see… .'

Muttering polite phrases, Vergil rose to leave. The Admiral accompanied him topside. Again, the trumpets sounded, the spearmen presented arms, and Vergil prepared to descend into the boat.

'You understand, then,' the Admiral said, 'that withholding the ship is not of my doing. Rules, you know. Regulations.'

'Yes, yes. Certainly. Thank you for—'

The face of the Lord-of-the-Sea grew redder than usual. 'Then perhaps you'll be good enough,' he said, in a low bellow, 'to give my wind back! I've got to make my inspection tour of the damned fleet, and—'

The wind flapped into the sails with loud cracks. The flagship gave a lurch. Vergil almost tumbled into the boat.

Sergius Amadeus shouted his thanks. "'Ware the Huns!'" his voice came over the widening gap. 'No quarter! And don't pass up the Temple! Two thousand ...' His voice vanished into the wind, but his gestures were unmistakable.

The Bay of Naples was, for once, its famous blue. Rocked, but not violently, by the wind and water, Vergil pondered. The subject of his thoughts were the words of old, mad Allegra, which he had almost forgotten. 'It's the Empire that's wanted.' By Cornelia? It had made no sense at the time. How could the widow of an obscure frontier king, daughter of a provincial doge, aspire to the Empire?

But if Admiral Amadeus should be right, if his scuttlebutt was correct, if the Imperial Consortium was going to break up by reason of the Empress's inability to accept the Emperor's infidelity, then – then, perhaps more than just a gleam of light could be shed on the cat woman's quasi-oracular pronouncement. If there was a chance for a new consort to the August House, then there was indeed a chance at the Empire. The current consort had no interest in politics, had never used her influence for any more than the award of minor posts to members of her not very influential family. Nothing interested her greatly, except the Emperor – and she could not bring herself to recognize that he was not, could not, be separated from his appetites. An aging, angry woman ... *and a barren one!*

Surely, though, it was absurd to expect that Cornelia had any hopes of wearing the crown matrimonial herself? She must be older than the one who wore it now. Though was not barren ...

Of course. Of Course! *Of course!* Vergil saw again the curious, calm look that had passed between Cornelia and the Viceroy Agrippa at the stag hunt, when Doge Tauro – displaying Laura's miniature and so loudly boasting – had hinted, broadly, that he and Cornelia's daughter would wed. What could be more natural than that the daughter of a doge of Naples should desire to see her own daughter its dogessa? Why, that she should desire to see that daughter Empress; that was what.

The reigning sovereign never desired more than an excuse to slough off cares of state. How natural, how inevitable, that he should – via a new, young, and beautiful wife – let those cares slip into the hands of ... say, the Viceroy Agrippa. *He* would not object to becoming the husband of the ambitious dowager, the step-father-in-law of the Emperor. Oh yes, it began to make sense; more and more sense ... if an Imperial marriage were intended for the Princess Laura, then a great deal more was involved in finding her than maternal concern (which appeared nonetheless genuine) and keeping open the Great High Road ... .

There was a polite cough. He looked up, blinked, suddenly conscious of his sodden, filthy robes; of the fact that he was tossing on the Bay of Naples, a quarter of a league (or almost) off shore.

'Pardon me, Captain An-Thon,' he said. 'I'm obliged to you for your efforts. In fact, if I hadn't been lucky enough to find you and your ship's boat by the Water Stairs—'

'Yes. Right.' The Red Man continued to call the strokes, beating with his bolt of wood upon the gunwale, and, although absently, as deftly as any water bailiff. The oarsmen bent to their tasks, the cedar-skin skimmed swiftly over the sea. Vergil returned to his own thoughts, did not emerge from them until they were almost in port. Grain freighters in from Sicily and not yet unladen wallowed heavily in the clotted waters of the harbor, and then the oars flashed and the boat glided beneath a figurehead carved in the shape of a grotesque and heavily stylized bird.

'What ship is this? Why are we here?'

But An-Thon Saphir was already balanced on one foot

in a line, grasped Vergil's wrist, did not so much help as haul him aboard. 'Mine,' he said. 'Why not?'

Vergil suddenly had neither mind nor stomach for displaying his present sorry condition again to the whole of Naples. Clean clothes and a chance to wash off blood and grime were certainly available on board the Red Man's ship.

The Red Man led his guest to a cabin carved in cedarwood that came from scented Lebanon, and did the valet's part while Vergil stripped off his clammy garments and bathed in water containing nard and calamus. Offered his pick of the captain's closet, he chose a suit in the local and current mode – fawn-colored shirt and tights, and a black doublet with silver laces.

This done, 'I smell fire,' said the host, leading him to a place on deck where the sail had been rigged as an awning, for shade. They took seats on the cushions spread out upon a red rug, and the Phoenician poured wine and held out a platter of olives, raisins, and small dried cakes.

'I do not doubt it.'

'Each fire has its own odor ... and this one stinks of Byzantium. Have you been there, by some mage-like art? Or has Byzant fire been brought to you? A gift, I should say, which you did not request, and which brings to my mind what one of the priests of Tyre, Léo-Cohan by name, said during that fatal siege: "Beware the Greeks when they come bearing gifts."'

Vergil, nose dipped into wine goblet, reflected that mad old Dame Allegra had shrieked of Greek fire, and he told the Red Man so. The latter listened to his account of the conflagration at the House of the Brazen Head, then said, 'Well, certainly, it's possible that it was a salamanderos. But it's not likely. It takes seven years to hatch one, and, besides, who in Neapolis had the craft to carry out such a project? You and Dr Clemens. It wasn't either one who did this day's work.

'No – I think your man Iohan was correct. It must have been done with a projectile – a bolt of iron, likely, wrought to carry tow steeped in the Grecian fire. As to who is so skilled in artillery that his catapult could find your house at first attempt, I cannot say. An appeal or at least an inquiry to the Doge's Master at Arms might produce results. In the meanwhile you appealed to Admiral Amadeus. Do you care to say with what results?'

The bosun of the ship alongside, a black man, came to the cancel and, leaning upon his massive arms, exchanged greetings in the Punic dialect with Ebbed-Saphir; and stayed there, at rest, regarding them with untroubled eyes.

'He said I would have to appeal to Caesar, but that Caesar was disporting himself in Southern Gaul, beyond the vexatious reach of appeals.'

'Where will you get your ship, then, for Cyprus? Do you know of any private shipmaster who might agree to such a perilous voyage?'

Vergil shook his head, looked at the Red Man.

Who said, 'I understand your mind. And I am agreeable. It would be a straight commercial transaction – one thousand ducats for the charter, and the customary demurrage fees if we remain in Cyprus longer than a fortnight. The risk is great, and I can't chance – without protecting myself – missing my customary cargoes by reason of a late return. What do you say?'

In reply, Virgil gave him his hand. The man took it, then said, hesitating a moment, 'There is a condition. I can't afford trouble with the copper cartel. My connection has to remain a secret one. We'll have to rendezvous off Messina, and off Messina is where I'll have to leave you upon our return ... if we return.'

The Phoenician's ship seemed a good one. It would not be easy to get another. Vessels piled constantly between Naples and Messina, and it was worth the inconvenience. He asked one or two more questions; then gave his hand once more. 'Remember,' said the Red Man. 'No one must know. *No one.*'

'No one need know. And no one shall.'

The black bosun of the Sicilian freighter rowed him ashore. He spoke a word or two of Latin, not more; and, though declining with a grin Vergil's offer of money, accepted with an even wider grin a jack of wine when put before him.

The Street of the Horse-Jewelers had not quite returned to normal when Vergil got back. Though the ox was reduced to bones being cracked for marrow, the wine still flowed. Allegra's cats lay about her feet, too stuffed to move. She waved him a greeting, so busily finishing a spit of tripes that she couldn't talk. Flagons were lifted toward him as he passed, and winey voices pledged his health and commended his generosity. One or two offered to put out as many fires as he cared to name, at the same reward.

He felt a tug at the hem of his doublet, and, looking down, saw one of the swarming children who had gathered around the ox roast like flies. Doubtless they, too, had been given their share; if not, they would have stolen it. The state of this one's face – grease over the original grime – indicated that he had no complaints in this wise.

'Child, have you eaten enough beef?'

A vigorous nod. 'Enough for this whole year, lord.'

Acting on what he thought was a reminder that hunger, unlike ox roasts, was a frequent visitor, Vergil put his hand to his purse. The gesture made him think that he had made it more than once before that day. Boncar, the black bosun ... who else and where else?

'You are the boy who ran to tell me of the fire!' he exclaimed. The child gave a vigorous nod, looked at him with keen, bright eyes, large in his pinched face. 'What is your name?' he asked.

'Morlinus, lord.'

'I offered you money before and you did not take it. There is, in fact, scarcely enough money in Naples, to pay you. Have you a family for whom you want something done?'

Morlinus shook his head. 'I work the bellows for Lothar,' he said, naming a small baker of the district. 'He gives me bread and a place to sleep. But what I want – I'd like' – he hesitated, then words came out in a rush – 'lord, I'd like to be a magus, too! And I can't even read.'

The smell of the fire hung heavy in the house. To Iohan, Vergil said, 'I hope the damage was not great.'

'No, sir. Fortunately. But there was a loss of good seasoned timber.' Behind him, in the murk, an apprentice sat, still weighing bits of charcoal in the scale, still checking the hourglass before adding them to the fire beneath the closed vessel.

Vergil pointed to him. 'Was much time lost from that?' Four years the steady fire had burned, and there were two yet to go before the year in which the heat would be slowly reduced, then the six months of cooling.

'Sir, no time was lost from that at all.'

Vergil looked at the man's back. Thus he had sat and performed his careful tasks in the early days; thus he had sat, concentrating and carrying out when the projectile came sounding and crashing; and, while the flames rose and the smoke billowed, he – not knowing but what the very house might burn around and above and beneath him – or, rather, utterly confident that his master's craft and cunning would prevent any such thing from happening – had continued to sit, intent and diligent.

'Have him take his pick among the small instruments in my cabinet,' Vergil said. 'Astrolabe, horlogue, or be it what it may. If it is silver, have it enchased in gold. If gold, in silver. If neither, then in both. And upon the chasement let the engraver write the single word *Faithful*.'

He turned to the boy at his side. 'Morlinus, could you serve like that? Carefully, and without fear?'

The boy hesitated, then said, 'Sir – lord – I would try to be very careful-careful. But I would probably be a little bit afraid.'

The Magus smiled, 'Iohan, start this one off as a forge boy, and have someone teach him his letters – just Latin ones for a start. Greek, Hebrew, Etruscan, Saracen, Runic, the character of Bouge, and the others can wait till he has encompassed ciphering. If he learns well, advance him. If he learns ill, he shall have a place at the forge as long as he cares to keep it, with food, clothing, lodging, and wages.'

The boy gaped, wide-eyed, said nothing.

'If you learn well,' said Iohan, voice rumbling in his great chest, 'then you shall lodge with me. And if you learn ill' – he bent his huge arm till the muscle swelled – 'then I shall beat you until you learn well.'

Morlinus rolled his eyes, trying to take all in at once. He swallowed, Adam's apple bobbing in his scrannel throat, and in a thin voice he said, 'I give you leave.'

Again, Vergil smiled. 'Iohan, send word to Dr Clemens that I am leaving soon and would like to see him even sooner. Perrin, Tynus, judge when it is best suited that I speak to the men about affairs during my absence, and tell me a while in advance. You have helped me arrange my gear for a journey before, and I will have you help me for this one.'

But he had never made a journey like this one before, and deeply and dismally he knew it.

NINE

The phoenician was engaged in telling tales from his lost home's voluminous history once again.

'Our chief demigod was named Melcarth,' he said. 'In other words, Melec-Cartha, or King Arthur, the one who ...'

Vergil sat placidly, certain that no response was expected of him and that as long as he sat in a posture of listening, An-Thon would be content. Having many thoughts of his own, he remained quiet, not moving enough to have tinkled a hawk's bell. The ship rode well, the sea was clean, the sun warm. He had left Clemens in nominal, titular charge of the preparations for casting a speculum majorum – without ever stating or even implying that the charge was not intended to be actual. Left to do all by themselves, the chief artisans, though intrinsically capable, might well have become divided and resentful among themselves. This way, they would combine as one against the basically harmless vagaries and idiosyncrasies of the alchemist.

If Clemens had any notion of this, Vergil did not know. But some mild stirrings of reproach kept him from refusing the one favor on which his friend insisted.

'I am sending my gargoyle with you,' the great-bearded, shag-pate savant had said. 'It is a sacrifice, I must admit that, but I will be safer here without him than you would be. Up, Kiss the Magus' hand. Guard him in all things, obey him in everything. Vergil, may the Fair White Matron and her consort, the Ruddy Man, both shine favorably upon you. If you meet any in Cyprus who are skilled in the Spagyritic Art, inquire concerning antimony. I, in return, will oversee the work of preparation for the making of the maiden mirror. Since there will thus be no time for me to engage in any major work of my own, I will pass the few hours available to me, lightly – my editing of Catullus, my Galenical studies; and my transposition into current *modes* of music of the ancients. ... Up, Gunther! Up!'

The gargoyle had lumbered onto his hind legs and, with a slaver and a slobber, kissed Vergil's hand, then sank with a grunt to his common posture, and mumbled the ruins of a blood orange – his favorite tid-bit. It was long since that Clemens, returning from a consultation with the Druids of Transalpine Gaul, had come upon a rachitic mountain hamlet where he was obliged to spend the night. The place was in some degree of excitement – a party of hunters, out after wild goat, had met with a horde of gargoyles on a windswept plateau. The creatures fled incontinently, leaving behind one sickly whelp, which was captured without difficulty. The horde father, following at a distance, growling and lowing and making fierce gestures, was at length dissuaded by a shower of stones from further pursuit. Clemens had gotten the whelp for half a ducat and a flitch of bacon; and, by means of infusion prepared from the humors of bullocks, effected a cure.

Gargoyles proverbially seldom lived long in captivity, but Gunther was now in his second decade with Clemens. Great tongue lolling far out, bat ears either a-prick or a-flap, tushes sharp and given to clashing noisily, as near to no neck as made no matter, back covered with broad shoulders and forepaws (on the back of which he walked), short hind legs bowed, the talons on their spatulate feet clicking and clacking as he sloped along, casting suspicious glances from side to side, Gunther was worth a cohort in protection by his looks alone.

Vergil made the voyage on the Messina carrack without

molestation, arriving there a day before the rendezvous. He had acquaintance and other claims to hospitality there, to say nothing of what he might demand by reason of his letters of state. It seemed, however, easier all around to stay at the Great Serail, widely known as the finest inn in Sicily. The table was excellent, the gardens beautiful, the chamber well appointed and comfortably furnished and clean. He had had a curious dream that night, of a marble slab sinking back into the wall, and a hand coming out, of Gunther rising ponderously from beside the foot of the bed, shutting out his view. Everything was, of course, in perfect order the next morning when, first warm water, then breakfast, was brought in. Aware of some minor annoyance, however, Vergil, frowning, had looked all about before realizing what it was: a noise which Gunther had been making.

The gargoyle sat on the floor contentedly enough, chewing and sucking something. He glowered when his surrogate master demanded it, but finally and reluctantly spat it into his hand that Vergil held out.

It was a human finger.

Vergil finished his own breakfast rather thoughtfully. All in all, Gunther, though certainly useful on occasion, had better go; and go he did, on the Naples carrack, supplied with a hamper of blood oranges, which he crunched and swallowed, skins, pips, and all.

As agreed, Vergil had taken to water from Messina's Tartis Port, a small boat carrying him and his gear so far to sea that the City of the straits became a mere blur. The scent of oranges grew fainter, and a touch of a hot, dry wind passed over his face.

'The Saracen wind,' the Tartisman coxswain said, observing the effect on his passenger. 'It blows from Libya. It blows no good.' And would say no more, but only shrugged.

Presently a dark patch showed against the sea. Vergil

thought it was An-Thon's ship, but it was merely his boat – a tiny thing, no bigger than a scull, with scarcely room for two; the other being, to his surprise, the black man, Boncar. The Tartismen turned about with no word of parting, Boncar smiled his welcome, and the little craft skimmed along the sea. like a fish in search of sprats. The Red Man's vessel waited on them in the lee side of a tiny island which was all rock and offered only concealment.

'Greetings, patron,' said the Phoenician, directing, with a gesture, the lading aboard of the scant baggage. 'You left your lion ashore, I see.'

'My lion?'

'Rumor credits you with having embarked from Neapolis with a creature variously described as a lion, a gryphon, or a mandrilla.'

'Rumor, I fear, is scarcely as accurate as he is rapid. No, Captain, the creature was my friend Clemens' tamed gargoyle. I sent him back to his master, thinking that the longer sea trip might not agree with him. You have a new bosun, Captain.'

'Yes. The old one unwisely chose to dispute possession of a wench with someone younger, stronger, and more agile. Boncar, meanwhile, had become bored with ferrying sacks of wheat. Thus do the workings of the Major Principles arrange all things in ultimate order. You may have my cabin, I prefer to sleep on deck. In good weather it is pleasant and in bad I dare not stay long below anyway.'

The bird prow lifted oars, dipped its nose into the sea, and was off. The Straits were unusually quiet, for which all were thankful, and a loaf of bread was thrown over for the Prince of the Sea – one of his emissaries, a dolphin, appearing at once to claim it. A small sea monster broke water some leagues off, once, but made no attempt to break the sacred peace, merely staring at them with its great moon eyes before diving again. The waters were the color of lapis lazuli; in the distance rose mountains of a smoky blue-gray; the nigh shore was a dim green, and the off shore – far, far across the white wave seas – lay dun and gaunt. Clouds paced across the Heavens like giants' sheep, newly washed and fleeces combed; their dark twins and double-goers grazed upon the seas beneath. Here and there from time to time a flash of lime-whitened houses and thin plumes or clouds of smoke marked the settlements of mortal men

who must till the soil for bread, or perish.

Once the Tyrian lifted his red hand and pointed toward the crag shore. 'In that cave, patron, do you see ... ?' Vergil, carefully following the long finger, saw on the drab escarpment a black speck which might have been the mouth of a cave; he nodded. 'In that cave dwells a puissant guardian, the Cherub Dys, upon my life! When voyagers over the sea, being of good intent, such as lawful trade and traffic, are beset by that cruel fey which haunts the shores of that sharp rock – do you see, patron? there – so Dys, with his flaming sword, sallies forth and saves them. But if they are of bad intent, bent on war or plunder, or fleeing from the just wrath of the All-Maker, the Cherub does not help them. No, if any are able to escape the shade or djinn or daemon which dwells on Sekilla – meaning, in my language, the Rock – then Cherub Dys assails them, too, and serve them right, say I.'

Vergil listened, vaguely aware that the Red Man's tones and words now seemed, as he half-said, half-sang, these legends of his kith, far different from the manner in which not long ago he had spoken crisply enough of cargoes and charters, of fees, and demurrages. He realized, rather less vaguely, how little he knew about the man, his wishes, his concerns, and his brooding desires.

Presently the sun in his fiery ship (to use the figure of the Phoenician) descended along the equinoctial wheel (to use the tongue of science). The bird prow put into shore, the natives of the region assisted the rowers and the other sailing men to pull her up upon the sands for the night, received their customary dues, brought wood and water and some handfuls of capers – all they could spare in the way of victuals. The voyagers gave thanks to the Giver of all Things, blessed their ship's hard bread, dipped it in the salt, and ate their meal of oil and tunny, capers, wine, and cakes of figs. One of their number was picked by cast of die to stand first watch, the others hollowed out in the sand spaces for hips and shoulders, scattered herbs against fleas, rolled themselves in their cloaks, and sank peacefully beneath the weight of that grateful weariness welcomed by men who have taxed but not overtaxed their own abundant strength.

The dark came, the moon rose and set, the Ram trampled the black soil of the sky of night.

So simply and sweetly passed the first days of the voyage.

They had reached the wide waters of the Ionian Sea. Captain Ebbed-Saphir appeared upon deck with his astrolabe, as usual, and had returned to his cabin to consult his charts, when Vergil joined him. He indicated the chart just unrolled upon its ivory finials and said, 'A present from the Doge of Sparta. Where he got it I do not know, but certainly such a prime specimen of cartography never had its birth in that rude province. ... I intend, patron, to make for Zanto, or Sacynthius, for water and supplies. There we can decide upon a course for Candia ... and in Candia, concerning Cyprus.'

Vergil shook his head, and, while the Red Man looked at him in surprise, placed his finger on the map.

'Corpho?' cried the Captain. 'It is leagues and leagues out of our way.'

'We cannot continue as we are doing,' Vergil said,

'hugging a shore like a bait fisherman. At such a rate we might be months reaching Cyprus. I had not informed you, but inform you now, that my purpose is to demand of the Delegate of the Sea-Huns – who has his office in Corpho – a safe-conduct to his Kings, and to obtain from them a safe-conduct to Cyprus. That way we can travel on the open seas. The time required for these two side voyages will thus be more than made up.'

The Phoenician hesitated, considered. It was a bold venture, and a dangerous one, he said. He compared it to asking a riddle of the Sphynx. 'Nevertheless ... there is danger in any case, and if we succeed we will indeed save time. Very well, we set our course to Corpho.'

And he gave orders to the man at the helm.

Ernas, or Ernalphas, the Delegate in question, was a half-Hun, his mother having been a woman of the Goths or some other tribe of the sort. His residence was in a shore-front villa half surrounded by the groves of that fragrant citron tree for which the island was famous, but Ernas himself lived in a tent in the courtyard, surrounded by unshipped masts, old and new sails, grappling hooks, and other gear. He wore a silk robe and a cap made from the mask of a wolf, and as they entered he was standing an oar.

'Well, Pune,' he greeted the Red Man, in a tone contemptuously affectionate or affectionately contemptuous, 'what are you peddling today?' Then, turning to Vergil, he said, 'Shaman-i-Rume, can you don the bear's skin? If so, I will have the drum beaten for you.'

Soberly, Vergil replied, 'There are things, my lord Ernas, which a man might do which he would be a fool to do.'

Ernas squinted at this, pursing out his lips, then nodded. 'True for you, Rumi Shaman. Time I was a boy, it's recalled, Tildas Shaman, wise man of the Hun-folk in Atrian Sea, donned the bear's skin at Old King's funeral

104

feast. They beat the drum for him, I tell thee, and the spirit of the bear took him hard and held him hard. Grew shaggy and shambled, did Tildas Shaman, nails came out as 'twere claws. The drum beat, *tum-tum! tum-tum! a-tum! a-tum!*'

Ernas, as he imitated the sound of the Hunnish tom-tom, rose to his feet, half sank into a slump, and took on the exact stance and posture of a dancing bear. His eyes rolled up till only the whites were visible, his hands drooped from their wrists like the paws of the bear, and his feet, one by one, came up, came down, stamped upon the ground. Deep, harsh growls disturbed his chest; he coughed like a bear. Vergil felt his flesh shaken by a chill of fear. It seemed as though what pranced and snarled before him now was less a man imitating a bear than a bear wearing a silk robe. At length the man-bear slowed, sank to the ground, slept like a bear. Still Vergil stared, jumped back as the 'bear' leaped to its feet, once again a man enacting a story (so had history been, swift the thought came, before first drama and then writing had sundered the unity).

'By and by Huns grew tired. Time to get on with it! "Ahoy, Tildas, Shaman! Avast! Weigh anchor and make the neap tide!"' He kicked at the ribs of an invisible man on the ground. '"Awake, awake! Arise, Tildas Shaman, and prophesy for us! What said to you our Old King's ghost, and what said the ghosts of our fathers and our Sept-mothers?"'

Suddenly the man was a bear again, it rolled over onto all fours, snapping and clawing; it was a bear. It was a bear ...

Skimming the sweat of his endeavors from his face, Ernas took his seat again. 'Not another word spoke Tildas Shaman, ever. The spirit of the bear took him hard and held him hard and holds him yet. He put on the bear's skin and he cannot take it off. So! Shaman-i-Rume! It is a good thing that you said *no*, but it is also a good thing you did not say no as no, into my face, for a Sea-Hun does not care for that. Letters of state, why and wherefore?'

The abrupt transition did not catch the Magus off balance.

'To show you that I am on the Emperor's business as well as my own, and to obtain from you a pass to visit your Kings in order to obtain from them, friends by treaty of the August House, a safe-conduct to Cyprus and back.'

Ernas shrugged, picked up the oar on which he had been working. 'At this time there are no Kings for you to see. Ottil King is off somewhere, harrying the coasts of Little Asia. Osmet King is in Axand-i-Rume – how do you call it? Al-Axandria – dickering for more tribute. So, no Kings, no pass, no safe-conduct. Go.' His arm was half raised to point the way of their departure, when some recollection of his official role seemed honestly to settle down upon the man. Slowly and ponderously he dropped his arm, ponderously and slowly he said, 'If I can in any way, as Delegate of the Sea-Huns, assist the bearers of letters of state from the August House, of course I will do so.' But his eye was on the oar.

Promptly, Vergil said, 'You can. A pass to your King.'

Angrily: 'Haven't I told you? There are no Kings about!'

'There is one King about, as I assume from your not having told us he was away.'

Genuine amazement spread over the man's face, he frowned a second, puzzled. Then his face dissolved into a mass of moving muscles and he cried, 'Bayla King?' And he burst out laughing into their faces.

Afterward he had said, amusement still breaking his voice, 'So – you have heard of our famous monarch, eh? In all your great cities – Rume, Axand-i-Rume, Byzant-i-Rume, and Jerus-i-Rume – resounds, eh? The fame of Bayla King? Be so. I will give you your safe-conduct. May it be of much profit to the August House.'

And so he had ... two of them, in fact. A white horsetail to tie to the Red Man's mast, and a man of his own household to shout particulars to any Hunnish vessel which approached to find out what a Punic vessel did in those waters with the heralds' emblem at its mast. This man had the weazened, ageless look of all his folk, and refused (with a look too contemptuous to be scornful) to go below decks at any time. He passed the voyage squatting on the quarter-deck wrapped in a half-hairless old wolfskin. No one knew what he drank, if at all; for food he had in a leathern pouch with him some dark lumps of dried dolphin's flesh – a diet which horrified the Red Man's crew. 'The dolphin,' they said to Vergil, 'is the friend of man, and what man eats his friend? The Huns are no men at all,' they argued, 'but daemons, and this proves it.'

The shore camp of the Sea-Huns on the island of Marissus lay in a state of semi-somnolence. The guide indicated, with a grunt and a gesture, where they were to moor. It was deep water there, the broken crater of some drowned mountain, and the figurehead of their ship cast its shadow on the rough shingle of the beach, over the weed-slimed stones and the broken gray pillars of long past days. The hawser was passed through the eye of a stone post, the guide leaped ashore, a small crowd of pot-bellied children and old women gathered; and no further attention was paid to them. On the whole they thought it best to follow their former voyage mate.

Tents were pitched seemingly at hazard along the shore and into the pine and cypress woods, but there were few of them in comparison to the ships. Some of these had been beached for so long and were so unfit for sea that doors had been hacked in them and grass grew on their slanting decks. Here and there a man of fighting age sat, knees up, against a hulk or doorpost, honing a spearhead or a grappling hook or engaged in some other pastime work. But always, they noticed, he bore a wound which prevented his being out with the fighting fleets. There were few old men. Hunmen tended not to live until very old, preferring to perish in battle. But there were old women, and the old women were hideous. Withered, toothless, half-hairless, half-naked, their dried old dugs flapping as they nosed, bent over, about the camp, filthy and shrill, they epitomized the other side of the life of a race which despised what little they dimly understood of such concepts as love or grace or beauty.

Here and there captives of some other nation paused in the work of fetching wood or water and gazed dumbly at the visitors from the half-forgotten world which had not thought them worth the price of redemption; then went again about their labors. A stench of night-soil and stale urine and rotten fish, of ill-cured hides, dried sweat, old dogs, unwashed clothes, sour mares' milk, and other elements defying analysis hung over the camp. The Sea-Huns were said to bathe but once a year ... and on that day, it was told, the fish in all the circumjacent seas died in great multitudes.

Vergil felt he could believe it.

Like sea-wrack long after some great storm, the decayed fruits of their pillage and plunder lay strewn about the camp. Gilded furniture crouched broken and peeling, bolts of fine dyed linen served as casual close-stools, unstoppered jugs of vintage wine sat turning into vinegar, against a torn codex illuminated in glowing colors a scabby dog lifted its leg ... so it went.

The guide mounted the steps of a ruined temple and vanished. The Phoenician and his patron followed. The roof was totally gone, and in the interior was the largest tent either of them had ever seen. An avenue of horsetails, dyed red, dyed purple, black, and gray, led up to it. Through an opening in the top which let in a stream of sunlight, the two visitors, their eyes adjusting, observed the guide prostrating himself, rising before he was fully down, going through the motions of gathering dust and casting it on his head without ever actually doing so, advancing a few steps, repeating the process. And all the while he mumbled and muttered, yawning as if ineffably bored; and presently, raising his voice a trifle impatiently, but never ceasing his chant, he squatted on the great, and gorgeous, and filthy Bactrian carpet with which the pavilion was floored. He held his arm out horizontally as if to bar their further progress.

They halted, peered, squinted. Before them on a pallet of greasy sheepskins, clad in a doublet of filthy samite, mouth open to show a set (incomplete) of brown stumps which had once been teeth, a man lay snoring. They realized, after a moment, from the golden circlet topping the pole from which hung the last horsetail, and from the muted but still patently purple color of the doublet, that they were in the real presence of Bayla, King of the Huns.

Shabby as it was, the Presence was not altogether without its train of state or some notions of hospitality. Three scarred and limping men of his nation arose from the shadows at his bark (or snarl) when he awoke to find the strangers standing before his bed; these warriors-in-waiting, as it were, had been sharing the afternoon siesta with their King, and now added their own yips and yelps. Slaves and other members of the court came, though they did not come soon, and by the time Bayla King had cleared his nose and throat and laved his eyes in a little water and performed the other brute details of his scant and nasty toilet, something resembling a reception or audience had begun to be in progress.

Vergil and Ebbed-Saphir sat on sheepskins piled ten deep and covered with robes of fur-lined silk (doubtless once the property of some plundered Scythian magate). Wine had been brought, and splendid goblets, which did not match, fresh water, kymyss, ships biscuit, and pastries of colored sugar-flour which had once been soft. In one corner a woman sat cross-legged and sang something through her nose as she banged discordantly upon a timbrel, the while suckling a great child in her lap.

The warriors-in-waiting approached, introduced themselves, held out their hands. Baron Murdas had but one eye, Baron Bruda lacked most of his left arm, and Baron Gabron leaned heavily upon his spear to compensate for the severed Achilles tendon of his right foot: all three of them growled, 'Give. Give. Give.'

The bag of purple silk embroidered with the Imperial monogram and containing the letters of state was produced. Gabron seized it, gave it to Bruda, who handed it to Murdas, who opened it and dropped the documents in Bayla's lap. The latter stroked them with his grimy fingers, held them upside down, flipped through them as if looking for filthy pictures, then allowed them to slide from his hands. In a hoarse voice, which seemed faintly disappointed, he said, 'Emperor books, very beauty, very sweet. Great honor. Rume, Hun, big friend. Drink, eat. Meat, fish, soon. What name you got?'

His Thallasic Majesty Bayla, son of Bayla, son of Ottil, son of Ernas, of the Sea-Huns King, Great King, King of Kings, co-lord of the Seas and the Isles, was a flabby, pudgy little man with tiny and rufous eyes, a scant and drooping mustache. The left side of his face had been much worried by a knife, but not recently.

The Phoenician introduced himself ('Punic man good sailor, but all time peddle, peddle,' said the King, mildly amused. 'No peddle here. Hun not need buy, just take.') and his patron. Scarcely was he done when Barons Murdas, Bruda, and Gabron commenced again with their hands outstretched to growl, 'Give. Give. Give.' The guests produced their presents for the monarch. The Red Man gave a long knife, in the Sharkskin scabbard of which were fitted a small knife and a whetstone; Vergil's gift was

110

a pair of garters done of golden thread and adorned with Baroque black pearls.

Having donned the garters as bracelets or armills, and having picked his teeth awhile, meditatively, with the smaller knife, Bayla scrambled to his feet, beckoned them to follow. His warriors-in-waiting promptly sank down to resume their rest, and the woman (she was, they learned later, Sept-Mother of the Fox Sept and the hereditary Court Singer, and had incidentally – very incidentally – presented Bayla with his youngest child) the woman instantly ceased banging and shrilling, and adjusted her left dug to the babe's slippery mouth.

The sun seemed brighter. Back of the tent, following the King's gestures, they came upon an enclosure in which something was chained to a pillar.

'Vergil Shaman,' the King said, 'I give you good word. Take care. Not be like bad shaman. *Louse's bastard!*' he shrieked, suddenly, his scarred face going red with rage. *'Eater of swine's turds!'*

The thing in chains raised its head and then its body. It was the oldest, mangiest, shabbiest bear Vergil had ever seen. It grimaced and blinked and champed its almost toothless jaws and made little, feeble noises, then covered its face with its paws as Bayla, in a hysteria of fury, pelted it with sticks and stones. At that moment it seemed like a very old man clad in a very old bearskin, and despite the hot sun Vergil once again felt the cold sick touch of uncommon fear.

'Tildas Shaman? This?' The words were jerked from his mouth.

'Tildas Shaman yes! Tildas whoreson! Hangman Tildas! Tildas pox!'

Here it was, the bear which the whole Sea-Hun nation believed had once been a man. 'Why do you hate him so?' he asked.

'Why?' the voice of the King rose to a squeal. *'Why?*

Why hate? Why?' His mouth spittled and his filthy small hands clenched and unclenched in fury. Rage deprived him, almost, of his little Latin, and it was a while before he could make clear his meaning. Which was, seemingly, to the effect that Tildas the Shaman, by failing to assume his human and articulate form – and thus being unable to convey from the Old King's ghost and the ghosts of the puissant Sept-Mothers a message favorable to the pre-eminence of Bayla – had allowed Bayla's brothers Ottil and Osmet to usurp the royal power and reduce Bayla to his present impotent position.

'King!' he howled, beating his pigeon breast. 'Bayla, King, too! Ottil, King, and Osmet, King, but Bayla – Bayla, King, too!'

And so he was – King of the stinking shore camp, King of the old women and the potbellied children, King of invalids and cripples; of rubbish, flies, and scabby dogs – King. Bayla King.

There had been a sacred well used by the Greeks before the Sea-Huns had come crawling up over the horizon and squatted on the island like thick clots of locusts. The sides had fallen in through neglect, and moss was grown upon the rocks. Here, in the green and the cool, alone and unbothered, too solitary to be chafed by the comparison of what he was to what he might have been, Bayla sat and talked (calmer, now, after his outburst) to his visitors.

Would he give them a safe-conduct to Cyprus?

He would if he could – but he did not dare. His brothers – ('May they both have boils, piles, scurvy, saddle, galls, seasickness and black pox!') – his brothers would be furious. No ... no ... he did not dare.

A pity, Vergil observed. They had been looking forward to seeing the famous Cyprian city of Paphos. Bayla, at this, pricked up his dirty little ears. Paphos, eh. Where the great Temple of Aphrodite was, eh. Paphos – so they were going *there*. Ah-mmmm. Paphos.

'Yes, King Bayla. To Paphos, where the Great Temple of Aphrodite is – *and* the seven hundreds of beautiful priestesses – or is it seventeen hundreds? – all skilled in the divine arts of love and ready to make each devoutly amorous pilgrim a lover by proxy of the great goddess herself. It would be a meritorious deed to worship the goddess, would it not?'

'Worship goddess, eh. Mmm-ah …'

Vergil's eye met that of An-Thon; the latter at once declared how proud he would be to carry King Bayla to Paphos on pilgrimage. The little monarch refreshed his drooping lips with his tongue. His mind was working, at a slow and ponderous, but highly visible, rate. '… worship goddess …'

A scowl crept, draggingly, over his face. 'Ottil,' he growled, 'mmm … Osmet. Rrr …'

On the point of asking, rhetorically, he hoped, why the other co-Kings should object to such a pious journey, Vergil abruptly changed his plans. 'Unless, of course, King Bayla is not allowed to leave the camp without permission. … If he is a prisoner, in effect, of his brothers—'

So quickly did the *regius tertius* leap to his feet, so furiously raise one fist, so swiftly reach for his knife, that the Magus had no time to say more than, 'I die for truth!'

Out flew the knife. 'Up, up!' cried Bayla. 'Vergil Shaman, Ebbed Captain, up! To ship, to ship – now! We go Cyprus.' Rage a bit abated, determination not one whit, a corner of his mouth lifted the ruined side of his face in something which was not quite a smile and less than a leer. 'Paphos ho!' cried Bayla the King. 'Worship! We worship goddess!'

He drove them before him, as a dog drives sheep.

*

113

The three battle-battered barons were so dumfounded by the decision that they had not a word to say to their excited liege-lord. The situation, however, obviously required that they say something to someone; and they turned, therefore, upon the two visitors, hands outstretched again, palms up, fingers slightly curled in:

'Give, give, give.'

It was no time to hold off giving. They gave Vergil's writing case, Ebbed-Saphir's pocket astrolabe, they gave belt buckles and buskin clasps, knives, purses, amulets, combs, caps, cloaks. Vergil later commented that he had given everything but his virtue.

Supplies were swiftly laden aboard by the crew, and the horse's skull with black ribband through the nostrils fastened to the bowsprit – no Hun would ever presume putting to sea sans this potent talisman. They found the sea as slack and windless as a pool in the bottom of a cave, but the oarsmen rowed with their hearts and their bended backs, and scarcely let up the driving pace till the stench of the Huns' camp lay far behind with the smudge on the horizon that was Isle Melissos.

Free of the decaying influence of his court, such a court it was! – Bayla seemed another man. He proved himself a good sailor and even a brave though clumsy fighter, helping them through a gale off Farther Greece by his prompt seizure and careful handling of the tiller when the duty helmsman lost his grip and went tumbling arse over ale mug, and was the life and soul of the crippling and beating-off of a Sard freebooter south of the Cyclades. Time and time again Hunnish vessels approached, wet and pitchy-black sides gleaming with malice, sails the rusty color of old blood; but the royal standard of the white horsetail surmounted by crown, plus Bayla's stumpy figure on the quarter-deck, got the ship through every time.

But when the winds failed, Bayla could do nothing. Indeed, he went to sleep.

*

'Of course we can row, we can always row,' the Red Man said, more than a trifle impatiently. 'But my men are not slaves, to be used up, cast aside, and replaced. Hence, the amount of sea that we can cover by rowing quickly is limited. And there is the question of time. Always there is the question of time.'

It seemed almost as though he had taken Vergil's problems for his own.

'If it is the question of being back in Naples to pick up a charter,' Vergil said, stroking his short and pointed beard, 'I can only assure you again that, should you miss your customary cargoes by a late return, you will not be the loser by it.'

But the Red Man denied that time, though it must always be paid for, could always be paid for in money. 'And, sometimes, Ser Vergil, it has no price that we would willingly pay. Can you not raise the wind?' he demanded, abruptly.

No price that we would willingly pay. So well had his hired captain summed up his, Vergil's, own feelings. Caught up full, for a moment, in the never-for-long subdued anguish caused by the missing portion of his psyche, by the betrayal of the woman he loved most among women, he shook his head. Then, quickly regaining control, said, 'The influences are not favorable. But—'

Swiftly, An-Thon: '*But* then there is … something else? Then, do it, man. Do it!'

It was dim, down there in the cedar-scented cabin. From within a great chest of ebonwood Vergil lifted out a smaller one made of the puissant horn-beam tree, and out of this he took one of several caskets cleverly worked from tortoise shell. He placed it on the cabin table.

'This may not be pleasant,' he warned. The Red Man made an impatient, scorning sound in his chest, watched Vergil as with long fingers he carefully unwrapped layer

115

and layer of costly vine-wool brought from Hither India; soft and white as newly fallen snow; and uncovered something sere and forked and brown, and tied up hand and foot in a series of scarlet, silken knots.

Marveling, the Red Man said that he had never from his younger days till now seen any such a thing as a knot so utterly strange as (he indicated without touching) this, and this, and this, and this. 'And I am a sailor,' he said, 'and thought that by now all knots were known to me.' His voice grew lower. 'These are of another order altogether, I see. Are they the ones that bind the winds? No! You have here a ...' His voice ceased entirely. He watched.

The item was perhaps half the length of a pen, and of the thickness of about two fingers. It might have been the tiniest of mummies ever seen; it was thinly covered with a nap of hairs, and the legs were wrapped one around the other as if it had no bones. Certainly, it had no toes. 'I have here one of those called *al-rune*,' said Vergil. 'Also called perenose or perestupe.' He had poured red wine into a shallow basin and earth into a deeper one, and now, quickly, he dipped the thing into the wine and plunged it – feet first – into the earth and tamped it firmly down.

'Also,' he said, standing back and observing it, 'called mandrake or mandragon. It has many names. And many powers.' He watered the earth. He found the loose clew of the end of the scarlet silk and gave it the one tug that loosened all the knots. The mandrake moved. A faint shudder went through it. The tiny eyelids fluttered open and it peered here and there dimly and blindly and it grimaced like an idiot thing and the tiny lipless mouth opened and made a thin, dry sucking noise.

Vergil picked up a silver bodkin and pricked the ball of his left index finger and squeezed a drop of blood, which welled and swelled without dripping as he put it to the mandrake's mouth. The creature sucked and butted at the finger like a lamb at the dug. He pulled the finger away.

116

'Enough, homunculus. See clearly and speak plainly and obey me in all things.'

The homunculus smacked its mouth. Its gaze as it turned its tiny head this way and that was keen and no longer witless. It smirked and chirped and played among its hairs with its hands, which were single, root-like digits, each.

'Speak plainly!'

'The Queen of Candia cuckolds her lord with a stable-boy,' it said, piping, thin, yet surprising strong. 'Miso Yanis has a new customer for the red-haired girl. The boatman Carlis bends and strains, but not to his oars. Her name is—'

'Enough of that,' Vergil interrupted. The mandrake snickered and smirked. 'Scan the circle of the seas. Do you see wind? Do you smell wind? Do you feel, hear, or taste wind?'

The mandrake mused, considering. 'I see sardine and flounder,' after a moment, it observed. 'Also calamary and much sponge and—'

'Wind. Only wind. Seek wind.'

The tiny nostrils twitched in the bridgeless nose. 'I smell it,' the thing said.

'Where?'

'Off the coast of Little Asia, and it reeks of burning towns and rotting blood and the fearful sweat of violated maidens.'

The men exchanged swift glances. 'The Sea-Huns,' said the Red Man. 'Ottil King is busy there at work.'

'Not that wind, homunculus. Another.'

The mouth paused and pursed. 'I taste it,' the thing said.

'Where?'

'Within three leagues as the sun now goes, and it tastes of salt and spray.'

An-Thon shook his head. 'Rocks and shoals,' said he.

'Not that wind, homunculus. Another.'

The mandrake fretted and nittered. Then, it leered. 'The daughter of the Constable of Athens,' it began. With deliberation and without delay, Vergil thrust at it with a bodkin. The mandrake shrilled its alarm and twisted and tugged. 'A wind!' it cried, protestingly. 'I see a wind!'

'Where?'

'Two leagues and half again a league,' the thing whined, 'to the south and east! Between the south and the east, two leagues and a half again a league – a wind! Oh, warm! Oh, swift and sweet! A wind!'

The Red Man turned and bounded up the steps, crying orders. The feet of the men bounded across the deck and oars thumped at the tholepins. The water bailiff began to call the cadence. The ship leaped forward. 'Now,' said Vergil, to the man-dragon, 'you may suit yourself while you can.'

The eyes of the tiny creature gleamed like snail slime, and it spewed forth its sightings of centaurs and shepherd-esses, fisher-boys ravished by mermaidens, deceived uni-corns, dracos cozened of their treasures by non-draconian wiles … it piped and chattered and mewed. Then it paused awhile; then began again, in a tone of infinitely less inter-est, to talk of other things. Vergil listened, inclining his head on his hand, while, with the other, he occasionally incised a note on the wax of his tablets.

Suddenly the rhythm of the rowers was interrupted. A cry went up, again the running of feet, and now the hasty hoisting of the sail. The sail snapped and cracked loudly – once – twice – a third time. The men shouted in triumph. Vergil arose without haste and with his stylus scratched up a bit of wax, working it between his fingers. The mandrake eyed him with great unease as he approached, then opened its mouth wide. But before that fearful, fatal, maddening cry could issue forth, Vergil had (seemingly at one and the same time) popped the bolus into the tiny mouth, looped

118

the silken scarlet thread around the muted figure, and tore it loose from its fitting in the pot of earth.

The thing collapsed in upon itself with a convulsive motion. Another second it writhed. Then the knots once again bound it safely, physically and metaphysically, and it seemed no more than an ugly, curiously twisted root. With a flick of the bodkin he removed the gagger of wax, wrapped the perestupe in the vine-wool, restored it to the tortoise-shell casket, placed the casket in the horn-beam box, and returned the latter to the great chest of carven ebonwood. And then it seemed as though half the life went out of him, and he half sat, half fell, onto the chair. His face was ashen, and he gagged and retched dryly. Feeling as he had on realizing what his lady had done to him, he raised trembling hands to his face, winced, grunted in sudden pain. He looked at his left hand.

The index finger was angry, swollen, and red – except at the cushiony part of the first joint, where it showed a gray and purulent spot. Long he looked at it, with a wasted expression on his twisted face, before he felt strong enough to wash and dress it.

'I'll do that no more this year,' he said, at last. 'If, indeed, for many a year ... or ever again.' For a moment resolution showed on his face. Then, with a wry mouth and a shrug, it went.

'Cyprus!' cried someone on deck. 'Cyprus! Cyprus ho!'

TEN

Cyprus was another world.

The city of Paphos might have been designed and built by a Grecian architect dreamy with the drugs called talaquin or mandragora: in marble yellow as unmixed cream, marble pink as sweetmeats, marble the green of pistuquim nuts, veined marble and grained marble, honey-colored and rose-red, the buildings climbed along the hills and frothed among the hollows. Tier after tier of over-tall pillars, capitals of a profusion of carvings to make Corinthian seem ascetic, pediments lush with bas-reliefs, four-fold arches at every corner and crossing, statues so huge that they loomed over the housetops, statues so small that whole troops of them flocked and frolicked under every building's eaves, groves and gardens everywhere, fountains playing, water spouting ...

Paphos.

The air lay scented and heavy over this lush, sub-tropical scene, scarcely did a breeze vex the waxy red blossoms of the pomegranates, and Vergil, observing a slight frown upon the Hun King's open-mouthed countenance as he placed his grubby hand upon his chest, was suddenly made aware that he, too, seemed to experience a slight – just the slightest – difficulty in breathing. And wondered if it was really the grossness of the perfumed air ...

There was a man on the jetty, surveying with a languid interest the newly come ship and people. Vergil addressed him in his best Cumaean Greek, asking where the port officials were, and if porters might be obtained to unload.

The man answered in the slightly archaic dialect of the island, 'Surely, lord, anon ... tomorrow ...'

'Why not today?'

'Today, good my lord? Today is an high festival.'

Everywhere were evident the signs of neglect occasioned by the de facto blockage of the Sea-Huns. A fig tree heavy with ripe purple fruit grew in the middle of a roadway, a flock of long-tailed sheep grazed upon the docks, a wagon had overturned and smashed its wheel and lay where it had fallen, and moss softened its sides with velvet green.

'Aye, today, gentles, today is the natal day of Our Wee Lord Ichthys, own son to Sea-Born 'Ditissa, and folks have gone to feed the sacred spratlings in the Temple pools in his honor. Go you, too, get you bits of sweety-cake in the stalls, join the worship—' He gestured toward the great Temple, looming over the dreamy town. His speech put Vergil in mind of old Dame Allegra, and made him reflect that he knew nothing of her origin.

The problem of porters and port officials was settled after a while and after a fashion by the arrival of one Basilianos, the Smyrniote director of Paphos' far-famed Golden Hospital, that grand serail where pilgrims of rank resorted to be lodged in grace and comfort during the period of their devoirs. Secular visitors of sufficient wealth or status might of course be accommodated too – merchants, officials, young men on the grand tour, tax farmers, and so on. But the Golden Hospital, like everything else in Cyprus, felt severely the lack of traffic occasioned by the advent of the Sea-Huns over a generation before.

'Times were, Doctor and Captain,' Basilianos said, his litter borne between theirs by bearers who walked as languidly as lovers, 'when the Golden Hospital had an hundred guests of an average or common night – perhaps twice that amount at festival times. But today? Today, sirs, guests do not average more than one or two a night, and they mostly from Chitium, Amacosa, and other Island towns. Guests from off-Island we rarely have of more than that number per month, save, of course, what time the Great Fleet comes. We keep the Golden Hospital in first-rate condition, of a surety, we don't need to depend upon our guests for income, having our own ancient endowments. But,' he said with a sigh, and a wave of his hands, 'it is hard not to be restive when I recall our old great days of glory.'

They left behind the streets and their present scanty supply of people, most of whom were of an uncommon comeliness, an uncommon languor, and a most curious cast of countenance which impressed the Magus rather uneasily, the more so that he was unable to interpret it. They were about to turn onto a lane which led through the greenest sward imaginable to a dark wood of golden-fruited trees amidst and partly above which something seemed to float and shimmer and glister in the sparkling sunlight. A howl of such intense rage, of such horror and grief, as made his nape go chill and stiff, arrested not only his attention but the bearers in their tracks, and stumbled them to a halt.

An old man with unclad arms all bone and suntanned skin over rope-thin muscle had raised his fists to the level of his ears and now howled forth again from in his great gray beard. 'Wolves!' he cried, moan dying in his scrannel throat with visible shake and audible catch. 'Wolves and men! Men and wolves! Wolves like men, lord! Lord! And men like wolves!'

The bearers had recovered themselves and now started forward once more, with muttered comments and shaken heads. Vergil turned to Basilianos, who said at once, 'Do not, I pray, distress yourselves. Tis but that poor half-mad sectary, Angustus the Ephesian. I fear me for him and his little flock, their meeting-place is known to the Soldiery and cannot long remain unvexed by it.'

'Woe!' Angustus howled as they passed by. 'Ah, sinful city and oh, Island of sin!' His voice died away behind them. 'How beautiful! And how corrupt!' he was crying. Basilianos began to speak of the cool grove through which they had now begun to pass, telling of its origins, how it was of golden quince trees, descended from the very fruit which Hercules Lion-Slayer had obtained of the Daughters of the Hesperides, having killed their dragon sire in the beauteous and distant Garden. The voice of Angustus the Ephesian sank faintly into the scented air behind them, *'Oh, men! Oh, wolves! Oh wolves like men! And men like wolves ...'*

And then they were out of the grove and then the lineaments of the great Golden Hospital itself burst upon their sight. 'I have assigned to each of you a suite of rooms,' Basilianos said. 'Baths are being drawn and the servants will take your sizes and supply you with clean clothes from our wardrobes. Food will be waiting for you in your chambers. Our porters will go presently to fetch your gear and baggage from the ship.'

'Our interview with the King of Cyprus?' Vergil asked.

'His Sacred Majesty the King of Paphos is, by the rota, the present High King of Cyprus. I will arrange an interview with the hallowed Crown.'

'When?'

'Anon, Dr Vergil,' Basilianos said, urging him gently forward to the servant woman waiting to conduct him to his rooms. 'Perhaps soon. Perhaps tomorrow.'

Copper? It had taken the host some little while to consider if he had ever heard of copper. To be sure, it was possibly the chief industry of Cyprus – but what had the director of the Golden Hospital to do with industry? Copper magnates, ah yes, copper magnates had stayed at his premises often, when the Great Fleet was in. So ... copper? Ah yes. Copper. What did Dr Vergil have in mind concerning copper? Dr Vergil had in mind to obtain ore of copper? Indeed. Most interesting; one had not known that copper came from an ore. As to where copper might be obtained, Basilianos had no idea at all. One presumed that it was obtained at copper mines. And where were they?

Basilianos had no idea at all.

So, putting aside for the moment all thoughts of copper, as he had been obliged this while to put aside all thoughts of tin – and of the bird of gold and her message, and the two guardian falcon-eagles, and, indeed, the whole matter of the mirror and those royal ladies Cornelia and Laura – Vergil decided to join in worship at the great Temple of She Who Was Born of the Sea at Paphos. And immediately recollected that one of the signs and symbols of Aphrodite – and not one of the least – was a mirror.

'Do you not regret the waste of time, woman?' he asked, stiffly.

In the dimness of her cell-like chamber she shook her head, continued to pass her hands along his naked skin.

'After all,' he said, 'I did warn you.' Her touch aroused no more trace of passion than if he were an infant, but, just as an infant might, he found it comforting. He began to relax. For the first time since the horrid scene with Cornelia, he thought it might be possible for him to obtain complete rest ... despite everything.

'You are built like a greyhound,' she murmured. 'Slender legs and hips, huge chest. ... Warned me? Of what? Oh, of that. Greyhound, I didn't need your warning. Do you think I've been priestess of Our Holy Mother Aphroditissa all this time and can't recognize a man ensorcelled when I see him? Who is she? – the woman who has stolen that one of your souls? It has to be a woman. I can't imagine a man doing that, even thinking of that. And if a man did think of it, he'd shudder away from it, his stones would crawl. Wouldn't they, Greyhound?'

He even managed a short laugh. 'I don't know any

more. Have I still stones? The woman – you are right, of course. You are very keen. I'm not sure I care for such keenness, some things a man placed as I am now prefers not to have known – the woman beguiled me with talk of certain mysteries. I was weak enough, unwise enough, to yield. And thus came my undoing, priestess.

'Thus I lie next to you and stroke your breasts and your hidden parts and it is no more to me than if I stroke a kitten. ... Smite my lying tongue, O Thunderer!' he burst out in anguish, holding her tightly to him. 'It isn't true! It might perhaps not be so bad if it were. But although my flesh does not respond to yours, although that soul of mine which counsels that flesh is gone from me, still, still, enough memory remains, enough is shared in each soul and each part by every soul and every part, that still I do remember! I do, I do ...'

Her lips, her hands, her soothing skin, caressed him into silence. Great, indeed, was the power of Aphroditissa, sweet-smelling goddess of love, she whispered. But some things were beyond that power, and this ... as he must know ... was one of them. 'She can't help you,' the priestess murmured softly, pityingly. 'Any more than she can help the Paphos King. For he, too, you know ...' Her voice died away at his ear.

No. There was no great amount of rest for him here after all. No one, nothing, but his own efforts could help him. With something more than a breath and less than a sigh, he rose to dress.

'I can't help you, either,' she said, looking at him with her painted eyes. 'Or can I? I will, if I can.'

'Perhaps you can. I need ore of copper. Where can I get it?'

Her painted eyebrows rose in two great arches. Forgetfully, she cupped her breasts to him and rolled her hips. 'Ore?' she repeated, puzzled. 'Copper?' The absurdity of the question broke through her pose and emerged as a giggle. 'Good Mother, man, how should *I* know? Ore of copper. ... I meant, if I could help you with something important ...'

Entering the palace of the King of Paphos – who was, like so many Eastern kings, priest as well as potentate – was reminiscent of entering a temple. The air was still and hushed, what little speech there was was done in whispers. But the parallel was not exact in all things. 'Ditissa's worshipers had entered her great shrine in awe, true, but it was a pleasurable awe. There was no trace of any similar atmosphere in the palace of Paphos.

Vergil had been in fanes tended by men and in fanes tended by women, priests and priestesses alike were familiar to him. But at no other time in his life had he ever been in one where the attendants were hermaphrodies; indeed, outside of Cyprus, such creatures were scarcely known. And in Cyprus they were more than merely known: they were well-known. The strain ran in entire lineages of families, who tended to marry among themselves and perpetuate it. It was not regarded as a curse, it was not regarded as a blessing – it was a sacred circumstance, taken for granted, thoroughly accepted. How else were the semisacred priest-kings to be served, if not by the equally semisacred hermaphrodies?

They received Vergil with an intent, rather preoccupied calm, naked to the waist, small but full breasts and scanty beards providing a testimony to what they were, more decorous but scarcely less emphatic than complete nakedness would have been. They guided him through the ritual of preparation. Here he must doff his shoes, here wash his feet, here his hands, there perfume with incense both feet and hands, there deposit his gift/tribute/offering. The ceremony was long and intricate, probably none of them could have explained why half of it was done, and the explanations for the other half would probably have been thoroughly incorrect. And the Paphiote courtesies were but the prelude, for the Sacred King of Paphos was this year in addition filling the office of High King of All Cyprus: a special retinue for peripatetic hermaphrodies were charged with the rites appropriate to this higher office, moving from court to court as the office changed from throne to throne.

Preceded by sistra and cymbals and the tinkling and tapping of tambours, rather than by trumpets, the Paphos King at length made his appearance, his manner as bemused as that of a sleepwalker. Hermaphrodies surrounded him, their breasts rouged and their beards curled; they held his elbows and his sleeves and his cuffs, guiding him almost like some man-size puppet. In this manner, he spoke words which were not heard, he anointed, aspersed, spooned incense, fed lamps, touched with his sceptre, seated himself on his throne. It was a long time before Vergil was summoned.

His letters of state were shown to the King, who did not so much as touch them; indeed, he scarcely seemed to see them. At first, Vergil thought the man might be drugged. His eyes were glazed, his mouth was parted. A hermaphrody gave the royal arm the very slightest of touches, and the royal voice responded with the very slightest of sounds. It was indicated to Vergil that he had been asked a question.

'I thank Your Sacred Majesty for his gracious interest. The voyage was both safe and pleasant. We were accompanied by Bayla, King of the Sea-Huns, who, desirous of causing Your Sacred Majesty no inconvenience, is here incognito in the capacity of a pilgrim.'

A polite lie, in part. But Bayla would scarcely prove a figure congruous to the elaborate smoothness of this strange and hieratic court.

A ripple passed across the face of the Paphos King. His eyes seemed to focus on the man who knelt before him.

'The Sea-Huns ... we have heard of them ... when we were young.' A smile trembled, faltered, lapsed. A certain look passed between the hermaphrodies, and they turned their faces to Vergil, encouraging him by winks, by nods, to continue speaking. So might react the parents of a sick, sick child, he thought.

He did his best to interest the King, and to further his own necessities as well, by degrees turned his remarks to the subject of his visit here. ... Copper.

'Copper' – the King's thick voice grew mildly surprised – 'we ... we do not know why one would come here for copper. Is there no copper in Italy? Is ... is there copper here? In Cyprus?'

This was no mere bemusement. So removed from actuality was the numinous King that he really did not know of the rich mines which were the island's chief resource, which had given the island its very name. Next to copper, the chief reality of Cypriote life was the all but complete blockade which the Sea-Huns had, a generation since, flung around its coasts and seas. Yet the King, who was perhaps no more than thirty (a fair and heavy man), had not even heard of them since his childhood.

Before Vergil could reply to this, a terrible change passed over the King's face. A sob broke from his chest, and a low cry of unutterable despair. Features writhing, hands clenched on the arms of his throne, gently but no less firmly urged by the clustering hermaphrodies not to rise, the man cried, 'I am being bewitched! Bewitched!' Then words failed him, and he slumped down and forward and gazed numbly at the patterned floor.

At a gesture from one of his attendants, music was struck up, strange and alien music, and hermaphrodies came and danced before the throne, twirling their skirts and stamping their shoeless feet so that their anklets clingled and tinkled like tiny, tiny bells. The King watched vacantly, his head nodding a slow, infinitely sad accompaniment to the movements of the half-naked, half-numinous dancers. And the attendants began to sing in their curious, epicene voices, a song whose words were in a language which had probably ceased to be a living speech long before the children of Europa had first set foot upon the soil of Cyprus.

Presently the King rose, unhindered now, and, clapping his jeweled hands, went down the steps of the throne and joined in the quickening steps of the dance. Faster now, and faster, faster, faster whirled the King, flinging his head and rolling his eyes up till only a thin rim of color showed in the staring whites. The music stamped into a quicker, frenzied beat. The King leaped like a stag set upon by dogs. There was a hand laid gently on Vergil's arm. The hermaphrody gestured toward the chamber's door. There was a gray hair in the thin, whorled beard, and the breasts were fleshless and limp. The expression of his face was sad, patient, resigned. Hermaphrodies never lived to be old.

Moving down the long corridor, Vergil heard behind him a series of quick, sharp, rhythmic screams. He was sure that the voice was that of the Paphos King.

And so the time went on and continued to go. For a while An-Thon the Red Man made daily, fretful visits from the harbor, then he ceased to appear. Bayla was totaly absorbed in his devotions. Basilianos answered Vergil's urgent treaties with invariable politeness and assurances that he was prosecuting inquiries about copper with (he said, languidly) the utmost vigor. And the representatives of the copper cartel informed him that messengers had been sent upcountry on swift mules to make inquiries about the very small amount of ore required.

But nothing actually came of any of this.

It was not to be expected that he would be long content merely to sit still and wait on others. He hired mules himself, and set off alone. The palms gave way to pines

129

and cedars. Roses burned in great crimson clusters by the roadside. Here and there were the crude little shrines of the country people and their old, original religion – shapeless cairns usually set up alongside some low tree or large bush bearing fewer leaves than shreds of knotted rags, blossoming with the prayers and petitions of those who tied them there. Off in the fields the peasants, with long thin staves, urged the red oxen to bend to the yokes and pull the wooden plows. Chestnut and carob trees fed the black swine and brindled sheep. It seemed that nothing could really go much wrong in this Arcady-like landscape, stone bridges over brooks of bark-dark waters, cobs and pens and cygnets arching their necks like lily stems as they glided along the streams.

Nothing really much did go wrong, except that his mules cast a shoe each, it required a day to find the smith, find charcoal, heat the forge, find iron, heat the forge again, and shoe the beasts. He passed an impatient night, scrupulously followed the directions to the mines given him at the inn ... and, after another day's journey, found himself back in Paphos again. When this happened in similar wise a second time, he was bound to pause and wonder if he himself might not be bewitched.

Likelier – almost certainly – the copper agents simply did not believe him and his story of wanting no more than the small quanitity of ore for a scientific and philosophical experiment. Why should they? No one had ever come to them with such a story before. They might even have had word by a swift, many-oared blockade-runner, before Vergil arrived, from Thuraus Rufus; warning them that some plot to overturn the copper monopoly was under way; that Vergil, the prime mover, was not to be openly flouted, but subventuresomely to be thwarted in every way.

There was no consolation to be had from this logic, of course. The agony of his condition was not abated.

Impatient, here, he – what must be Cornelia's state of mind in far-off Naples? by nature yielding, by way of life imperious, unused to anything but immediate gratification, unaware of the difficulties in the way here at the scene. There was no assurance but that at any moment she might, either in a sudden rage, or by a deliberate calculation, or by direction of someone else, commence to torment that part of him which she held captive.

He remembered Tullio's words with a shudder. *Do her work, and I return it to you. Refuse – fail – I destroy it. Tarry – I punish it. Dally – but I do not think that you will dally....*

Yet now, in effect, despite himself, that was what he was doing.

Angustus the Ephesian received him half propped up on the narrow trestle board which evidently served him as a bed. The old man did not bother with conventional apologies or greetings, merely looked at him with his burning gaze and invited him by a curt gesture to speak.

'I have been informed that the meeting place of your group is known to the Soldiery. It might be wise for you to arrange to meet elsewhere.'

The old man at first said nothing. Then he said, 'Can it be that you have made it known?'

His visitor showed his genuine surprise. 'I, sir? No, sir. Not only would I have no inclination to do so, I could not do so, for I do not know where it is.'

Still the eyes would not relinquish their gaze. 'That is strange ... seeing that you have been there with us.'

'No, I assure you,' Vergil said, more astonished than before.

There was a pause. 'I do not feel that you are lying,' the old man said. 'Either you are mistaken, or a veil has been placed over your memory, or – or I may myself be mistaken. Wait, wait ...' He ran a thin hand over his long gray beard, reflected. 'Either you have been with us,' he said after a moment, 'or else it is the future I see, and not the past. In which case, you *will* have been with us.'

The room was small and bare. Vergil was faintly aware of something that confused him … perhaps only because he could not identify it. 'I do not understand,' he murmured.

'Nor do I. But I will. And so will you.'

It had not been the easiest thing in the world finding this strange old man. It was, however, obvious that no help was to be expected from anyone in established authority anywhere in Paphos. Therefore it became equally obvious that help must be sought from someone *not* in established authority … and the more distant therefrom, the likelier the success. Vergil had thought of attempting to contact the criminal level of Cypriote society, but – supposing such to exist in this easygoing island – it would be more sensible for those in it to take his money and then reveal the matter to the overlords, than not to. Who, then, was in such irreconcilable hostility in regard to the establishment that betrayal need not be feared and assistance might be hoped for?

The answer was Angustus the Ephesian.

Who now said, 'You came here like a trader, with intelligence in one hand and the other hand outstretched to receive intelligence in return. But that day has come when no trademen are seen in the Temple. Nevertheless, I shall give you the knowledge which you desire – give it you as freely as our Lord and Savior Daniel Christ gave His flesh to be torn by the lions in order that we might be saved and have everlasting—'

He broke off and gazed at the suddenly speechless man in front of him. 'Ah,' he said. 'Now you remember.'

'Yes. Now I remember, it was in a dream.'

The old man nodded. 'Then it has not yet come to pass.'

'No, sage. Nor need it.'

Softly, gently, 'Yes, it need. It need ... Now I see it all, I know it all now. Captivity, chains, torture, the arena, the mocking crowds, the lions. The lions! Think you-of-the-paynim that I or any of us would have it another way? We are not worthy only' – he lifted his clasped hands and tears filled his sunken eyes and broke his voice – 'if our blessed Lord Daniel desires nonetheless to grant us, freely, of His grace, the same death – oh, blessed gift and charity! – the holy privilege of dying as *He* died, the sweet and sacred bounty of the lions....' His face seemed radiant and trans-figured by joy. He bowed his head and moved his lips in prayer.

After a while he said, almost briskly, almost cheerfully, 'So now I will tell you that which you must know, though why you must know if I know not, nor is that among the things which I must know. All knowledge now is but imperfect. We see but the dim and dark reflection in the bronze mirror. Such is the life of this world of illusion.

'You wish to know why you have not been permitted to pursue a journey into the interior, is it not so?'

Vergil nodded, dumbly. The countenance of the aged Ephesian settled into an expression of mingled sorrow and wrath. 'Because, my unsought guest, because the road to the interior leads past the terrible, terrible shrine of the daemon whom the paynim denominate Zeus-Leucayon. Know you that name? And what it means? Wolf-Zeus! Wolf-Zeus! Fearful enough is his form in that shape of humankind which he counterfeits in order the better to deceive humankind, but, O! how infinitely more fearful is he in his lycanthropous form! Woe! Woe! Woe! O sinful city, and, O island of sin! Men like wolves and wolves like men!' And again he raised his eyes, his head, his hands and arms, cried aloud.

But his cry was brief. Vergil interrupted. 'Why is it considered so important that I be not allowed to pass this shrine?'

'Because, my guest unsought, in that grim, gray fane erected of uncut rock and dark with the stains of centuries of evil sacrifice, preparations are underway for the horrid rite wherein the celebrant offers his own son as sacrifice and as sacrificial meal ... and, for his pains, his punishment, and – as they would have it – his reward ... is changed into a wolf! A wolf! Is changed into a wolf! He eats human flesh like a wolf! Such are the paynim's ways, and their own records describe what happened when this was first done by King Lycaon, who killed a man and set the cooked flesh upon the table. Have you forgotten?'

The aged prophet began to chant the fearful lines. 'The King himself flies in terror and, gaining the silent fields, howls aloud, attempting in vain to speak. His mouth of itself gathers foam, and with his accustomed greed for blood he turns against the sheep, delighting still in slaughter.

'His garments change to shaggy hairs! His arms to legs! *In villos abeunt vestes, in crure lacerti-fit lupus et veteris servat vestigea formae.* He turns into a wolf, and yet retains some traces of his former shape. There is still the same gray hair, the same fierce face, the same gleaming eyes ... the same picture of beastly savagery... .'

'They say that this metamorphosis was ordained by their daemon Zeus, or Jove, or Jupiter – accursed by the evil names, all of them, he bears! – to punish that beastly and evil deed. And yet that daemon so delighteth in it that again and again throughout the years he requires it be repeated. Thus, the filth the paynim worship! O sinful city and O ...'

No moral hesitations were involved in the urgent desire that Vergil neither see nor learn of this ceremony. It belonged to the realms of the oldest payanism, where concepts such as good and evil did not pertain, where magic had no division into black or white. The deed was neither fair nor foul; it was potent; it was at the same time both fair *and* foul. Forbidden – abhorred – detested in any other time at any other place, in the time set and at the place set it became necessary and desirable and infinitely potent. The greater the sin, the greater (in this case) the blessing.

'And he,' said the aged Ephesian, shaking his gray head, 'he who became a eunuch for the sake of the Kingdom of Satan, he is so blind as to think that this will benefit him.'

Vergil, for the moment confused, could only show his bewilderment by his face, and murmur, '*He?*'

He, Sylvian, Chief Priest and (by definition) Chief Eunuch of Cybele, and head of the third side of the triangle which was Paphain religio-politics. Cybele, whose worshipers called her Magna Mater, the Great Mother, denying that title to Aphroditissa. Cybele, whose cult had come, shrieking and dancing, out of the darkest depths of Little Asia.

'Ditissa, indeed, was not the oldest of the Cypriote deities. These had long ago lost their names, perhaps had never had any; naiads, dryads, faint and fleeting little spirits of the woods and of the streams. But 'Ditissa's advent was both local and historical, she had been born of the foam gathered between the offshore rocks and the coast of Paphos, and had been worshiped long and contentedly. Pilgrims had come in entire fleets, passing o'er the white-waved seas, to offer to her great Temple and to embrace the Mother in the persons of her priestess-daughters. Throughout the changeless years the processions had passed slowly, chanting, through the Paphiote streets, group after group bearing palanquins surmounted by 'trees,' each leaf of which was made of a pastille of incense, smoking fragrantly in the languid air.

'Ditissa had been the Mother of all the land of Paphos; he who was both king and priest had been the Father; she, all goddess; he, partly god. The Greek and Roman pantheon had come to be represented, too, but in lesser wise. And then the Sea-Huns had swooped down, burning

Chitium and ravishing Machosa, as they did a hundred cities and a thousand towns elsewhere than Cyprus. They were at last bought off, but the price was paid in more than tribute; it was paid in semi-isolation, in gathering silence, in slow decay. In such a time the old religions seemed to flourish, but familiarity and tradition could not forever satisfy the need for excitement and stimulation, now no longer met by foreign intercourse. And in the stagnant pond, strange things came to grow.

Critics claimed (though not often openly, and never loudly) that Cybele's cult had been implanted in Cyprus by small groups of merchants trading in from Little Asia at a time before the Great Blockade had fallen across the horizon, and that in those happier days it had met with no encouragement from the peoples of the land. But the orthodox doctrine had it that 'Mother saw the children of the Island languishing in loneliness and grief, Mother spoke to her Sisters and her Brothers, saying, "Will none arise and go and succor the sorrowful children of the Island?", but none would speak and none would go. Therefore Mother herself arose and, gathering around her priests and *galli*, dervishes and devotees, took ship at Tarsus. The Sea-Huns clamored, the Sea-Huns threatened, the blood-red sails and death-black hulls of the Sea-Huns gathered around the Mother's ship like flies, like lions, and like dragons. But none dared approach, none dared attack. Silent and abashed and wholly stricken with awe were the corsairs and the pirates, overwhelmed by the heavenly beauty and the fear and dread of Mother Cybele ...'

And so on and on. What needed neither faith nor dissent to believe was that for years, from time to time, the peace and quiet of the opulent Island had been rent apart by the Cybelean theopomps – pouring down some startled street like a maddened torrent, the image of their goddess surrounded by screaming and ecstatic religious, tambour, horn and shaking systrum; and, drawing to them each fascinated eye, the *galli* – the priests! the priests! painted faces and thick falsetto voices, prancing, dancing, jiggling and jigging, ranting, chanting, gesturing, cavorting, prophesying and giving tongue in the unknown speech of the sacred madness: the priests of Cybele.

The gelded *galli*, the eunuch priests.

All this was quite enough in itself, but there was more. For these castrati did not hesitate by every conceivable (any by many almost inconceivable) means to inflame others with their own mania. It was chiefly of the women that they sought and received alms, but their main appeals were ever directed to men and to boys. And seldom had it failed that at least once in each hysterical, ecstatic session some deluded youth would be caught up out of himself and, yielding to the frenzied cries of 'Cast off the flesh! Cast off the flesh!' would seize the sacred knife and geld himself ... forever and forever after by this hideous consecration a priest of Great Cybele.

In its very horror, in its monstrous denial of nature, in its utter irrevocability lay much of its appeal. Men and women alike, to be sure shrank from the thought, but still they came to watch, to wonder, to worship. The thought that all this was for nothing was too much for the average mind to grasp. So great and terrible a sacrifice must surely signify something, something great, something marvelous. And so, meanwhile, the cult and mythos grew and grew and grew. 'Ditissa was still worshiped, and from her clergy little hope or adherence could be expected, they being women, all. Therefore the greed and guile of Sylvian was perforce turned in another direction.

He had never known what it was to be a man, his discarding of the flesh which makes men had been done before the first hair grew upon his flesh. His body had never developed, nor his mind, in the fashion of a man's. His desires therefore remained in many ways those of a child – but magnified and amplified and aggrandized by adulthood and the increased power of distorted maturity. It was not altogether strange, then, that it was not 'Ditissa and her women who aroused his envy and his hatred. The desire to increase his power, to place the cult of which he was the head on a higher footing, fell instead in enmity and implacable malevolence upon the figure of the sacred king – a man – and the figures of his servants the semi-sacred hermaphrodies who were his servants – and who were both man and woman in the same person, unlike Sylvian, who was neither.

'He is undoubtedly one of the heads of the great dragon which is called Harlot, Babylon, and Beast,' said Angustus the Ephesian, waggling his beard, his eyes now shining with a joyous hatred. 'Rome makes one head, Hun makes two heads, two and one maketh three, sacred by the es-chatological numeration. Sylvian is one head, Paphos is two …' He counted on his fingers and he smacked his lips.

'Your pardon, sage,' said Vergil, with infinite civility. 'I do not willingly interrupt your sacred mensurations, but I should like to know what connection you imply between the Royal and Sacred Paphiote Court and the shrine of Wolf-Zeus.'

Angustus looked at him with astonishment. 'Why, is it not clear? Sylvian wishes to crush the King and to destroy his influence. He also desires to entreat the assistance of the abominable older gods – they be but daemons – in assisting him with some privy matter that I know not, any more than I know yours. Who then do you think it is that is to perform the abominable rite of offering his own son as sacrifice and sacrificial meal? Who then is then to be translated from the world of men and changed therefore into a wolf?

'It is himself the King of Paphos. It is he.'

*

The moon had risen, a great yellow moon, riding the clouds over the yellow marble of the villa; the moon had set and the great stars burned and melted in the velvet blackness of the sky. The dog had barked in his hutch, the babe wailed in his bedlet, the ox had lowed in his stall. The ass had yet to bray in his yard or the cock crow on his roost, otherwise the audible watches of the night had been told as the Heavens wheeled around the earth.

Vergil had slowed his breath and lessened the beatings of his heart. For hours he remained immovable ... but not altogether motionless ... Vergil was being a shadow in a doorway ... and, as the moon moved, so the shadow moved ... slowly ... slowly ... slowly. One could no more observe the actual motion in motion than that of the hand on the dial of an hour horlogue. It was long, long before he restored breath and heartbeat to their normal rates of speed. Then he waited for his body to restore itself to its wonted tone. Having thus passed the hours in something close to stasis, he felt no fatigue. Some distance more or less directly opposite him the guard lounged and yawned at his post, leaning now and again upon his halberd.

Behind the guard at yet another distance burned a torch, smokily.

Underneath Vergil's long cloak, spun and woven and cut and sewn in Herborean Cymmeria and there dyed into that nameless color which is darker than black, was the device called a pembert, of which only Vergil himself and one other had the art. It consisted in a tiny lens-lamp and a tinier mirror set upon gymbals and a swivel. The parts responded to the slightest touch and tremor of a finger.

The lamp, a minute version of those globes of light which – never needing oil nor wick – illuminated the House of the Brazen Head, now answered to the finger's touch. A shutter slid away. A beam of light emerged, passed though a lens, was greatly magnified. At the same instant the tiny mirror, shifting on its movements, sped into place at a calculated angle. The man in the shadows made a practiced movement with his throat. His lips did not move. The guard looked up sharply ... looked straight into the eye of the lamp. Vergil's throat moved again ... his finger, too. The tiny eye of light vanished. The guard shook his head, puzzled.

But the shadows had moved forward.

Once again the voice which was less than a voice and other than a voice came from Vergil's throat. His finger shifted slightly on the pembert. The light appeared again, was not reflected in the tiny mirror, moved ... right ... left ... up ... down ... around, slowly, slowly, around.

And the guard's eyes followed It ... right ... left ... up ... down ... around, slowly, slowly, around.

He watched the moving light, his face slack, and did not seem to see at all the shadow slowly moving forward. The light presently vanished, the shadow moved past him, the torch guttered in its socket; the guard remained unmoving, staring. Staring. Staring.

Vergil expected to find obstacles, impediments, and delays standing between him and an audience with Sylvian; he was surprised to be told that no audience at all could be granted. There was no attempt at procrastination masked by oblique consent, no honeyed words urging postponement – the information was stated flatly, devoid of visible malice, but firmly:

'Lord, Sylvian sees no citizens of Rome.'

Basilianos was of no help. And when Vergil, with some half-formed notion of going by sea to another Cypriote port and trying to accomplish his purpose there, began to speak out his thoughts to Ebbed-Saphir, he found the Red Man, from some unknown cause, too tense and preoccupied to listen.

There seemed no other way open than the dark and mystic way he was now pursuing, although of course to

him it was based not on mysticism at all, but plain philosophy and science.

Through the grounds, first, then the corridors of the
Chief Priest's great villa he proceeded, leaving behind him
a train of bemused guards in a state between wakefulness
and sleep, partaking somewhat of each, but in its entirety
neither; and came at last to his destination.

There was a painted room, brightly, almost garishly
painted, as it might have been by a somewhat talented
child, with the figures of people whose faces – eyes round
as circles rimmed all about with long lashes, red spheres
for cheeks, double cupid's-bow mouths – were turned full
frontward but whose bodies stood sideways underneath
trees almost their own size and alongside flowers even
taller; with the pictures of striped and dotted birds, blue
dogs, red cats, green marmosets ... an almost insane panorama which yet arrested rather than repelled.

In the midst of the painted room was a vast bed and in
it lay a figure with waved hair and full lips, a figure which
was human-like, but as a great doll might be human-like.
This figure, which was neither man nor woman, made an
agonized face and turned the face away from him. But
when the creature groaned and opened its eyes a moment
later – hopefully, fearfully – Vergil was there again in
front of it.

'Still there,' it said. 'Still there,' moaned the epicene
voice.

Vergil said nothing. He had again been struck by shock,
as, when with Angustus the Ephesian, the cloak curiously
fallen over the sights seen when he, Vergil, had 'gone
through the Door,' had suddenly been lifted, and full
memory of that one scene returned. Now it had happened
again. It seemed that as he approached in reality the things
observed in the visions of the night, recollection of them
left him in order that free will might be reconciled with
predestination; in order that his choice of what he would

do be not influenced by his prophetic knowledge of what must be done. He reached back, now, in memory, to strive to recall other details, for surely the work of preparation called 'going through the Door' was intended to assist him: else of what use was it?

Rome! It snapped into his mind, almost audibly. The key was Rome.

'You have had this dream before,' he reminded the whimpering figure on the bed, sexless as a doll. 'You know you have, and you caused it to be written down and you referred it to the Wise Men and the Chaldeans and you consulted learned Jews and even the women who serve 'Ditissa. But no one has given you a good interpretation, not one.' It looked at him, consumed with woe and self-pity and a measure of genuine foreboding and horror. It wept a little and it sniveled.

'But now, Sylvian, this time it is no ordinary dream.'

He reached out and touched the soft hand. Sylvian jerked back as if burned. He screamed. He screamed.

'No one can hear you, Sylvian. No one can come to help you. It is now that you must come to terms. And I will tell you why you now must, in one word, Sylvian. *Rome!*'

The eunuch drew his breath in on a note of long, shuddering fear. His face became waxy and pinched. Vergil recalled to him the might of Rome, made the room echo with the strokes of the oars of the great armadas, with the rhythmic tramping of the feet of many legions. He thrust the forefinger of his right hand toward the bed screen, and instantly it reflected the shadows of a besieged city. On its crenallated walls the outlines of figures waved their arms in defiance, but nearer and nearer crept the great siege-engines, the armored towers, battering rams, catapults, lumbering on relentlessly, crashing and pounding. Then the darkness grew bright with flames, and billows of smoke veiled the scene.

142

'Shall I tell you what follows, Sylvian? The capture, the degradation and the shame, the fetters, the darkness and the stinking wet at the bottom of the prison ship, the marching in chains through the mocking crowds of *Rome*, Sylvian! A prize figure in a Roman triumph, Sylvian? How soft the soles of your feet are, Sylvian! How hard and how harsh are the stony streets of *Rome*, Sylvian!'

Inert, the recumbent figure rolled up its eyes and made little gasping moans like a woman in terror. Relentlessly, Vergil pressed on. 'But that is not the end, Sylvian. Common captives, they merely sell into slavery. But the chiefs and the princes, the leaders of rebellion and defiance, Sylvian, them they strip before Caesar, Sylvian – and they flog them, Sylvian – and then they kill them, Sylvian.'

'They fling them from precipices, they behead them, they crucify them, they give them to be torn by wild beasts in the arena, and sometimes ... though perhaps not often ... they dip them in tar and then they burn them, Sylvian.'

The Chief Priest of Cybele flung his arms over his eyes as if to shut out the sights. 'Why?' he cried. 'Why? Why?'

'Why? Only thus is mastery and empire maintained. It is not in the nature of any people that it should willingly endure being ruled by another people, whether it is ruled ill or ruled well.'

Sylvian cried, '*No.*' He rose in his bed and came toward Vergil, crawling and lurching, protesting that this was not what he meant. Why should Rome wish him ill? It was true he feared Rome, this was why he feared Rome, but why should Rome hate him so, why intend him harm? He came, humping and groveling to the foot of the bed, and there he cowered, begged an answer.

Vergil gave him a question.

'Why have you bewitched the King of Paphos?'

The eunuch sat bolt upright, his figure ungainly and unnaturally tall, his face askew, his mouth working.

'*Why?*'

Sylvian stammered that it was to destroy the King's resistance.

'He need not in any case resist,' Vergil said. 'He shall have nothing to resist. Rome will not countenance the ceremony to which he is intended to submit. How could you presume to think it would? Or did you? What! Rome, city-empire of the Sons of the Wolf! Is Rome to endure an ally king's consuming the flesh of his own child, slain by his own hand, and then to be changed into a wolf? No, by the wolf that suckled Romulus, the wolf that suckled Remus, it shall not be!'

The eunuch babbled of Zeus-Leucayon, but was cut short. From beneath Vergil's cloak came the bag of purple silk embroidered with the Imperial monogram; from this he produced the documents of vellum and parchment, lettered in glossy black, vermilion, and purple; here with seals affixed to the page, and there, with seals dangling upon ribbons tied through slits – each page embossed with the Great Imperial Seal of the Eagle and the Wolf.

'These Sylvian, are my letters of state. Do you see these syllables? *Himself, the August Caesar.* Read these documents if you like, but, read them or not, defy them at your absolute peril. In the name of *Rome*, Sylvian, and by the power which *Rome* conveys through me and through these letters, I now place the Royal and Priestly House of Paphos under my protection.

'And that protection, Sylvian, is the protection of *Rome*.'

The hermaphrodies bowed down and kissed his knees and feet. How much they knew, how they had learned, Vergil did not know, but it was clear that they knew something which was enough. How much the King himself knew was even more debatable. But obviously he knew that a dreadful thing had threatened, that it threatened no more, and that in some way the foreign wizard was responsible.

'My head is not very clear,' he said, dazed yet, but

thoroughly happy. 'But my faithfuls' – he gestured to the clustering hermaphrodies – 'tell me that copper ore is needed for your white wizardry. What this may be, I do not know, but I have ordered one hundred tumbrils to be put at your diposal, Lord Vergil.'

'Sir, my infinite thanks, but not even one hundred palms are needed. Sufficient ore to fill an ordinary bowl will be quite enough.'

The King pondered a moment. Then, with the some-times wisdom even of fools, he remarked, 'But if you take more, lord, then you will not be put to the trouble of coming for it if you should need it another time.'

Vergil blinked. So vexed had he been with the matter of this one major mirror, it had not occurred to him that it might be possible for him ever again to wish to make one under less troublous circumstances. It was, to be sure, not likely. But it was not impossible. He thanked the King for his generous thought, and agreed to accept as much as could be carried by a fast mule without slowing its pace. A pace, as it soon turned out, which was not long in delaying the ore from almost present appearance, from its storage place nearby. Now that circumstances had so quickly, abruptly changed, Vergil found everyone willing to discuss the mining, grading, transporting, and working of copper in all its aspects. Unless he exercised great control, it was clear, nothing would prevent them from telling him much more about copper than he cared to know.

He dined in the King's atrium on boned quail wrapped in grape leaves and the tender tripes of young beef dressed with nuts and herbs and young onions. Spiced wine was mixed with cool spring water and poured onto roasted figs, the mixture heated again in a closed vessel and poured into goblets of gold engraved with antique scenes. The conversation of the King was neither deep nor wide, but it had the interest of the curious; also it was a pleasure to observe his almost incredulous good feeling, the joy of his relief. And now and then he called a child of his to the table and fed him with his own hands of the choicest morsels.

It was while host was making polite discourse of local scenery, in particular of certain grovy hills on the road to Larnaca, that a thought which had been rolling about in Vergil's mind came to the surface. 'There is a hill, sir,' he said, 'not on the road to Larnaca, but on the road to Chirinea, at the foot of which there is a triple arch. Can you tell me anything about it?'

The reply was brief, politely disinterested, provoking. 'The phoenix sometimes honors it,' said the High King of Cyprus. But it was then that the copper arrived, in chests of carven olivewood, and there was no time for further discourse.

Messengers had already been sent for Bayla, and he was there, enjoying the rare pleasure of a hot bath, in the Golden House, comely serving maids rubbing the soles of his feet with perfumed pumice stone as he grunted delightedly. He had evidently worshiped the goddess to his heart's content, and put forth no objection to an immediate return. Now the company lacked only its third member, and word was brought that An-Thon was not at his ship in Paphos port. Where was he? Certainly not still at that hill concerning which Vergil had asked of the King – that hill, marked at its roadside base by the triple arch, on which Vergil (going to Sylvian's villa) had observed the previous night a great fire, and heard a cry of ecstasy; that hill from near where he might have seen the Red Man coming on his own return ... but so far was the distance and figure, so dim the now dying fire, that he could not be sure. And perhaps never would be.

But even as he used, pacing the tessellated pavement of the Golden House with growing impatience, growing – once again – the familiar ache and pain of loss within him, the Red Man appeared on the scene. He was quiet now, subdued, rather different from the tense figure he had been before.

'Ready to leave?' was all he asked. 'Right.'

The rich, drowsy city was apparently prepared to see them depart as placidly as it had seen them enter. But, just as there had been a disturbance of one sort only at their arrival, just so there was destined to be a disturbance at their leaving; and of a similar sort. Out from a narrow lane in the poorest part of the lower town poured a group of the Soldiery, pressing around on all sides and pushing on a smaller group of captives, who, far from seeming cast down at their situation, were braving the blows and curses of their captors by singing a hymn.

Yom shel chamath, yom hazeh
Hoshanna, Oseh felleh —

And there in the midst of them Vergil recognized Angustus the Ephesian. At his sharp cry the Soldiery halted, scowling at first, then merely sullen. The hymn broke off.

'Sage, I will speak immediately to the High King and have you and your conventicle released. Meanwhile, have no fear,' said Vergil.

But the old man, his eyes wide and his lips moving in protest even before Vergil had finished, broke immediately into a spate of earnest disagreement, the burden of which was, 'I forbid you!'

'I am not to be forbidden, sage, and I—'

'I! I! Accursed payan, is it not always *I* with you? You think to gratify your greed for power by interfering with the work of that dragon serpent which is called Harlot, Beast, and Babylon – but we will not have it! We will *not* be released, cheated of our promised reward in the arena. As much as we are for the lions, the lions are for us. I adjure you, in the name of Daniel Christ, not to interfere!'

Vergil took out his book of wax tablets, quickly and firmly incised a message with his stylus, handed it to the captain of the Soldiery. 'Take this to the King,' he ordered.

The old man broke into a cry of dismay. 'Do not do so, do not do so! Is this the reward for the good usage I have shown you? I desire this death, and no other. I have desired nothing else since that day when, seized by the spirit as I neared Allepo, I—'

'Sage,' said Vergil, a trifle coolly, 'it seems to me that in your own speech as well, there is overmuch of *I*. Farewell, then, and if one is not mistaken, you will contrive one way or another, sooner or later, to engross the cruelty you both condemn and court – if not on this occasion, then on another.'

The voyage back was neither marred nor marked by any untoward incidents. The winds were fair, the weather well. The only thing of especial note was the growing uneasiness of Bayla. Evidently the thought of his brothers' displeasure was now coming home to roost, ousting even the complacent satisfaction with which he looked back on his exceedingly vigorous pilgrimage in Paphos among the priestesses of Venus. And when the home island came into view, like a cloud at sunrise pink upon the horizon, he began to utter soft and plaintive little moans which grew increasingly anguished. At the approach of the first Hunnish ship, he made as if to bolt for the cabin, then bravely drew himself up and stood in full view at the bow.

There he was seen by the ship's occupants, and a great shout went up. 'Bayla!' the Sea-Huns cried. '*Bayla King! Bayla King!*' No trace of either wrath or ridicule was in their voices. He stood in surprise, and, as the men on the ship were seen to bow down and to strike their heads re-peatedly and resoundingly upon the dirty deck, his mouth sank open and his round red tongue popped out and licked his dry lips in bewilderment.

'What do you make of this, Captain An-Thon?' Vergil asked.

'I don't know. I don't know. I've never seen them behave this way except for Osmet and Ottil.'

'Osmet and Ottil …' The stumpy little king muttered his brothers' names, muttered something else, shifted uneasily from foot to foot. Signals flew between Hun ship and Hun shore, a triumphal dance of welcome broke out on the deck of the former, and now it seemed as though every vessel of the corsair fleet was making for the incoming ship which bore Bayla. Who cast questioning glances all around, continued his continuous questioning mutter, and seemed much relieved when Vergil and the Red Man took stands beside him.

Great was the multitude awaiting them onshore, where a platform of sorts had been hastily improvised. Some of those thereon were immediately recognized by mage and master as Bayla's chamberlains: one-eyed Baron Murdas, one-armed Baron Bruda, limping Baron Gabron. Plucking up courage from their presence, Bayla pointed to two other figures, a huge and hairy, rather ape-like person – 'Ottil, Ottil King' – and the thin one next to him, gaps between his long and yellow teeth, his bald head rising almost to a point – 'Osmet brother, Osmet King.' Bayla's finger moved, rested in the direction of an old and somewhat mangy, somewhat bearish man … and there the finger remained, while Bayla's mouth again fell open with utter shock. The one he pointed to observed the gesture and gave voice to an absolute howl, began to move his legs up and down in a shambling and curiously familiar way.

Bayla found his tongue. 'Tildas!' he cried. 'Tildas Shaman!'

The black boatswain tossed a line, Osmet ran to catch it, the oars backed water, the ship slowed, floated, Ottil hastened to tie it to the canting old pillar which served as mooring.

They walked ashore.

Suddenly, it seemed, no one was willing to meet them, everyone avoided their eyes. Then stepped forward the squat figure of the Fox Sept-Mother, the sometime quasi-morganatic-concubine of Bayla and ex-officio Hereditary Court Singer. She gave three claps to her timbrel, all fell silent, she began to sing. Bayla at first regarded her much ascantly, as if comparing her to the priestesses of Aphrodite, but then the burden of her song – evidently composed for the occasion – began to come through to him. Vergil, afterward, was inclined to give the little, squinting, red-eyed King considerable credit that in this infinitely important moment he bothered to try to translate for his hosts something of what it was all about.

Tildas Shaman, wise man of the Hunfolk of the Atrian Sea, had 'donned the bearskin' at the funeral feast of Old King, father of Ottil, Osmet, and Bayla. The purpose of his doing so was to obtain the final message from the Old King's ghost, and any message going from the ghosts of the puissant Sept-Mothers. But Tildas had not 'taken off the bearskin,' Tildas had remained a bear, Tildas had conveyed no messages, as a result of which the kingship had become a triumvirate – a triumvirate, however, in name only, with Osmet and Ottil sharing the power and Bayla receiving only titular honors. Honors which did not prevent his being despised, mocked, abused. So it had gone, this much they already knew.

But while they were off to Cyprus, something had happened. The Fox-Mother was awakened one morning by the slave whose daily chore it was to bring food and drink to the long-chained Tildas-bear, and, following the frightened servitor, found chained to the pillar no bear at all, but the bewildered and angry figure of Tildas-man himself. Why the metamorphosis had been so long delayed, neither he nor anyone else knew ... or cared. It had occurred; that was sufficient. And the message so long delayed was more than sufficient.

Videlicet, that it was and had been all along the pleasure of the defunct Old King and the ghosts of the puissant Sept-Mothers that Bayla alone be King, and that Osmet and Ottil serve him in all things.

The shrilling of the song and the banging of the timbrel came to an abrupt end. The silence was shattered by a great cry of 'Bayla! Bayla! Bayla King!' And Bayla drew in his breath and drew himself up and looked at his usurpatous brothers and they cringed, they groveled before him.

'It would seem,' said the Red Man thoughtfully, as Bayla proceeded to give them each a hasty, hearty kick and a sidelong look and snarl, which promised more close attention at a later date, 'it would seem, Ser Vergil, that you now have a powerful friend at court indeed.'

ELEVEN

But there were no great tidings awaiting them as they made their last landfall, although from the once again increasing tenseness of the Red Man, who might have thought he expected such. No visible disappointment showed in his ruddy face, however, and Vergil – after reflecting briefly that, did he but know the Phoenician's worry … did the latter but know his … it might well be that neither of them would exchange – saw only the well-remembered beauty of the Bay, Vesuvio's white plume and Capri's purple rock, ancient and teeming Neapolis climbing her steepy hills above the harbors thick with shipping. In order that they should not be seen together on ship in Naples, they set a course for Pompeii, where Vergil was to go ashore.

A breeze touched their faces. 'And I smell the rotting garbage and the man-stale in the streets,' he said.

'This, too, is life,' said Vergil, after a slight pause.

The reaction astonished him. An-Thon Ebbed-Saphir's face twisted and suddenly he seemed a thousand years old. 'Oh, Melcarth!' he groaned. 'Oh, Tyrian Hercules! Life! Life!' He gazed inland, mouth open in silent pain, as if seeking an answer. But none came; nothing and no one came – save only the harbor master's clerk, seeking the manifest of the vessel, a possible bribe, and a probable free meal and at least a glass of wine.

'What is this?' the clerk exclaimed, surprised. 'You left in ballast and you return in ballast? No cargo? No cargo? What kind of business—'

Vergil flicked the corner of his cape, showing briefly

the purple silk pouch with the monogram. 'Imperial business ...'

'Pardon, pardon, pardon ...' The man's voice died away as he stepped back, raising his hands and his eyes. But he was a true son of the city, and genuine reproach was in his voice as he said, 'You might at least have brought a few women ...'

All that Captain Ebbed-Saphir said as he and Vergil parted, was 'We shall see each other again.'

And, 'We must see each other again,' with a slight emphasis on the second word, Vergil answered; adding only that payment was ready at any time in the House of the Brazen Head. The curt, bother-me-not nod he received put him in mind at once of the Phoenician captain's comments, when they were becalmed, of time and the payment therefore not being always tellable in money.

When he was in his own familiar street again, at his own house, 'Watcher, what news?' he asked the guardian Head.

Whose eyes and mouth opened, moved, focused, spoke, saying, 'Master, news from Tartis.'

This was confirmed soon enough by Clemens himself. The alchemist was seated in his favored corner of Vergil's favored room, his leg crossed at an angle which put his left foot almost under his right ear, and he hummed and tutted to himself contentedly as he read from a small book. Looking up brightly at his friend's entrance, he sang out, 'What say you, Vergil, shall we attempt to employ ash of basilisk in this process? Ah ... before you answer and before I forget ... it's come. What was sent to Tinland for. Now ... ash of basilisk ...'

But Vergil was not yet ready to discuss ash of basilisk. He sank into his chair with ineffable relief. 'The bird of gold, the messenger bird, it's returned?' Clemens slowly revolved his massy, maned head. A touch of cold was felt on Vergil's heart. Had he now, having after all obtained the copper by going himself to Cyprus, to attempt himself the more than fabulous journey to Tinland? 'But you said—'

'I said not "What was sent to Tinland," but, "What was sent to Tinland *for*." That is, the tin itself. No, sadly, that curious and so useful creature never returned, and only one of the guardian falcon-eaglets … sadly battered, sadly torn, but bearing a purse of ore. The Tartisman called the Master of the Air was sadly bitter, I'm afraid. Now, concerning ash of basilisk …'

Concerning this substance, the great authority Roger of Tayfield felt it necessary carefully to distinguish between cockatrices and basilisks. The former hatch from the tiny eggs laid by old cocks on rare occasions, and are merely venomous, their ashes being antidotes to poison: but being thus dangerous – that if no poison were actually present to be counteracted, the patient might die instead from the poison of the cockatrice ash. Basilisks, however, were hatched from the eggs of certain hens, which, not withstanding they be so old that the cocks no longer tread them, in their unnatural lust seek out and gender with toads. That these unions are approved by the King of Hell – says Roger – is shown by the chicks having a tiny crest in the shape of a crown, whence their name from *Basil*, king. However, as the gaze of the living creatures causes almost instant calcification or petrification, it is customary to put them into opaque containers just before they hatch … else it is necessary to approach them from behind, walking backward … looking into a mirror … If these basilisks are burned to ashes they are of great effect in the making of gold and in other great work among metals. Thus, Roger.

'No,' Vergil said, bitterly, 'I think not. The whole thing is far too chancy and uncertain. There is so much which *must* be done. Concerning which, my Clemens—'

The alchemist, who had been nodding assent, lips pursed, now lowered his leg and sat up straight, rubbing

154

his hands. 'I think you will be well pleased with the preparations. We have, first, enclosed the larger portion of the yard and thus created a new workroom, untainted by the residues of any previous works. I have had windows installed of thin panes of alabaster which will admit a light clear and yet not harsh. Lamps have been hung and new ones, too, also chimneys of the same alabaster. The furnace is prepared, the hearth, the wood and charcoal, the kiln, the tools and implements, anvil and forge, sand and clay and wax, benches and wheels and iron. We have gotten ready, also, vessels of the finest earth, almost like glass, but less fragile. There are liquors of lye and potash, and pickles of aquafortis or oil of vitriol, as you may prefer, even sawdust of boxwood.'

Softly, Vergil said, 'Good ... good ...'

Stroking his huge beard with his huge hand, Clemens said, cheerfully, 'I shall think the less of you if you do not check every item as carefully as if I had never seen to it, and you may think the less of me if you find anything not just as you would have it.'

Vergil nodded. His pain had now reached a level at which it almost acted as its own anesthetic. Even more softly, he asked, 'Any other news?'

Clemens reflected. No. No, no other news. Cornelia had been poking about once or twice, with Tullio, the latter looking ready to order all hands flayed and flogged at the slightest excuse. But the fact that preparations were always and obviously going on helped allay her impatience and his wrath.

'Oh.' He suddenly looked blank. Vergil raised his eyebrows in inquiry. 'You're back. By Poseidon's codpiece! How silly of me to have forgotten that you'd gone somewhere farther away than, say, Elba or Ischia. Welcome, then, Vergil, and praise be to the Fair White Matron and her Consort, the Ruddy Man, for having obviously protected you in your journeying.'

Something tugged at Vergil's mind. Surely he knew well enough that phrase, expressive in the ornate symbology of alchemy of the Moon and the Sun, Silver and Gold, and of their supposed 'wedding' in the alloy electrum and elsewhere; then *why* ...

But Clemens was speaking again. 'Forgive my babbling on, and begin to tell me of everything that happened.'

Vergil smiled faintly, 'It is here, as in most tales, that I should say to you that I am tired, and that my account must wait upon tomorrow. It is true that I am somewhat tired, but tomorrow will not find me less so, and, besides, tomorrow must see the beginning of a long and intensely careful unceasing toil. I had better tell you now. Yes ... let us have in some flask or two of that fifth essence of wine engendered in your alembic, and I shall tell you now.'

Old Tynus nodded his snowy head. 'True, master, some have always said that Friday is unlucky, but I cannot either see that this would hold true of our work here ... if it ever held true of anything. For Friday is the Day of Venus, and Venus is not only a benefic – as is Jupiter – but she rules copper, brass, and bronze. Therefore today is an auspicious day to begin the work. Moreover, and mayhap most significant of all, as you point out, the sign of Venus is the sign of her mirror ...' He scratched it with his staff on the cleanly sanded floor:

'The sign of lesser fortune, yes, but the sign of fortune nonetheless. From lesser fortune, appropriate to the beginning of a work, we shall ascend to greater fortune as we progress. The sun can only be seen in its own light, "*By light, light,*" therefore ... and, by mirror, mirror.' He stroked his long white beard. 'Venus ruling copper, brass, and bronze, Saturn ruling "form" and timing, also lead, of which copper ore will contain somewhat, and Mars ruling molten things. ... Yes, master, you have chosen well and rightly, with Mars, Venus, Saturn, and also the Moon, all making good aspect to each other in the Heavens. Because of the various rulerships involved here, the question then, of course, becomes one of which hour – Moon hours? Venus hours? Mars hours? Or even Saturn hours. ... But your decision is a quite proper one, for in horary-electional astrology, reading the augury of a given moment, it is the Moon which is, as we say, Significator of Change, and thus a Moon hour is preferred. Mars and Saturn conjoined in the mystical sign Pisces, well-appointed by Venus in the magic sign of Scorpio, a most creative relationship indeed, and none retrograde in motion, but all well-disposed toward the Moon in her own demesne of Cancer, and she translating the light of Venus unto Mars and Saturn – thus favoring secrecy of workmanship and the power of prophecy ...'

His voice died down and he murmured of Planetary Hours, and of Day and Night hours and rulerships; then he fell quite silent. All present seemed to breathe more lightly. And in this silence the slow, measured *drip ... drip ... drip* of the water clock was heard, its seconds melting away into minutes. Vergil raised his white wand, everyone ceased to draw breath, the hollow ball in the basin of the clepsydra touched the bottom with a clear, faint chime; he whipped the wand downward in signal; a dull, heavy, thudding blow followed immediately, no less startling for having been quite expected. The work of crushing the copper ore in the mill had begun. Up and down the Street of the Horse-Jewelers the deliberate sound penetrated, and, as the recurrent sensation, felt as well as heard, drew their attention, the people paused and looked at one another. Many things might have been read in their expressions, but fear was not among them. The owner of the House of the Brazen Head gave them no cause for uneasiness.

The green copper stone was hard, but gradually it yielded to the importunities of the huge, pounding pestle, like a vertical battering ram. This first treatment was intended only to reduce the pieces of its mass in size. *Stant quatuor lapides in modum crucis,* four stones are set up in the form of a cross: so began the ancient direction for the construction of a furnace; this had been done during Vergil's absence under Clemens' direction, and on this foundation the work erected immediately afterward of iron rods crisscrossed in squares. Over these a hearth was laid of Babylonian clay well-kneaded with horse dung, three fingers thick, in a circle, punctured with holes by a round stick, and left to dry. Around and up from this hearth, of the same clay and of small stones, a wall was built up *in modum ollae,* in the form of a pot.

'Narrower from the middle upward, you will observe,' Clemens pointed out for perhaps the tenth time, 'and higher than wide. So I have always built my furnaces, and so I built yours. The clay was macerated and triturated and washed and strained, believe me, fully an hundred times. The horses were all maiden mares, pure white in color, fed upon mallows and apples and grass plucked – *plucked,* mind you, not cut – from rocky hilltops such as we might be perfectly sure had never been tilled, for three days, after which we might be certain that they had thoroughly passed all gross fodder. As for the four iron bands binding the outside of the furnace, they were, needless to say, newly forged. For tempering them, I obtained an oxhorn from one of the sacrificial animals and burned it on a fire of *lignum vitae,* scraped it, mixed it with the purest salt I had in my elaboratory a third part, and ground them vigorously together. I put the irons in the same fire till they were white hot, sprinkled the preparations over it on every which side, opened out the coals and quickly blew all over, but seeing that the tempering did not fall off. Immediately I withdrew the bands and quenched them evenly in water, took them from there, and dried all gently over a fire.'

'As for the water, ha ha!' – he chuckled and he rubbed

his hands together – 'I did not use ordinary water, all corrupted with gross earths and impure salts and what-have-you, no. Instead, I procured a three-year-old goat and tied it up indoors for three days without food. On the fourth I gave it fern to eat and nothing else for two days. Then I enclosed it in a cask perforated underneath and under the holes I placed a separate water-tight container and for two days and three nights I collected its urine. With this same water I also tempered all the tools of steel and iron.'

Vergil said that this was well done. He hearkened a moment to the pounding of the mill, then added, gravely, 'It is fortunate that there was fern.'

Promptly, Clemens said, 'Had there not been, I should have tempered with the urine of a small boy.'

Small Morlinus, who had been listening at odd moments, looked up expectantly at this; but Clemens, who had not observed him, amended, 'A small, red-haired boy,' and the face of Morlinus, who was dark, fell.

Vergil raised his wand and the mill fell silent. The green ore was removed and piled in a heap and burned like lime. It did not lose color, but it lost much of its hardness; after which it was cooled, returned to the mill, and broken up small. It was then ready for the furnace.

Vergil addressed his adepts and their helpers. 'We are now approaching the more delicate parts of the work,' he reminded them, 'although the casting and founding will be, of course, next to the burnishing, the most delicate parts of all. You have all bathed and prayed and sacrificed. More than a willingness to work together is required. Any degree of impatience, any loss of temper, might, at a crucial moment, result in irreparable damage. Are all things well with all of you at home? Reflect, and, if not, then withdraw. Your wages shall in any case continue, and there are other works you can engage in until this one is complete.'

He paused. There was silence. No one withdrew.

His voice was very low but very distinct. He looked at each in turn with his clear, gray-green eyes. 'We have now to go on with our task of making a virgin mirror. It is important to the honor of this house that we do not fail. And it is important to me in another particular as well. I know it is not necessary that you should know how or why, that your merely knowing it is so will be sufficient for you. If I have offended any of you at any time, forgive me. If any of you have offended me at any time, forgive you I freely do. And if any of you have offended against each other, will you not declare it now? – if any of you feel that another has given you cause for grievance, will you not reveal it now? – so that we may proceed in perfect purity and amity and confidence of heart.'

There was another silence. Then followed a few low-voiced conversations, several shook hands and returned to their places. Vergil had half turned his head as if to give directions, when the thin, piping treble of Morlinus was heard. 'Iohan, when the Master told you to take me and instruct me and you said that you would beat me if I learned ill and I said that I gave you leave—'

Iohan, in some surprise, nodded.

'So I had no right to curse at you when you did beat me because I smudged my letters or wrote them backward or drew pictures instead. And I ask your forgiveness for cursing at you when you couldn't hear me and for calling you a bear with a sore cod and a son of a whore and a dirty old fig-polucker and a blind bawd's pimp and a hussy-hopper and …'

His vocabulary was both remarkable and extended. Iohan's face beneath his bristly beard grew red as wine, and his thick and hairy fingers began to twitch. At length when the boy drew a breath, and began anew with, 'Also, I ask your forgiveness for having said about you and your wife—' Iohan, his vast chest heaved up and his nostrils round with rage, bawled out at the top of his voice.

'Enough, enough! I forgive you for everything you said and you don't have to say any of it all over again!'

Then, as if suddenly aware of the echo, he repeated, in a small, abashed tone, 'I forgive you, boy.'

Red-hot coals were now placed in the furnace and small pieces of ore spread out on top, then more coals, then the ore again, and so on until the furnace was filled. All was swift, sure, silent; no foot slipped upon the carefully sanded floor. Some time passed and Vergil drew Clemens' attention to a vessel placed some way below and apart, where unto a flow of metal was directed by channels graved for the purpose. An iridescent sheen was on its thick and scummy surface.

'Now the lead begins to separate,' he said.

'Some will still remain, unless—'

'Some *should* remain, to serve to hold the tin and copper together well, and to help give the bronze a good polish.'

The bellows were not now needed, for the wind, entering into the opening below, drew the flames well. Clemens said, 'This should now remain heating a very long time, and although we have a proverb: "*The eye of the Master melts the metal*," still, the Master's eye is not needed at the moment. Come and sit down and let me read something to you.'

A divan had been set up against the wall and spread with carpets and cushions and fleeces. The colors clashed, Vergil noted abstractly. A woman would have seen to it that they didn't, but it had been long since there was – except for brief visits – a woman in the House of the Brazen Head. He seated himself and, catching the eye of Morlinus, he beckoned him.

'Yes, lo … yes, master?'

'Tell them in the house to prepare me a small bowl of hot pease soup with thin dry bread grated on the top, and a slice of fried sausage … Now, Ser Clemens, what is this that you have to read to me?'

'You sound like a pregnant woman, with your sudden and specific urge for a snack.'

'Yes, I daresay I do. I suppose in some way I am.'

Clemens shrugged. 'God send thee a good delivery, then. What I have to read to you?' He held up the little book which he had been engaged in reading on Vergil's return. 'This I found in my own library. It is called *On Cathayan Bronze*, and it is as full of good things as an egg is of meat. Let me read you the chapter I have marked.

'*Concerning Mirrors.* Sorcery works against Nature, magic works with it. Of all the means of magic, the most important are the sword and the mirror, the ordinary uses to which warriors and women put these objects being of little significance to the Superior Man. Concerning swords and their power to compel daemons, we will speak in another chapter. The learned Covuvonius sayeth, "*When you look at yourself in a mirror, you observe only your own appearance; your fortune or misfortune can be read by seeing yourself reflected in other.*" This reminds us that mirrors ought not to be used for such foolish purposes as merely looking at one's self, but rather for the Eight Essential Functions, and these are they: to ward off evil influences, confuse daemons, assist physicians by reflecting the interior of the patient's body, protect the dead by giving light to the graves in which they are placed, to assimilate and simulate the brightness and power of the Sun and the Moon, reflect inner thoughts and moods and elevate them to happier ends, for divination, for reflecting in visible form the shapes of invisible spirits haunting the earth; and similar works of moment and magnitude. Emperor Hisuanuanius –

'A curious tongue,' said Clemens, leaving off and looking up. A sharp hot smell was in the air. 'Like the hissing of serpents.' He sniffed. 'It comes along all we now.'

'Serpents mean wisdom,' Virgil pointed out. 'Furthermore, in the Hebrew tongue the word *nachash*, which is "serpent," also means "copper" or "bronze" ... also "magic" – or' he asked himself thoughtfully, 'is it "sorcery"? Pray, read on.'

'Emperor Hisuanuanius had thirteen mirrors, one for each month of the regular year and one for the intercalary month of leap years, the particular month of each being indicated by the zodiacal animal thereon and the asterism to which it corresponded; and each successive mirror after that of the first month was increased in diameter by one inch.'

Clemens interrupted himself to comment that this was mere artsy trickery, for, after all, no one month was more or less important than any other month.

'On the back of each was graven the Four quadrants of the Uranoscope, thus: the Sombre Warrior in the north, the Vermilion Phoenix in the south, in the east the Azure Dragon, and in the west the Milk-white Tiger.' ['Now, *that* idea, I rather like,' Clemens said. Vergil nodded.] '(Others say that locusts were also shewn, the winged locusts meriting a numerous posterity because they live in harmonious clusters.) 'All magic mirrors must reflect the Six Limits of Space, comprising the four cardinal points plus zenith and nadir. They must be round as the heavens and yet square as the earth, and he who makes one must conjure it, *Be thou like the Sun, like the Moon, like Water, and like Gold, clear and bright and reflecting what is in thy heart.* Some authorities further distinguish between sunlight and moonlight mirrors. We will now explain the art by which the design on the back of a magic mirror is cast upon a wall or screen when a light strikes its front or reflecting surface ...

'If you would safely capture tiger cubs, you must carry with you a large mirror and place it in the path to be followed by the tigress, for, great as is her rage and grief, on perceiving her reflection, she is sure to forget all else and linger to admire it till the fall of night. ... 'The best alloy for mirror bronze ['What?' asked Vergil. 'No more tigresses?'] ... will consist in seventeen parts of copper to eight parts of tin ['This is rather less tin than we in Europe are accustomed to use for ordinary mirrors, but it approximates Egyptian usage quite closely, as well as our bell-metal.'] ... Moonlight may be obtained by hanging a well-prepared mirror on a tree during the full of the moon and then distilling the dew which forms on its face. If this is done properly, a translucent container of it will give bright light in the darkness at any time; but if not, it will only shine according to the phases of the moon itself.

'Solar fire for kindling the sacrificial flames may be caught in a concave mirror cast at high noon exactly on the solstice.

'And now we will speak of molds and wax and stamps and clay and potter's wheels to shape the curved surfaces ...

'The bronze-founder borrows from the sculptor and the woodcarver borrows from both, the potter imitating the bronze-founder and in turn being imitated by the lapidary who influences the sculptor; thus turns the wheel, bringing up water to quicken all the fields and furrows ... Suquas sayeth that, in casting mirrors, the ancients would give the large mirrors a plane surface and the small ones a convex surface; for all mirrors will reflect a man's face large if they are concave and small if they are convex; and by reflecting the human face in reduced size, a mirror may be small and yet take in a man's face complete, though the reflected image will correspond in size to the size of the mirror.'

Clemens looked up from his reading. 'This is an important passage,' he said.

Vergil's small bowl of pease soup had just arrived, he took a mouthful of it. 'Yes, most important,' he said, rising and starting across the room toward the furnace.

'Surely it is cool by now,' he said, with a curious air, to his inquiring friend.

Clemens took hold of him by the sleeve and drew him to a halt. 'Cool by now? What ails you? You look strange and fevery. It is not even sufficiently heated by now ... Or do you mistake the soup for the ore? First the copper must be baked, then smelted, there are the crucibles to make, the residual leads must be further purified, the molds have yet to be designed, let alone made ... This is for the moment enough, surely—'

'*Enough* ...' Vergil repeated the word with a sick look and a low sigh. But, Clemens representing to him the bad effect that any display of impatience would have upon the adepts and the workmen, he returned to his seat, and to a discussion of the little book *On Cathayan Bronze*; a copy of which he presently directed his scribe to make.

Thus, with due precautions both mechanical and astrological, with attentions alchemical and metallurgical, the work slowly proceeded. The crucibles were made, of two parts of raw clay and three of fired clay, kneaded in warm water with hammers and hands to the sound of a rhythmic old Etruscan chant, on the principle that 'the voice is good for the mixture'; and the clay molded on wood, covered with dry ashes, and placed near the fire. Meanwhile, the tin was being attended to in accordance with its own peculiar needs. Copper and coals were next put in crucibles and set upon the furnace-hearth, stirred carefully with the wooden-handled long and thin and curved rod. From time to time each crucible was lifted with long tongs and moved a little to prevent its sticking to the hearth, and, by and by all the copper melted and was poured off into the trenches.

'Observe, adepts and workmen,' Clemens pointed out, in a deep, moved voice, 'the philosophical lesson which this process teaches us. The metal must die in order to live. It must be destroyed in order for it to be created. Burned in the fire which utterly annuls all manner of form and life, in order for it to be given new form and new life. Where else do we see anything like this? Why, in that seed which is cast into the very earth itself, there to die and there to rot, and there nevertheless to quicken with life again, to grow and to come forth and to flourish. Don't think, then, when it comes your time to be given to the flames or to the earth, that you will remain ashes or earth forever, for nature and philosophy alike combine to teach you better …'

Vergil listened as carefully and as humbly as the forge-boy seemed to, and for all his attention yet something stirred in a corner of his mind and he could neither focus on it nor hear what it had to say. Clemens went on to declare that to alchemy there was no distinction between organic and inorganic life, that the ore which came from the earth and the seed which came from the earth were but brother and sister; so, listening, Vergil gradually allowed the oddly summoning thought to vanish once again.

The speculum proper consisted of two parts: the actual reflecting surface and the cover, fastened to the surface with screws and studs and clasps and catches; the entire product rather resembling a large locket. Some of these smaller pieces would be wrought by hand, some cast in molds like the larger pieces. In preparation for making the molds they now began the refining of the wax. Tallow, coarse and stinking, would not do; nothing but pure wax of bees would do. In many matters concerning the artificing of a major speculum, The *Text-book* of Rufo, the *Chalceocicon* of Theodorus, and *The Manual of Mary of Egypt* differed, but in this one point they were unanimous: the wax must be gathered from the combs of bees that had fed on Mount Caucasus – and nowhere else. *Certain virtue hath the soil of this Great Mount*, Mary had written. *Great is that virtue, and is passed along to all plants and herbs nurtured in that soil, and from nectars of said plants passed on to the wax of bees feeding thereon, and thence to all things molded therewith.* Rufo said that certain substances derived from the mineral content of the mountain passed into the clay molded around the wax at the time that the wax itself melted in the fiery heat of the kiln, and were in turn passed on to the metal founded in the clay molds when the heat of the founding activated these residues once again. Theodorus attempted to connect the matter with the blood of Prometheus, shed upon the crag of Caucasus when the eagles tore at his liver for his presumption in bringing fire hid in fennel stalks to the children of men – the flowers thus fructified by this blood forever after retaining what Mary called *virtue. And certain it is*, he concluded, *that no other fire but that of fennel will do for working this wax if it is to be of most effect.*

Now, if the only use of such Caucasian beeswax was to be employed as 'lost wax' in casting virgin mirrors, it might have remained forever among the mountaineers – except when some rare, infinitely rare, artisan chose to engage upon the work of such a speculum. But it happened that wax of Caucasus had other employment as well … for example, in making a supporting medium for the fashioning of those silvern cups which in an instant turn black when any poisoned drink is poured into them … or for waxing the ends of threads (the better to pass them through a needle's eye without fraying) used to sew cerements intended to preserve bodies from corruption … and sundry, and costly other uses.

There was, accordingly, a certain trade in it, and this trade in Naples was in the hands of one Onofrio, an apothecary, whose combination ware- and counting-house seemed more like some strange and odorous cave than any place of business. 'We have it,' he told Vergil, winking and nodding. 'We haven't much of it, of course. Our wife was saying to us not a week ago, "Onofrio, put Caucasus on the list, it's running low." So we did, we're sending out work, there'll be a bit more by and by. A year. Or two. Or three. Eh?' another wink. And, 'How much? Hmm.

Mmm. A lump the size of a man's head. Don't know its present weight, been scraping at it here and there and now and then as the need arises. Why? How much d'ye need, Dr Vergil? What? All of it? Impossible. Impossible. Impossible. Impossible. Can't be entirely without, no, we can't.'

In this he was certainly sincere. When, however, it was represented to him that part of it could be recovered and returned, it suddenly became no more priceless – but its price was considerable – and not to be calculated in gold alone. There were certain things which Onofrio wanted to know and which Vergil could tell; and certain things which Onofrio wanted done ... and which Vergil ... only Vergil ... could do. Fortunately, the apothecary, though desirous, was not covetous. He drove a hard bargain, but he did not insist on payment in advance; the precise degree and amount of payment would, it was mutually agreed, depend on the amount of wax returned. Vergil followed him past towering cabinets containing ambergris, musks, storax, balsams, jujubes, attars, essences and elixirs, azoth, ointments, theriacs and talequales, unicorn, ostrich shell, toads and toadstools, bats' blood and bats, vipers in treacle and vipers' blood and dried vipers, fewmets of griffins, mummy and mandgagora and mercury; scents and stenches and smells and odors; to where the essential wax was stored, locked up in an iron cage guarded by a dog who had not seen the sun, poor creature, since he was whelped.

The wax was dark, darker than common beeswax, almost black, but of no common blackness; shot through with tints of amber and red, did the light strike it a certain way. It was of a rich and overpowering odor, spicy and strong, and it felt unctuous and potent to the finger.

'We must have as much of it back as can be saved, Dr Vergil,' the muskmonger said. 'We can't spare a scruple of it to feed the fires wastefully, no, not a drachm. Those

168

other items we've spoke of to you, we value them, we'd gladly pay for them in gold or goods or any way ... we're prepared to pay in wax, yes, if we must ... but' – he ran his old, sere finger, like one of his own medicinal roots, over the great lump of Caucasus wax, lovingly and regretfully – 'but, we beg of you nonetheless, Doctor, don't waste it. Not any of it.'

The wax was melted slowly over a fire of fennel (and no small task to gather and dry enough fennel: fire to feed fire, tongs to make tongs, cycle upon cycle, wheels within wheels) and strained; washed with water, and again strained; purified and strained; refined and strained; ever with a cloth of an increasing fineness – these cloths, by direction of Master Workman Perrin, saved to be boiled to retrieve the residual wax. Vergil himself had neither thought nor patience for this – and the process repeated over and over and over. Slowly. Slowly. Slowly.

And the other tasks proceeded. Slowly, slowly, slowly.

Finally the wax was pure enough, pale enough, fine enough.

Page after page of parchment, and ink from entire schools of squid and forests of hawthorn trees and oaks, were employed in the ever-continuing work of casting the horoscopes. The question of the Moon's nodes was a particularly important one, the points at which the Moon's orbits cross the ecliptic, the north node being known as the *caput draconis*, or Dragon's Head, and the south one called the *cauda draconis*, or Dragon's Tail. *Caput* was fortunate, *cauda* was misfortunate.

'There you have it!' Vergil cried, despairingly, throwing down a pen. 'I should draw the entire nativity of the princess – cast it myself – not depend on the one Cornelia supplies – *when* was she carried off? Was her ruler of life conjoined with *cauda*? Should we wait six months for Venus to go around the zodiac to be conjoined with *caput* as an auspicious moment for the dragon to spew her forth?' Seizing the pen, he hastily sketched a diagram, only to have it arouse a host of speculations, many of them far from apropos, such as the resemblance and semblance of the dragon with *caput* at *cauda* to the Midgard Serpent and the Worm Ourobouros and Great Leviathan and the River Oceanos engirdling all the world. 'The chart of the Eight Houses,' he murmured. 'Saturn-adverse-Venus … disappointment almost certain … What is astrology but the study of cycles in time? Are our planets truly globes of light? Or are they, for our purposes, our present, particular purposes – are they instincts whose interrelationships is that which causes destiny?

'Let me erect the horary chart again,' he said, more calmly this time. He had lost weight, color, tone, in all this great work and worry.

He took fresh parchment, pen, ink. The shapes took on form. Here was the First House, showing the questioner; here, the opposite, the Seventh House, showing the problem or the (unknown) person causing it. Supposing Cornelia to be asking the question, this would have her represented by the First House, and Laura by the Fifth; thus Laura's problem was represented by the plane in the Eleventh House, which was opposite her own … 'Let me see, let me see,' he muttered, bending close. 'Jupiter is royalty, rules Sagittarius, so the chart for the moment is with Sagittarius rising … Sun in Sagittarius, First House denotes Queen … Sun rules rulers … sign of Leo, First House *could* be Leo, then the Fifth House would be Scorpio – *Venus beseiged!* Surely! Venus ruling love and beauty – the Princess Laura Now – interception of the sign, thus is with Taurus on its cusp, Venus ruling Taurus. And so the Seventh House, containing the problem and its causer, thus would be Gemini on cusp, or Mercury ruled. Saturn – no, no, Saturn will not do, will not go where I want him … Venus conjuncts Mercury in the

170

Eleventh House ... the Eleventh Cusp is Scorpio ... what is Scorpio? So, sign of magic, profundity, intensity, eagle, serpent, and phoenix ...' He repeated his words, drawn by a sudden conviction of a connection both present and invisible. What was it?

Eagle? The Empire? The Imperial House? Prometheus bound on Mount Caucasus? *Serpent?* This opened the way, surely, for whole torrents of possibilities: wisdom, witchcraft, copper and bronze, the cycle of Venus through the zodiac from Dragon Tail to Dragon Head, cycles, circles, rings, rings ... He paused, pressed his hands to his aching head. There *was* a ring there, somewhere. But it would not come up where he could see it. *Eagle, serpent, phoenix ... Scorpio – sign of regeneration – the Eleventh Cusp, Venus conjuncts Mercury in the Eleventh House. The princess and the causer of the problem. Mercury, ruler of the Seventh Cusp on the horary chart. Seventh House rules enemies and world conditions. Afflicting. Bad aspects ...*

No, no. It was still impossible. The chart would not work out. Too much was lacking, too much contradictory. It was best to waste no more time on it, and on other things.

Still ... it was certainly very curious. 'The sign of regeneration ... *Eagle, serpent, phoenix ...*'

They purified the copper further with three ranges of bellows working at the forge by night and day, night after night and day after day, and poured it finally into ingot molds. Before it was cooled and while it was still red-hot, they held it with tongs upon the anvil and struck it with the largest hammer. It cracked. They melted it once again, repeating the long process, drew it forth again, struck it again. This time it did not crack.

Vergil bared his arm, Clemens bound it. Clemens bared his arm. Vergil bound it. Iohan, Tynus, Perrin, and all those engaged in the work did the same. The veins swelled. The lancet passed between the mage and his friend. The blood spurted forth and was caught in the vessel. Each gave, none withheld. And then the vessel was full, and then they plunged the glowing ingots into it, and thus they cooled them and completed the work of the smelting.

It was that night that Vergil saw himself again 'pass through the Door,' and part of his mind shrieked in silent terror at the sight, knowing it had not been his intention to do this ... knowing too, the danger involved in this implied loss of control. But another part of his mind counseled calm and acceptance, and this implied that the loss of control was perhaps apparent only, and not actual.

He was in Cornelia's chamber. She sat at a writing desk, a branch of lamps beside her. She did not look up, but he could tell that she knew someone was there.

'I must cast a proper nativity,' he said – and her entire body recognized his voice, and – strange, strange, exceedingly strange – this intelligence quite dispelled the fear in her. Taut tendons relaxed in her neck; she let out her breath with a sigh.

'Of course,' she said, softly. 'Of course.'

'Write down the precise moment of her birth,' he directed, 'and the exact or even approximate latitude, if you know it.' She wrote. 'Now the nearest moment as you can recall it to the time you heard of her disappearance ... Now get up and leave me quite alone.' He watched her gliding step as she went from the room, the drapery at the door rustling yet another moment, then lying still.

He stared at the wax tablet and what was written thereon, committing it to memory. He wondered who it could have been that she had so much feared to find behind her. Then he seated himself and began to work. The natal chart took rapid shape beneath his fingers, he needed no ephemeris, all information welling up in his mind as he thought for it. He saw the type of danger likely to threaten in her life chart, and the direction from which it would come; even the probable time was there … yes … it fitted … the Progressions fitted … advancing the birth planets roughly one degree for one year on the principle of *A Year Shall Be as a Day*, events of the age of twenty were indicated by the thus-progressed planets twenty-one days after her birth, the first day not being counted as it equalled the birth year.

'Sometime during this week' – his finger pointed as he calculated aloud – 'and possibly on this day – she would be in grave danger from dark forces emanating from the north as shown by Saturn at her birth at the nadir of the chart, adversely affecting her Venus-at-birth by Progression when she reaches that age, but' – he scowled, calculated, smiled, became totally abstract – 'her Venus-of-birth being trined by benefic Jupiter posited in the zodiacal sign Scorpio, help would come to her through a wise man, philosopher, mage …'

Yes … it did fit … it was almost uncanny how it fitted. Scorpio, *sign of regeneration*, and, hence, naturally, of eagle, serpent, phoenix. Besides its other obvious possibilities, was not the eagle, with its uncanny keenness of vision, sighting its prey from leagues afar, a clear symbol of the magic mirror? And did the eagle not, when age had dimmed its eyes and heavied its wings, seek out the fountain of youth whose location was known only to its kind, soar over it until, 'within the circle of the Sun,' a potent beam or ray from the as yet undiminished Source of Light burned away the dimness? And, thence, diving from on high, deep, deep into that fountain, new its youth for lustrums more. Then, lastly, if one could so speak of lastly, there was the falcon-eagle, which had at peril and to its great cost borne from distant, distant Tinland the purse of that essential ore. And how had Clemens managed to miss the exemplum of the serpent in his little philosophical address? – the serpent which annually casts off its skin as the ore casts off its dross, serpent seemingly almost at the point of death, dull, dazed, struggling; serpent, finally, alive and quick; renewed. Last of the three was phoenix, that rare among birds, unique for its life-span and life cycle, enduring for five hundred or a thousand years, then building its nest and making its 'egg' fanning with its wings the fire which converts nest into pyre; fire consuming phoenix, fire hatching egg, out of the egg a worm, out of the worm the phoenix.

Out of the fire, the phoenix.

Models for the double discs had been carved of ordinary wax, studied, corrected, approved; then copied in the wax of Caucasus for the final model, copied so carefully and with such exquisite, agonizing care as to make mere painstaking seem slovenly: stroke by stroke and flake by flake and quarter inch by quarter inch. The wax must not be too warm, the wax must not be too cold; it must not melt, it must not sag nor slip, it must not grow brittle and chip. And everything in this doing was done in accordance with the celestial confluences. A separate horoscope was cast even for so pragmatic a matter as placing the waxen sprues. Finally, omens having been taken on the thunder chart, the entire modelings, save for the tops of the prues, were coated with the specially prepared clay; allowed to dry ... and dry ... and dry ... coated again ... dried ... coated a third time. When the hour auspicious and appropriate arrived, a fire was built, aspersed and censed with appropriate herbs, and the molds placed adjacent to it, over vessels of water to collect the precious wax, which, after it had melted and left its impression on the clay, was poured out through the sprue channels. Then, when a Sun Hour arrived, suitable for workings with fire, coinciding with a time acceptable to the chthonic Presences having jurisdictions over earth and things made with earth, Vergil and Clemens and adepts and workmen, chanting the strange, discordant Etruscan litany, reversed the molds and now placed them carefully in the fire with the sprue holes pointing downward. And in that position they remained until the clay was turned as red as Mars ruling molten things, as red as the fire itself ... as red as the red robes of the sun ... as red as the earth.

On a Thursday, fortunate period of benefic Jupiter ruling prophecy and things at long distance and beyond the veil, the Street of the Horse-Jewelers was laid end to end ankle-deep in tanbark to muffle sounds and concussions. The molds had been heating with a low fire kept in, and this was now increased, and the crucibles got ready. The bellows were fixed, with two strong men to each one. All now had to go with speed and precision. Fresh coals were arranged in the furnace for the molds and the molds set on them, supported roundabout with hard stones such as could not break with the heat of the fire, *lapidem super lapidem*, stone upon stone and with sufficient interstices until they were half a foot higher than the molds; and burning coals around them, and fresh coals over them to the top. They burned, they sank, were replenished, burned, sank; and again, till three times.

Vergil lifted the cover to peer inside, but the heat drove him back. Clemens, more used to it, peered quickly within, and the heat crisped and singed his beard. 'It is red-hot,' he said. Vergil hastened with deliberate steps to the crucible where the copper was waiting, and had it put inside and mixed with coals. At his gesture, the bellows began to work again, *primo mediocriter, deinde magis ac magis*. A green flame arose from the crucible. The copper had begun to melt. Immediately Vergil signaled for more coals to be added, ran to the mold furnace and oversaw the work of removing the stones and the fire and replacing it with earth. He ran back to the other fire, stirred the copper with a long charred stick.

'Now!' he said. And he threw in the copper fibula Cornelia had given him.

The tin was added, and carefully stirred and stirred until it, too, was all molten and all mixed, and meanwhile the crucible was with infinite care turned around from side to side in order to maintain an even temperature. Then it was removed from its own fire and carried to the molds, skimmed of coal and ash, and a straining cloth placed over the opening in the mold of the first half. Vergil threw himself down on the floor as near to the mold as he could stand the heat, his ear to the ground.

'Pour!' he said.

They poured, slowly, slowly, and he listened. He gestured them to pause. He listened. All was well, nothing murmured, nothing grumbled, nothing groaned. He gestured, he listened, and they poured. At length Iohan said, 'Master, it is done.' Vergil said nothing. They waited and they watched. It was quite some while before they realized that he was not still listening, and then, but silently and gently for the sake of the molten mass within, they lifted him from where he lay, insensible, and so they carried him to his upper chamber.

But Clemens remained below and directed the casting of the second half.

Presently, when Vergil had recovered from his exhaustion of body and spirit, they broke open the well-cooled molds and removed the two parts of the speculum. He then had them boiled in a strong liquor of potash until all residual dirt was removed, and rinsed in hot water and dried. The discs were then annealed in fire until red-hot, the utmost care being taken that they were not made white-hot. Should any dirt or impurities have remained, they were now gone, and the metal made softer and fit for the burnisher – but it was not yet his time. The bronzes were cooled and then placed in a pickle of one part of oil of vitriol and three parts of water. 'I prefer aquafortis,' Clemens said.

'Ordinarily, so should I,' Vergil said. 'But you wouldn't use "new" acid for this, and that which makes "old" acid desirable, namely the presence of much metal in solution, obviously disqualifies it for our present purpose. The entire status of this bronze as *virgin* bronze would be annulled.'

The pieces remained awhile in the solution, then were removed and rinsed in clean, cold water, thoroughly scoured with clean, wet sand, and then placed in a wooden pail of water. Thence they were removed for further dippings in strong solution and rinsings in water, and now care equal to that employed on behalf of the bronze had to be maintained on behalf of the workmen. The dipping was done in the open air, their clothes were covered with special, thick aprons, three, of carpeting; and while some dipped and quickly rinsed, others stood by with vessels of asses' milk – to drink, if the fumes affected the lungs, to pour on the skin, lest the acid at least stain it and at worse remove it, to dash instantly into the eyes to 'kill' any stray splash. But these precautions, perhaps because they had been taken, proved unnecessary. After the last dip and rinse in cold water, the bronzes were next washed finally with boiling water and then dried with dust of sawed boxwood, and then – care being taken that they at no time be touched with naked fingers, they were covered and wrapped in the softest of chamois leathers.

And now came the time of the burnishers.

Isacco and Lionelo were their names. Isacco was stooped in age, but blindness had come on him gradually over the course of many years, and he had gradually adapted to it. Lionelo was still in his time of vigor, and his sight had been lost to him suddenly by the kick of a runaway horse whose frenzied rush he had no time to avoid. Each had been a burnisher and each had been fortunate to work for good masters who had allowed him to continue in his craft; their touch was knowing, and – so the master burnishers had reasoned – others could always look and say where sightlessness had left some spot for further care. As the years went on, though, this outer vision was needed less and less. Lionelo said that he could tell by tapping and smelling, Isacco offered no explanation: he knew without knowing how he knew.

'I have hired your time from your own masters,' Vergil told them, 'but I shall pay you double for your work. A room has been fitted up for it, and I think it lacks nothing – benches and brushes and boxes, lathes and wheels and water and soap, hook, spear, round, and long burnishers, buff leather and chamois leather, crocus powder and dilute beer, vises and poles and sawdust and vinegar—'

'Ox gall, master? Is there …?'

'No, Lionelo, the work is, I think, too delicate to risk the strong stench of ox gall.'

Isacco said, 'Vinegar will do, it will do prime, and so will beer. Is there a good small fire, master, and pots with handles?'

'All that. We are not yet ready to commence burnishing the prime pieces, and in the meanwhile I want you to familiarize yourselves with the layout of the workroom. We will rearrange it any way you wish, and then there are items of lesser importance which you may begin with to try your hands, so to speak. I need give you no specific further directions, except this – and this is most important. *The door will open only from the inside and you are not to open it when the bronze is exposed. You must cover the bronze first.* And also note that the stove is set in a sort of cabinet or closet by itself – this, too, must be closed whenever the bronzes are uncovered. *You must polish them from behind.* No one can be here to check on you. I must – and I do – rely upon you utterly.'

They nodded. At first they groped, then they moved with confidence, later with absolute unthinking familiarity. Finally, when the Moon began to pass through Scorpio and Pisces, the discs and all of their smaller fittings (made from the superfluous bronze that had filled the sprue channels during casting), carefully wrapped and boxed, were handed over to the two blind burnishers and the door closed upon them ... and upon the light. There, within, the opaque surface of the mirror would gradually become fit for reflecting. But it would reflect nothing, and, even if by rare happenstance it did, no one there could see it. And there in the blackness the lid was fitted on and all the clasps and fastenings put in place. And so wrapped again, and boxed again, and returned to the world outside again.

Vergil placed around the box a series of knotted scarlet silken cords alike to those which bound the perestupe or mandrake. 'Pull' he invited Clemens. 'Try your strength.'

The alchemist shook his head. 'I thank you, no. I am an alchemist and not a magician ... Ah. What I desired to show you before I go – evidently there was a loose leaf in my copy of the tractate *On Cathayan Bronze*, as I found it last night in my library, it will not appear in your transcript. Listen:

Inscription on a Mirror
Round, round precious mirror,
Bright, bright on the high altar;
The phoenix looking at the mirror dances to its own
  reflection,
Reflecting the moon, the blossoming flower.
Over a pond, shining like the moon,
It appears to the beautiful one, to her.

'Lovely, isn't it? I wonder what it might mean ... Well! I have a multitude of things to attend to at home, but of course I will be on hand at the viewing, though Father Vesuvio himself intervene to prevent me. *Absit omen.*'

Again the phoenix, and once again the phoenix! It was

night and Vergil walked out on his balcony, thinking to try a sortilogy from whatever stray utterance of old Allegra's might come to hand. And her remark, crooned as she bedded down her cats and herself, was cryptic enough. *'On the sea, my lord, walk without water if you would find her ...'* The Woman of Delphi herself would have been satisfied. But, riddle it as he would, clear as its obvious meaning was, Vergil could read in it nothing about the phoenix.

There was a belvedere set into the upper part of one of the upper rooms in the House of the Brazen Head, with twelve windows, through each of which, during its proper month, the sun at its meridian cast a beam of light; and the tessellated pavement below was further marked off with annotated areas, some of them overlapping, for day and by day; so that the chamber formed one great sundial. Vergil had been at work with his astrolabe, checking and rechecking and setting and resetting his horlogues. His face was yellow and sunken and he did not even look up as Cornelia entered; then, suddenly, he did. It was their first real meeting since his return, and one might have admired the restraint she showed in not vexing him with the frequent visitations she must dearly have desired to make. Their eyes met now. It was she who, almost instantly, withdrew and broke the gaze. Almost, her look pitied him. Almost, she did not see him. Silently she approached the box and looked at it, extended her hand, hastily and almost fearfully drew it back. She was very pale, and the skin about her eyes was dark violet. She sighed, compressed her lips, clasped her hands, Vergil took hold of the clew and gave the silk cord the slightest of tugs, murmuring a word as he did so. All the elaborate cordings and knottings fell open and slack, the sides of the box parted slowly and settled back onto the table.

And the speculum was revealed.

Like a great locket, it rested there, shining and brightening. As if at an agreed signal, all began to walk around it. Its back was ornately and beautifully designed and inscribed, but no one lingered to examine or to decipher; all walked with eyes awestruck and unfocused. And, as they did so, an horlogue began to sound the twelfth hour and as it did the room began to darken, until at *eleven* it was almost black. Then came the stroke of twelve, Vergil reached out and snapped back the lid, and the bronze, resounding like a bell, encompassed and occluded the stroke of noon. Simultaneously the darkness was pierced by a broad shaft of sunlight and Cornelia pulled from the bosom of her robe a long golden pin and thrust it at the blank but luminous face of the mirror's disc. The pin touched, the surface of the disc went into flux like oil resting upon the surface of water when disturbed. The disorder became a whirlpool, round and round, drawing everything toward it and everything into it.

'*Laura!*'

And there she was, pacing slowly on great Cyclopean steps; near her, always near her, but never quite in clear range of vision, was something ugly and dreadful. Whose voice had cried her name, Vergil did not know, but it was Cornelia's voice which cried out now, cried no name, cried out. The whirlpool swirled reversewise, closed in, the scene vanished, and the last vanishing echoes of the stroke of twelve were heard. The mirror was a mirror now, and nothing more. Vergil, Clemen, Cornelia saw their own faces, but Vergil now *saw* what he had already *felt*: it was his own face, his true face, his face complete. His missing soul had returned to him. Cornelia – she who now stood staring, staring, staring – had kept her word.

To her it had been plain magic. To Clemens, a living metal had revealed a living truth. To Vergil, a focus had been provided to reveal in presently visible terms an event occurring elsewhere and at that moment impressed upon the universal ether, from which the virgin speculum (virgin now no longer) had received and revealed it upon its virgin surface. Vergil reached out his hand towards Cornelia.

Cornelia spoke. She did not speak, she was pointing at the wall, her face worked, her lips moved, her throat moved, a harsh and fearful cry came from her mouth. There on the wall in a luminous circle was the design of the four figures of the four quadrants of the uranoscope; around the rim, both clockwise and counterclockwise, the inscription in the curious and impressive letters of the Umbrian alphabet, so often written mirror-fashion, Widdershins.

Vergil seized her hand. 'Lady Cornelia, don't be afraid,' he said urgently. 'This is the so-called magic mirror effect, yet it is no true magic but an effect derived from purely natural causes. Come and see, come and see … .' He showed her the design, now reflected on the wall, on the back of the surface of the speculum, whence (he explained) by a seemingly inexplicable effect caused by atomical disturbances, it was cast upon another surface and thus gave the impression that the solid bronze was transparent as glass. 'I do not wonder at your surprise,' he said. 'No doubt you failed to observe, while looking at the reverse of the disc before, that it showed the heavenly configurations … the Somber Warrior in the north, and in the south, the Vermilion Phoenix.'

She tore her hand loose from his grasp. Fear now partially retreated and was replaced by rage, but did not vanish utterly; and outrage and hatred and despair struggled with them both. She turned upon her heel and left the room.

Softly, Clemens said, 'It is done.'

But Vergil knew that it was not done, that only a phase of it was done. The girl in the mirror, the first woman he had really seen in months – and he had fallen in love with her.

And now he had to find her.

182

TWELVE

The bull had bellowed that he would take Tartis Castle apart, stone by cyclopean stone, treaty rights or no treaty rights. But in actually approaching the castle with the Imperial Sub-Legate and a century of his own troops, Doge Tauro's voice had decreased in volume and increased in awe. The politely astonished Captain-lord had immediately granted permission to search not the castle alone but all of Tartis ward, and insisted on limping along with them. The building was huge, it was vast, it seemed to extend for half of forever beneath the hill. Most of it was gaunt and bare, and of the rest, most was half dust and half decay. Long before the search was done, both Doge and Sub-Legate were convinced that not the Captain-lord nor any of his men knew anything of the matter. It took until the end, however, for them to conclude, reluctantly, that no one and nothing had held Laura there – with or without the knowledge of the rightful occupants – at any time. And so the seekers departed, more baffled than when they came.

Vergil lingered a moment to thank the Captain-lord in person for the gift of tin. The man shrugged. 'It seems no good to have helped you. But why thought you that she was here?'

'I never thought she was. But she was clearly in a place as like to this as to make the others think that it *was* this … great blocks of stone piled by the four-armed Cyclopes in the Age of Dreams …'

The Captain-lord looked at him with shrewd and tired

eyes. 'I know of one other such, that in Mycenae. But it all of ruins is. It could no one conceal. You' – he shrugged again his massy shoulders – 'you know of more ones, I think. Yes? Then – Doctor – Magus – advise you, I have no right. But let me say ... go not yourself. Let another go. But you, go not.'

Vergil sighed. 'Sir, go I must.'

The snowy brows met in a frown. 'Pursue, pursue! Always must you pursue?' And the vast chest rose in a great breath which was itself both question and statement.

His departing guest nodded. 'Yes, Captain-lord. Until death conquers me. ... or I conquer death ... always, I must pursue. Farewell.' He turned to go.

Behind him, the low and weary voice said, 'Pursue ... pursue ... I would be content merely not pursued to be.'

The torches were burning low, the Doge, stamping impatiently, started off, asking over his shoulder, 'What did the old man have to say to you, Magus?'

'That in Mycenae is another castle which used to be like this. It's all in ruins now, though, and no one could be hiding there.'

The Doge swore. So much work, so much magic, and all – he asked – all for what? And the Sub-Legate, breaking his silence, said, 'I understand that the Emperor's patience cannot be answered for much longer.'

Although Tauro growled that it made no difference, that even the Roman legions could not find Laura if no one had any idea where she was, Vergil understood ... and knew that he, though not the Doge, was meant to understand ... not that Caesar, losing patience, would summon troops to seek the princess of Carsus out, but that he would simply turn his ever-wandering attentions elsewhere. There were other young women of rank suitable for marriage, should the Emperor finally decide to divorce his aging and ill-tempered consort ... should he decide to bother with marriage. And in that case, what worth were the plans of Cornelia and the Viceroy?

For that matter, in any case, what worth Vergil's own plans?

Clemens slapped his thigh in wrath and bawled from his chair that Vergil was acting like a concupiscent school-boy. 'I understand it clearly enough. You've seen nothing fairer than a furnace nor comelier than a crucible all this time. You were taut, tense ... wrought up, dispense me the need to display the other many adjectives. And then in that, admittedly magnificient, abrupt moment you saw what I concede without argument was the face of rather an attractive wench, and – Zeus! you weren't *thinking*, man – you were simply reacting. It wasn't your heart, it was your codpiece that the impulse came from!

'No, no,' he said, now in a softer voice, 'really. You had that damnable trip to Cyprus, followed by that damnable work of the speculum. True, you are now looking better, but you do not look well yet. It is madness to embark on another journey.' His arguments were long, vigorous, logical. They did not avail. Finally Vergil broke in upon them, looking up from his open volume of the *Cosmographia* of Claudius Ptolemaeus on his library table. 'I say that one of the things which compels me to do it is love. You deride this and say that it is lust. May I now remind you of your own words? "Love is for animals. Only human beings can appreciate lust."' Clemens, caught short, snorted, pawed at the air.

Recovering himself, he sidestepped the pitfall and asked what the other things compelling Vergil might be. He listened gravely, now and then sorting his beard, and finally said, 'It is a long way to go, Libya, because of what you think you saw in an astrological calculation.'

'She is in Libya. That is where she is. I know that we thought we saw her at Cornelia's villa, perhaps we were

185

mistaken, but the point is really only where she was, *primus*, when I drew up the horary chart, and where she was, *secundus*, when she was sighted in the speculum. Assuming that it was indeed she whom we saw at the villa that time, there is nothing which could have prevented her going subsequently to Libya. Or, being *taken*, subsequently, to Libya. Her mother's motives I do not know and I don't wish to involve myself at present in trying to know them. But I shall and must know them before I'm finished. At any rate, the chart, which was correct enough in so many other ways, clearly revealed Libya—'

Clemens closed the gigantic leather-bound codex with a clap. '"Clearly revealed Libya"!' he mocked. 'Aside from Egypt, Mauretania, and Ethiopea, most of Africa *is* Libya! And you intend to search this infinity of desert just because of what might be no more than a random configuration?'

Vergil straightened up and stretched on his toes. He was wearing one of his cloaks of sunset blue edged in gold embroidered work. In his mind he could see a certain rustic farm he knew well of old: the beehives, the spaniel-eared sheep, the furrows yielding to the plowman's pressing tool; in the oak and beechy woods beyond, the tusky boar besought by hunters. Too, he could see a certain village in the Calabrian hills, known to him in later times, the spare lean houses perching like eagles upon their crag, the rushing streams – incredibly cool, wondrously clear – the quiet pools where lurked the cautious fish, the sweet-smelling woods and flowery glades. How much he would love to visit either place, sink gratefully into the quiet, and float there forever … or at least until all his weariness and turmoil was laved and washed away. But it would have been at this time a wrong turning in the road. His labors on the mirror had restored to him his complete psyche, but this left him, after all, no more than he had been before. All the great questions remained unanswered, their problems unresolved. He had, so to speak, been forced to look into the sun; now, wherever else he was free to look, the image of a great, dark disc hung over and obscured his vision. And this vision must be made clear.

And also: 'Permit me,' he said, quietly, 'to know at my age the difference between casual attraction and that deeper feeling which is both rare and valuable. I must go ... to Libya. Chasing the stars.'

Told of the appeal to the *sortes* via old Dame Allegra ('*On the sea, my lord, walk without water if you would find her....*'), Clemens admitted, as though he grudged it, that this was likely enough a possible reference to the sandy waves of Libya Deserta. 'I have also heard of a Libya Petra,' he added, 'but of a Libya Felix? Never. So, a pretty face, the stars, the babble of a withered madwoman. What other auspicious omens impel you?'

Vergil walked off into the darkness of his library's farther end. 'Come and see,' his voice invited. As Clemens, muttering and grunting, advanced with caution, a square of light opened in the obscurity – a map on oiled parchment with lamplight thrown upon it from behind. Vergil had again his white wand in his hand and now used it as if it were a teacher's pointer. They had, in the newly opened surface of the major speculum, seen Laura pacing down a vasty flight of steps of unmistakable provenance. No hand of man or men had ever cut those great stony slabs and wrested them into place. The craftsmanship thereof was as unmistakable as the leopards' claws or the fleecy hair of the wise Ethiopeans.

'They were the work of the four-armed Cyclopes.' Clemens said, 'Granted. What then?'

'What then, did the Cyclopes erect so many castellations as to baffle us forever? It isn't so. Perhaps forging the thunderbolts of Jove occupied so much of their time, or wooing the beautiful females of the former age – Glaucus, for example – that the time they had for building was limited. But a record has, after all, come down to us.

187

All of those they set up in central Sicily, their first home, have been torn down with immense labor by the tyrants of that island, to prevent their providing strongholds for rebels.' The wand touched the map, now here, now there; the points touched glowed briefly. 'The castle of Mycenae, I've been lately informed, is a heap of rubble. The one occupied by the Tartismen here in Naples, we have searched, and found – as I would have expected – nothing. That in Carthage, as it later became, was with the rest of that great city destroyed by great Scipio and its very site sown with salt.' One by one the locations of each Cyclopean fortress became a tiny spot of blue-white light, like a wandering star, then vanished.

What was left? There was one other castle that the hideous Cyclopes made, each man glaring with his single huge eye, toiling and straining with his four arms. 'It is not marked for sure upon my map. All that I know of it is that it lies somewhere in Thither Libya. And it is there, Clemens, that I must go. Captain An-Thon Ebbed-Saphir will be my guide again, for he knows where it is.

Clemens sighed, sagged into a chair, waggled his huge mane. At length he said that he would not argue. 'At any rate, I suppose you may rely upon the Red Man as you did before,' he conceded. Vergil was silent here. The Red Man had made it quite clear that, for reasons of his own, which he would not discuss – let alone disclose – he would guide Vergil to within sight of the Cyclopean castle ... but no farther.

Whatever it was they had seen, without being able to see it in any way clearly at the edge of the mirror, whatever was with Laura, ugly and dreadful, Vergil would have to confront it alone.

The desert of Libya stretched on all around them, dry and glaring, red and orange and yellow and white. The sands undulated like billows. Already the coast lay far behind them, and its curious capital, where reigned Mahound, the god-king, a strong and ugly man; and Baphomet, the god-queen, his equally strong and even uglier wife. Behind them lay farmlands and fields and, at length, even the hills of scrub and thorn where only the scrannel goats found nourishment, and they only because they could climb the niggard trees like cats and browse upon the tiny buds and leaves.

It could not be said that Vergil and the Red Man followed a road. It was barely even a trail ... a faintly glistening streak was all it was, like a mark upon the flesh of a woman who has begun to put on weight. The camels snaked their long necks and gazed about with almost insufferable haughtiness and now and then lifted their meager tails and refreshed the sand with their strawy dung. Three oases lay behind them, with their green pools guarded by the date palm trees, and three more lay still ahead of them. Ebbed-Saphir squatted aboard the lead camel, gazing out over the sands as though from the poop of his ship, his reddened face muffled to the eyes, with a blue cloth, against sand and sun.

The rocking gait of the camel was not unlike the way of a ship, but a ship at least offered room to walk about on or to lie down. Vergil rode as long as he could stand it, then he walked until the sand became too hot to bear, then he donned the blue burnoose again and remounted. Now and then a rock stood out above the sands like a twisted chimney, polished by ages of sand until it glistened.

'Would it not be better if we pitched a tent and rested during the day, and then traveled by night?' Vergil had asked. But the Tyrean merely made a curt gesture and shrugged, silent. At night the stars blazed hugely in the blue-black velvet sky, each encircled by its own ring, and sometimes the rings intersected. Each night they drew a circle of their own around the campsite, and removed all stones found inside. One night one stone was overlooked and not discovered until Vergil, lowering his eyes from the stars, observed two tiny glowing circles moving slowly toward them through the darkness. His sudden gesture drew the attention on the instant of the Red Man, who advanced with ember and cudgel. The tiny lights blinked, retreated. A hissing was heard. Ebbed-Saphir blew upon the ember, tossed it, leapt, plied his club. There was the sound of stick hitting something soft and nasty, then it struck upon something hard.

The Red Man returned, tossed the something, with a grunt, at Vergil's feet; then kindled a torch and went searching. It was one of the hideous and deadly petromorphs, which came alive at night, loving to crunch the glowing coals of fires, but not disdaining to bite with their venomous jaws anything else which they encountered and which gives out warmth. Stony and chill was their bite, and stony and chill their victim soon became.

But there were deadlier things in that desert than the petromorphs.

There is nothing, perhaps, more disturbing than to see things one cannot hear and simultaneously to hear things one cannot see. The fourth Oasis, and its bibulous chieftain, Abèn-Aboubou, now lay well behind them, for all he had urged them to stay – unlike the other chieftains at the other oases, who, though charging gold and silver for water, food, and wood, seemingly begrudged every hour the strangers remained. At first, 'It is shadows, it is a strain of the eyes, it is the warping of the air by the heat' Vergil told himself: tiny things flicking and flickering around the corners and edges of his vision. He turned his head, they were gone. Then commenced and followed odd little noises, hissings and mummings and clickings and patterings. But when he drew his camel to a halt, they, too, were gone.

He had grown used to them, blamed them all upon the heat of the sun, looked forward to the night, the rest, the encircled, blazing stars. And then it was, no sooner than Ebbed-Saphir held his hand up and out and urged his grumbling camel to its knees; then, in the blue-red-purple dusk, it happened. Vergil gave a shout of alarm and fear and loathing as the host of figures seemed to swarm, all but silently, up from the sandy earth itself. Tiny, they were, and filthy-ragged, and hairy, and hideous to look upon, with snottled faces and pores like pockmarks; up they swarmed, up from all around, knives in their paws of hands.

The Red Man shouted strange words in a strange language. *'Tala' hon, tala' hon!'* – then, 'Hither! Come hither! Come hither to me!' Vergil ran, driving the alarmed camels before him – indeed, they might have bolted and been lost, had not at that moment the finger of Ebbed-Saphir, in an instantly well-remembered gesture, swept about in a circle ... and, in a circle, all about them, up sprang a ring of fire.

Now, in alarm and terror, the silence of the hideous Troglodytes was broken. They shrieked, tumbled backward. The few who found themselves inside the circle turned to look – The Red Man produced two swords and tossed one to Vergil. Up rose the encircling fire, too high for any Troglodyte to hurdle. The fiery hoop expanded, driving those beyond it back and ever back. There was no time to watch the fire, no time to watch the Red Man. Vergil, who had caught the thrown sword, unsheathed it and fell to defending himself against the three tiny imps who now rushed upon him with pattering, splay, and filthy feet. They darted around him, knives held in such a wise, stooping, low, that he knew at once their intention. From behind, to sever his Achilles tendon; from in front to pierce his artery at the groin – this was their aim. But those who depend on stealth and surprise as the chiefmost weapons are never at their best in an open fight. One, he laid apart his skull; the second failed to dodge a heavy stroke though much he tried, and, staring amazed at his severed hand, ceased to take part in the combat; the third continued to evade him as the rat evades the dog in the pit. They moved about and eyed each other, weapons poised. Then came Ebbed-Saphir, who had by now slain his two Troglodytes, and he and Vergil advanced upon the survivor. It would have been his death, then, had he not come upon one of his kind's hidey-holes, and, with a bray of triumph, vanished down it, where they could not follow.

And now once again the Red Man indicated with his finger, and a writhing, undulating serpent of fire sprang into being and slid down into the scape-hole. A dreadful screech of fear and pain grated upon their ears; then it was gone.

Across the darkling plains of sand the ever-widening circle of fire shed its ruddy rays. There was silence. Vergil said, 'Indeed, you have studied fire very deeply, Captain.'

Almost contemptuously: '"Studied fire"? You may say so! I worship fire! I know its secrets, and the secrets of its secrets ... Come! Tonight we will do as you begged, and travel. There are worse things to be feared here than the heat of the sun.'

The fifth oasis lay behind them. They had not tarried, nor had the chieftain urged them to, nor would they even if he had, remembering the bibulou Abèn-Aboubou, and not doubting that he had used the time to send out word alerting the murderous Troglodytes, lurking in their cool caverns below the heated sands. Likely he intended himself a share in the loot. And so Vergil was not surprised to find the remains – torn rags and gnawed bones cracked for marrow – of several men along the way.

'They were not lucky enough to have you with them,' he commented, turning the things over with the toe of his shoe. The Tyrean only grunted, waiting impatiently to ride on. Suddenly Vergil exclaimed, fell upon his knees to look closer. 'Surely,' he cried, astonished, 'it was only from Naples that this striped yellow broadcloth came! And it could have been only in Naples that this shoulder knot was tied!' His fingers pawed and combed the sand, came up with a blackened bauble. In a low and troubled tone he said, 'And none but a Neapolitan would wear this, particular charm against Evil Eye ... I don't like this. I've heard of none from Naples venturing into Libya before us. Who could they have been? Who *could* they have been?'

But An-Thon Ebbed-Saphir from the stork's nest of his camel saddle cried only, 'Ride! Ride! Ride! Ride on!'

The last oasis lay behind them, and none lay ahead; nothing lay ahead but more desert, and then the farfamed Mountains of the Moon, the Anthropophagai, with tails, the dwarf-like Pygmies, and the distant, distant shores of the Erythrian Sea.

'I go no farther,' said the Phoenician. The blue burnoose had slipped, showing his face, and it looked haggard.

He had been of little service as companion on the journey, but he had not been hired as companion, after all ... only as guide. 'You engaged to bring me within sight of the castle,' Vergil pointed out. 'And unless you do so, all has gone for nothing.'

The Tyrean lifted the stick with which he drove his camel, and he pointed. 'I have kept my word,' he said.

Sand had choked the castle's moat and either time or lesser enemies had pushed down its battlements and turrets. Certain rude lineaments still persisted, becoming clearer as Vergil advanced. The curtain wall was still largely in place and, rather than go around and seek a proper gate which might prove to be no longer there, he entered through a wide breach in the curtain. There had been a garden in that place once – in a sense, there still was: bone-white trees cast slant, thin shadows over bone-brittle shrubs around a bone-dry pool. A fine white sandy dust lay over everything, and on its surface, small and delicate, Vergil saw the print of a naked foot.

While he mused and pondered, somewhere on the dry, thin air, a single note sounded, clear and pure. After it came another, and another, then a rill, a cascade of them, and formed into a tune of a music unknown and strangely beautiful to him. He followed it as if it were the sound of a rill of coolest water to quench his long unsated thirst.

Through a broken arch he paced the sound of music, and down a huge and winding flight of deep-set steps, dark and grateful after the weeks of naked sunlight, and so, in the lower courtyard below, there at last she was.

Lovely Laura, dulcimer in one hand, quill in the other, kneeling and resting her coils of red-brown hair against the seamy sides of the castle's keeper, the huge and ancient four-armed Old One himself.

Whose eye was open upon the instant of Vergil's stepping through the inward-bending frame of the doorless doorway. Whose eye was huge and blazing-gold and shot about the white with tiny lines of red. Whose eye was set in the center of his broad and low and furrowed forehead. For eye other than this, he had none, nor had he space nor had he place for any other.

No one had the right to call him a *monster*, Vergil presently affirmed. The Cyclops' voice was deep and rich and slow and smooth, his words were civil and quite without threat or guile. A mind cultivated and distinctive lay behind that single glowing eye. He spoke of his loneliness without much self-pity, and even recited a few lines of his own verse-making. Laura, plainly, liked him, had no fear at all of him. But he was old, old, preternaturally old, the last of his race, and lonely.

'Man, you've come a long way, and if you are too new upon my vision to be my friend, I need not, at least, be your enemy,' he said. 'But I will not give her up. Do you love her?'

'Yes,' said Vergil.

Cyclops nodded his massy head, flowing with snow-white curls. 'I love her too,' said Cyclops. 'You have a world teeming with friends and fellows and kin, Man. I have none of such. Your duty and your pains, you'll think, have given you a claim upon her. Listen – have I not already rescued her from the Troglodytes when all her so-called guards were killed? I have. And I do not believe that they were truly her guards at all. I think they were manstealers, taking her to be the bride of that one whose pyring place is hard nearby. Oh – have I not watched often in anguish as some beautiful Man female was sacrificed to that one? And do I not hate that one? I do. What is your claim, Man Vergil, to mine?'

And Vergil said, softly, and not without respect, 'Old One, my claim is not my claim alone. Laura has a mother and a brother and a great hope among the lands of Men. Some Man will someday be her swain. You, Old One, never can.'

'I know it, I know it. I am wiser than my brother Polyphemus, whose bootless wooing of a female not of our kind drove him near mad. I do not think of Laura so. I would keep her with me, and I will keep her with me, as a lovely bird who might have perished on the burning sands, but found refuge here with me instead. Her mother has had her long enough. Her mother has a son, her brother has a mother – and, likely enough, wives and cubs. I have none of these. I have only Laura. I do not remember when last I had anyone, and I will not give her up.'

Laura herself remained silent, turning her gaze slowly from one to the other, saying nothing, showing nothing but a faint and passive smile; though now and then she touched a chord upon her dulcimer. Vergil argued as earnestly and persuasively as ever he remembered doing.

But the Old One only said, 'I will not give her up.'

He said, 'I was here when all you saw was green and fair. I saw the Titans sporting like whales in great pools where now is nought but sand. The Titans, where are they? I saw the prides of sphynxes come to whelp in the caves along the river. The sphynxes, where are they? And where is the river? The earth has grown old, like a garment, and I alone am left, and I am lonely in a way that no Man can know or has ever known loneliness. Do not speak to me of kings and queens and of princesses, Man. I will not give her up.'

Plainly, he would not. Vergil continued to talk, but his mind was now less on his words than on his thoughts, and his thoughts were on how he might overcome the Old One. It might be that his thoughts were read, or it might have been a caution of so long a standing as to have become habitual; however it was, the Old One had fixed him with his great golden eye, his huge and puissant eye, and gradually Vergil became aware that the gaze of this single eye was holding him. He was not paralyzed, no, but while the great eye gazed at him and bathed him in its golden light, he could not loose the string of his bag of tricks.

And yet, thought fathering the deed, as he bethought him of the metaphorical bag and purse and pouch, his fingers toyed with the actual pouch hanging from his belt, and his fingers let slip its cord and his fingers delved therein. He could not have, even had he desired, got therefrom a knife (if knife had been there) nor lifted it against the Cyclops. What he got, without hindrance, holding it unperceived, was so simple a thing as a coin. It had been fresh-minted not long before he left, and, in being new to him, he had put it aside from spending it at once, as people do, preferring instead to pass the old and worn, familiar coins while they lasted. So this one bright coin remained. He tossed it away.

The flash and glitter of it automatically drew the

196

Cyclops' single eye away for a second – long enough for Vergil, released from the eye's power, swiftly to stoop and swiftly scoop a handful of dust and toss it into that eye, that single, great, and golden eye.

Cyclops shouted. Laura cried out. Vergil turned and swept her up. He took her voice and his own voice, and cast them to the side. As he ran, with her in his arms, ran to the left, he heard his voice and hers coming from and dwindling down to the right. And the blundering, roaring Old One rushed with all four arms outstretched, now stooping and testing the ground, now striking his great and horny palms against the walls, down the wrong corridor, down, down, and away, following the fleeing voices; following the lying, traitor voices.

'Cyclops, farewell,' she cried, faintly. 'I did like you, Old Cyclops. I like you much – farewell!'

And: 'Forgive me, Cyclops,' Vergil heard his voice in the distance say, 'but I have done thee less damage than the Grecian did thy brother Polyphemus – farewell – farewell – farewell.'

Eventually, but before his tears had washed his eye clean, the Old One learned, too late, of their escape. From afar they heard a great cry of wordless grief, of aeons of loneliness.

THIRTEEN

The red man was seated, slumped, upon the ground when they reached him at last. The journey had evidently wearied him much, more than it had Vergil. Not until his blurred eyes focused on Laura did a flicker of interest show in them, and he slowly rose to his feet and prepared to mount. Vergil would have liked to take some of the scant food remaining in their packs, for, though he had drunk sweet water in a silver cup at the Cyclops' castle, he had not then thought to ask for anything to eat. But it was best to wait. Let them get well away. Only ...

'This is not the way we came,' he called out to his guide.

The Red Man shook his head slightly. 'Another route ...' his words came, faintly over his shoulder.

'That's wise. We will avoid the Troglodytes this time, I suppose?' But no answer came. He rode alongside of Laura, and spoke to her, but she had little to say. Her manner was as passive as ever. Indeed, she seemed so blank and docile that Vergil felt a pang of doubt concerning his feelings for her. Could she really be little more than a lovely doll? Had Cornelia's state and beauty sapped and stunted her personality? Or was this merely a sort of protective shock?

Presently she was enough aroused to answer one or two of his questions – or, rather, to explain why it was she could not answer them. 'I do not know why they took me from the Great High Road,' she said softly. 'They said that Queen – that my mother had sent them, and they showed me a letter from her.'

'A forgery, doubtless. But it is very strange … to have brought you so far, when convenient hiding places were so much nearer. One wonders why, for what motive. Ransom?' But Laura did not know. She gazed out of her mild and lovely wine-dark eyes on the passing desert. From time to time Vergil suggested a halt, but the Red Man pressed on. Sometimes he shook his head, sometimes he gestured ahead with his driving stick; he never spoke. They had grown so gradually weary that it took some time for Vergil and Laura to realize that their present route had taken them quite definitely out of and away from the Sea of Sand. They were now, and had been for some time, in a region of stones, the land rising gradually on all sides.

They were discussing this, in weary wonder, when he observed that she had closed her eyes and pressed her hand to her temple. He drew his camel in close to hers and reached out to support her. 'We must stop now,' he called out. 'The princess is very faint.'

Without turning his head, the Red Man said, 'We are almost there.'

'Almost there?' Vergil felt anger rising over fatigue. 'Almost *where*? I tell you, we must stop at once!' But Ebbed-Saphir spoke only to the mounts, and they would not pause now for all of Vergil's urgings. It was a slight shift in the wind which brought tidings of what their eyes soon enough beheld. A perfume, a fragrance, as of some garden in Cyprus … he thought, at first, he dreamed … Then he saw it.

But it was no garden. Up, up past a wilderness of polished stones glittering in the fading sun like giant gems the trail had led them, finally disemboguing into a high plateau. And there was a great pile, as large as a house, of logs: scented cedarwood and fragrant sandalwood and trees of myrrh and other odorous timbers of balsam and the like. Intricately carved and carpeted steps led to the summit and there was a pavilion somewhat furnished.

A clap of thunder, a blaze of light sounded and shone in Vergil's head. Fragments whirled and danced and, suddenly, like pieces of a mosaic, came together in a visible pattern. 'Man of fire! Man of Tyre!' a voice shouted as the Red Man dismounted and advanced. 'Phoenician? No, not Phoenician alone, but ...'

'*Phoenix!*' said the Red Man. His face blazed with fiery light.

Not just a Phoenician, but a Phoenix! Not, indeed, the symbolic, metaphorical bird of legend, but the actual being itself. Gone now was all semblance of fatigue; all was joyful haste, as of a man going to a long-awaited tryst. The words poured forth from him. He, too, was old – if not as old as the Cyclops – but he was mortal, and his mortality indescribably wearied him. Up and down the world and to and fro, he had been coming and going for centuries: and now his time was at hand, had been at hand for these two years past. Only the fire could liberate him from the fretting, chafing shackles of his flesh, and, by its destruction of his present body, enable him to renew his youth.

The sign of regeneration, Vergil thought. *Eagle, serpent, phoenix.*

Aloud, he said, 'If such is your need, Captain Phoenix, then it is not for me to stand in your way.'

But the other looked at him, teeth and eyes gleaming in his blazing face. 'You? You are nothing but a path on which I tread. The Phoenix has no need of wizards.'

'Then do what you must. Why you have brought me here, I do not at all know. Is it to kindle your pyre? The task likes me not, but—'

An-Thon Ebbed-Saphir laughed his brief scorn. 'I have little time to enjoy the irony of it, but I have brought you here to pull, as it were, my chestnuts from the fire. I know the Cyclops hates me. I was not certain that you would succeed in rescuing my bride from him—'

'*Your Bride?*'

The Red One nodded. 'Yes ... You spoke of my need. Little do you know of it, that you ask in such astonishment. Yes, *the Phoenix must have a bride!* And, as the Phoenix is always male, he must take his bride from among the daughters of ordinary men. Our marriage, my marriage, the marriage of the Phoenix, is not an act of venery – though in such sweatings and writhings we usually join as gladly as the rest of you. No – only the union of male and female in the fire's dissolution can result in the formation of the magical egg from which the new Phoenix will emerge. My bride!' – he turned to Laura, extending his hand – 'my bride!'

With a gasp and a quivering breath, she drew back within the shelter of Vergil's arm and cloak.

'You need not fear. The pain is brief and slight, the joy is exceeding great, and in these our wedding resembles weddings of mortality and flesh. Neither fear me nor disdain me, but come surmount with me our matrimonial pavilion on the pyre ... You still fear? Believe me that you need not! I will be patient a moment more, but I have not forever.'

Vergil said, as the setting sun cast its red reflection on the other's face, 'But why, Phoenix, out of all the world of women, have you selected *this* one woman? You see she does not wish it, nor should you wonder. But surely in all the world there must be at least one who would?'

'There is. She was. Long ago, as this girl measures time, the other pledged her troth to this mystic wedding in return for long life, for love, and for the potency to gain a throne. She gained that throne, she shared that love, she was to live as long as her Phoenix lived ... perhaps five hundred years ... perhaps more ... one can never be sure. But when the time to be translated and transformed came to her Phoenix, earlier than expected, this traitor woman shrank in terror. She refused to join me.'

Pale blue-green and cold were his eyes, but red, red his fiery face and skin. Vergil heard Cornelia's voice, so low. *My heart belongs to someone whom I dare not see.* He did not wonder. He would not have wondered if the sight of her lover alone caused her to burst into flame upon the instant.

'Oh' – the other's face twisted, his head went slant, in admiring love and almost hatred – 'she is cunning, in this one way she's strong! She was able to erect barriers against me for herself ... but only for herself. So—'

'What a man vows for himself, as all the world knows, can be fulfilled in his son; a woman, in her daughter. And thus it is now that I claim my promised bride. If it's not to be Cornelia, Queen of Carsus, then let it be her daughter, Princess Laura. *Let it be*, I say. Come, my bride. Come, my bride.'

He finished speaking, once more he extended his hand, once more Laura stepped back – this time too rapidly for Vergil to continue his protective vigil. And instantly the finger of the Phoenix moved, and two circles of fire sprang up, one around Vergil and the other around Laura. And when Vergil moved, his own circle flamed high and higher, imprisoning him.

Vergil stood there, motionless. The Phoenix beckoned. Slowly the fiery circle round Laura advanced toward its maker, and she perforce advanced with it. The sun's great orb touched its lower rim to the horizon. The air grew dark and blue and chill. The wind riffled the flames.

The Phoenix said, 'Come'

He extended his finger. He said, 'I was able to attend at the pyre of my fellow in Cyprus. None will attend me here. But that matters not. I need no epithalamium.' Vergil, staring through the leaping flames which enclosed him like pickets and palisadoes, watched as Laura, fire-encircled, advanced numbly toward the Phoenix, who held out his hand. And she took it. Together they approached the pyre.

The Phoenix turned. 'Farewell, Wizard,' he said.

But now it was Vergil's finger which moved, moved in a motion contrary to that of the Phoenix, moved widdershins. And the fire blazing hot around him flickered ... sank ... sank ... became a mere faint glowing circle on the ground. He stepped over it. Dumbly, the Phoenix stared.

'Phoenix of Phoenicia, I, too, have been in Phoenicia. Student of the secrets of fire as well as you. *But I studied them in Sidon and not in Tyre.*' A sound, half growl and half groan, came from the other's throat. Tyre, burned to rock and ashes; Sidon, still enduring.

Vergil advanced. The Phoenix turned to face him. Vergil said, 'My powers are the opposite of yours, and are not always deemed as useful. I am one of the few. Yet what think you quenched the blaze in my house in the Street of the Horse-Jewelers? Do you not know – you of all must know – that they err who say that the Salamandar starts fires? He starts no fires, *he puts the fires out!* It is this power of his which enables him to walk through the flames and the embers unharmed ... consuming, but not consumed.

'Go, Phoenix, confront your proper pledged bride in Naples, and claim her, if you can and will. But this woman here is not she, and her you must release—'

He staggered back. The night had exploded in flames in front of him. The rocks were fonts of fire. He flung out his hands. For a space about him there was an opacity, a blackness, and this spread. The fires hissed, fell back as though in pain. The rocks spat like griddle pans. A steamy vapor was seen in the air, and an unseasonal dew distilled upon the ground. Lightnings flashed and writhed, were quenched by rains. Fiery serpents large as pythons rushed upon him, met wet, black mists; the twain intertwined as if engaged in some dreadful, loveless copulation. The mists hissed, vaporized, grew thin. A cry of rage and triumph came from the Phoenix, he hurled out his fires, he blazed himself like a fire, he waved his glowing arms.

The mists thickened, became clouds, clouds and thick darkness, the air grew wet and thick and hot as a bath heated by a hypocaust. The nimbus-circled stars were obscured. The dark and steamy atmosphere was shot through with flames – white flames, blue flames, red and orange and yellow and green flames – but gradually there were less of them.

And finally there were none at all.

Vergil shivered, his flesh chill and trembling in the cold wind. Strange how the scent of the spicy wood, warmed by the fire, now came fresh and strong. Outlined against the pyre, slumped and shrunken, was the enemy.

'Phoenix,' said Vergil, 'mount.'

The Phoenix raised his head and drew in a breath and held it. He brightened, he blazed up, he glowed like a fanned ember. It was his last effort. Then, totally, suddenly, the light went out of him. Dull, dull and defeated, he seemed to hang there.

'Phoenix,' said Virgil, 'mount.'

It was painful, almost, to watch how he more crawled than walked up the carven stairs of the great pyre, how he dragged himself to one of the two furnitures there, half throne, half nuptial couch.

Round and round about the pyre Vergil drew with his wand a great circle, and blazoned it with rays. 'Now, Phoenix, hear my bane,' he directed.

'Within the circle of this sun
Shall no fire burn
Nor water run
Until my quest be won.'

The cold moon rose and the strange rocks melted into its shadows. Atop his cold pyre, the Phoenix stared, immobilized, motionless as a statue.

The camels for once, seemed less than haughty.

He dared not risk a return by the same route. There was danger that the hideous and treacherous Troglodytes might take them unawares. There were the petromorphs, stone things which came alive, reversing the process whereby living things became stone. Drink and baffled greed might well have turned the chieftain Abèn-Aboubou into a confronting instead of a stealthy enemy. And any other route to the coast he did not know and dared even less to hazard.

'We must turn south and east.' he said to Laura, having explained this to her. 'Unless perhaps you have thought of something else?'

She laughed, and wound her fingers in a long coil of hair which had come undone. 'I'm not used to being asked my thoughts,' she said. 'I shall have to bend my mind ... bear down upon it ...' She frowned her unaccustomed concentration. 'Northward lies the Middle Sea? Is that right? And westward ... ? The Western Ocean. That seems fair enough. But what lies south and east, Ser Vergil?'

He sketched a quick map for her upon the moonlit dust. South lay the mountains clove in two by the thick, black waters of the River Nigir, upon which was said to lie the great rich city of Tambuctone. Beyond river and mountains was the land of the Garamantes and Ethiopea Interior, the Equinox, the region called Agisymba, and the Terra Incognita whose extent and terminus not even legend had touched upon. A southeasterly course would traverse Proper Ethiopea, Nilus, the rivers Astapus and Astaboras, and so to the Sinus Barbaricus and the Erythrean Sea.

'South is more or less an unknown quantity, and southeast would consume an infinity of time. I think then, that we should descend sufficiently south to leave the hills, and then head east – hoping that, if we are fortunate, we may meet another caravan intending for Upper Egypt. There ...'

She apologized for yawning. 'You see I am like a servant girl of no manners, despite having been benefited by Queen Cornelia, daughter of the Doge and granddaughter of the Emperor. I was never outside the Carsus until all this began to happen. It's been all very terrible, and I'm very glad it's all happened. Shall we go to sleep now?'

Toward the end of the next day, in approaching the end of the foothills, they were fortunate in finding a spring of water welling up from a cleft in the rocks into a shallow pool. It could not have been called an oasis, for evaporation evidently prevented the moisture from ever spilling over onto the adjacent ground, and the ground around it was so rocky that only a single and small pocket of soil had survived the restless buffetings of the winds.

They drank their fill and let the camels drink and filled the leathern water bottles. Then they mixed with water the handful or so of parched ground grain, which was all their food, and ate the only faintly salted paste slowly. 'It is utterly tasteless,' she commented, licking her fingers. 'Horrible stuff ... I wish there were more.' She patted her pockets and examined their contents in her lap. There was a tiny handkerchief, a coney's foot amulet ('There's no meat on it, I'm afraid!'), some loose beads, and something brown and crumpled and smelling faintly sweet.

She smiled. 'The core of my last apple,' she said. 'The gardener at Carsus gave it to me when I left and I said that I would keep it to remember forever ... but by and by I got hungry, so I ate it. Those are only beads, they have no value,' she added, as Vergil picked them through with his finger. One seemed to catch his eye.

'Where did this come from?' he asked. It was a nacreous off-white, faintly iridescent, with tiny flecks of blue through it.

She shrugged. 'Why? I don't know ... oh, it was picked out of a river bed one dry summer. Has it a name, Ser Vergil?'

He inclined his head. The pebble seemed to weigh rather heavily in his hand. 'A river bed. One of its tributaries has evidently an origin far north of Carsus, for this seems to be that stone which the Sarmations call "Timebinder". ... There is scarcely any telling what might be done with it, if it is real ... but in our present situation we must make one certain experiment, and one only.

'May I break your bead?'

She made him a japing, low curtsy, dress spread out wide, somewhat disconcerting him. Immediately, she was all remorse, and begged his forgiveness. He murmured something, searched among the nearby rocks. He placed the blue bead upon one and, still murmuring, struck it with another. Twice more he struck, and at the third blow it severed into three parts without shattering.

'Now give me your apple core.' He took his wand and pierced the sod in the pocket of soil and dropped into the hole one single leaf of arbor vitae from the tiny packet he carried in his pouch, slightly widened the hole, dropped the apple core into it, tamped it down with the blunter end of the wand, replenished the hole with soil. Then he planted the three pieces of the timestone so as to form a triangle with the buried core in the center. Of what he did and of what happened next, she told him afterward she could never be clearly sure. She remembered, with perhaps somewhat greater clarity than one commonly remembers a dream, the sun and the stars and all four phases of the moon rising and setting and wheeling in retrograde and then back again, to and fro, but all this within what appeared to be a vast triangular embrasure in the Heavens distinct from the major portion of it. And, as she turned her astonished and bemused gaze from the Heavens to earth and back and again, she beheld a shoot break through the broken soil and become a twig. The twig grew apace into a sapling increased in girth and stature.

'Oh!' she cried, rapt, and clapped her hands. The dry and vacant air was filled with the scent of snowy apple blossoms, and then these, too, faded away like snowflakes. And presently the boughs of the noble tree sagged earthward like the breasts of a woman filled with milk, and the apples hung heavy upon the boughs.

They ate their fill of the food, which was also drink, and they let the beasts have their satiety as well. Then they filled the saddlebags and made sacks of their blankets and their cloaks, and filled them, too. And then, refreshed and supplied, they set off once more.

In Garamanteland the climate was so hot by day that water exposed to the sunlight boiled at noon, and by night so cold that the same water, if poured out into a shallow vessel, froze at midnight. The rigors of the climate were fortunately not matched by the severity of the people, who neither hinder travelers nor help them. The Garamantes are so shy and eremitical as to be willing to greet strangers only from a distance too great for voice to carry; often Vergil and Laura would see their strange, cloaked figures, arms upraised, outlined against the hill or sky. Always at their sides were their dogs, which the Garamantes love more than they love humankind; and this love is returned, for when the Numideans carried off captive the King of the Garamantes to hold for ransom, no less than two thousand of his own dogs followed his trail by scent and by stealth until they burst upon the sleeping camp to destroy the captors and release the king.

In Outer Nubia they were perplexed by what they at first took for the ghost of a woman who had died in trying to abort her child – doomed forever to seek the babe unborn, weeping and wailing, forever following, never seen, sobbing and calling out. But it did not respond to exorcism, and so Vergil realized that it was no human ghost after all, but that inhuman loathsome creature sometimes called *Jaekal* and sometimes *Hyaena*, which imitating the human

208

voice like a perroquetta, or Indian jay, it often lures men and women to come in search of it; whereupon it leaps upon them from behind and laughs as it devours them.

At last, alternately burned by heat and numbed by cold, they met up with a caravan which led them into Meroë on Nilus, a river port famous for its trade in the hides, ordure, and tushes of cocodrilli. By one of those paradoxes in which Nature seems to delight, these stinking beasts pass perfumed dung exceeding the primest musk, much sought for in confecting ointments and scents; its teeth are in demand for treating pains and affections of the bones and joints, as well as being aphrodisiacal. In Nilus Meroë they obtained places on the downriver packet boat, and allowing only for two or three stops en route, would be in Alexandria as swiftly as the current flowed.

To eyes used to the mountains, hills, valleys, isles, and coastlands of Europe, the Nilus and its banks could not but seem somewhat samely and monotonous, but to Vergil the mere greenery was grateful after the fret and glare of the desert. And to her it all had a charm for being new. The bending trees all a-gaze at their reflections, the vasty hippopotami – once, even an oliphant appeared, and gnashed its enormous teeth at them – the incredibly rich fields full of heavy heads of grain, the ornately carved entrances to the caves yielding the precious and essential balm called mummy, and perhaps above all the huge pyramidical structures which were the treasure houses of King Pharaoh ... treasures which continued to baffle the searching zeal of those who would find them.

He thought that she was entirely absorbed in these sights, and it was with surprise that he was roused from his own musings by her question, 'Ser Vergil, why did you come to look for me?'

Some foolish compliments hesitated at his mouth. And yet, fatuous as it might have been for him to have said, Your red hair with its glints of brown, your brown eyes with their glints of red, your white skin with its tracery of blue veins, your delicately formed and coral-colored lips, the gracious arching of your brows and the sweet rise of your bosom – all, all seized hold of my eyes and heart, and beguiled me from the bitter reek of my elaboratory and the musty but beloved scent of my books. ... Was it not the truth?

He stammered a bit, then told her instead that he desired to follow the matter of the mirror to its conclusion.

'And not leave it unfinished,' she summed up.

'Yes ... and not leave it unfinished.'

She nodded, seemed to follow this well, be satisfied; then she grimaced. ('What ... ?' he began.) 'The Queen,' she said. ('Oh,' he said. 'Yes. The Queen ... Don't worry.') She looked at him and raised one brow. Then she smiled faintly. 'I won't, then,' she said.

FOURTEEN

He had made no point either of informing Cornelia that he was going to Libya or of keeping the information from her. He rather thought that she would have learned, though, but as he and the Red Man had taken their usual precautions against departing together, he rather thought that she would not have learned of that. Tullio he met in the villa's hall of entrance as Vergil swept in, the girl behind him. The seneschal's eyes and mouth opened wide at the sight, but a gesture and a glance from the Magus sufficed to close them. A further gesture and a further glance, and Tullio meekly led the way.

Cornelia was occupying herself with small rectangles of ivory, parchment-thin, on which curious designs and pictures were limned in color, evidently by a skilled miniaturist. Her face had a familiar look of faraway thought. She had laid a number of them out in several even rows, and the rest were in her hand. 'Rota,' she murmured. '*Rato. Arot. Otar. Ator. Taro*—' She looked up and saw him and the pack leaped from her hand and scattered and fell.

'*Magus* ...' she whispered. A girl sat on a low stool next to the table, the same servant maid he had seen when he first saw Cornelia, the day of the manticores. For a moment, as Cornelia saw him, as she saw the girl who now entered behind him, it seemed that she – the seated one – would exclaim a word or two. But, quick as he observed this, much as he had startled and shaken Cornelia, Cornelia was quicker; quick to recover self-possession sufficient to place her hand on the shoulder of the seated girl ... whose face set in composure ... but whose eyes fell.

Now Cornelia arose and faced Vergil and his companion. One brief moment her eyes, filled with joy and triumph and malice and passion and awe, met his. Then she embraced the girl he had brought and, closing her eyes, rocked to and fro. Then she released her. The girl had yielded to the embrace, returned it passively.

'I won't ask now what has happened, or where you have been. I am too full of emotion. Besides, it is of no importance compared to your return. What a welcome we shall prepare for you, daughter! But – now – oh, let us be alone together!'

She put her arm around the girl and started to lead her away. The other girl had already turned her back and now made as though to precede them.

'Madam—'

'Only a few moments together, Magus. You can understand, and then—'

'Madam—'

She sighed, and turned around. 'I can refuse you nothing,' she said.

'It is of my reward, indeed, madam, that I wished to speak.'

He felt he had no reason to doubt her sincerity when she said, 'It may be anything you ask, any price you choose to set. Money, jewels, in any amount. This villa, if you like, or my dowerlands in Carsus – even the estates which are my patrimony from my great-grandfather the August Caesar – anything ... anything at all ...'

He bowed his head. Then: 'These are noble offers, madam, but my heart desires none of them. May I tell you what it *does* want?' Cornelia nodded. Vergil said, 'Nothing but the gift of that servant maid.' He held out his hand toward her.

Cornelia's face went pale. Then it blazed ruddy. She lifted her hand as though to strike. Then she regained

212

control of herself. 'I ask your pardon,' she said, with an effort. 'You have done me ... done us ... a service which is almost beyond price. But, I must repeat, only *almost*. The ... servant girl ... her name is Phyllis ... has been with us since she was born. She is like one of our family. In fact ... I need not lie to you, you have eyes to see that she is of our very blood. It would be impossible to dispose of her as if she were a common servant, or slave.'

'I understand and I respect your reasons. Then I urge you to send for the lictors without delay and let the Phrygian cap be placed on Phyllis' head, and when she is freed, my word upon it, I shall marry her. Am I unworthy to wed a freed woman?'

Cornelia was now fully composed. 'Far from it, Magus,' she said. 'It would be a condescension on your part. Child,' she asked, 'do you wish to accept the honor which Dr Vergil offers you?'

The girl said, in a low voice, 'No ... I do not wish it.'

Cornelia shrugged slightly and spread her hands a bit. 'You see. There is too much devotion. What would you do? Surely not to force her.'

His head sank upon his chest. Then, after a moment, he said, 'As I cannot look down, then I must look up. Lady' – he addressed the girl beside him – 'would you, despite the differences in our stations, would *you* be averse to considering me as a suitor?'

The Queen raised her eyebrows at this, but no more, and looked at the other girl as if awaiting an answer which could only be a negative one. And when the other girl said, 'I? Oh! No ...' The Queen began to nod her approval, only to stare in incredulity as the girl went on to say, 'No, I would not ... be averse to considering it.'

Having had (it seemed so long ago) example of, and experiences with, Cornelia's moods, he was aware that her emotions had barely begun to stir when she said, swiftly and confusedly, 'You forget yourself, Wizard. Forgive me, there may be daughters of royal and Imperial lineage who would be permitted to wed you – though I doubt it – but mine is not one of them. Nor, if I could permit, never would my son, her brother the King of Carsus, permit it. Other arrangements are being made.' Once again she mastered her emotions, smoothly turned the apparent rebuff into something softer. 'Arrangements involving – I cannot say more – someone of very high station. So my daughter's guardian could hardly permit it to be said that we have broken our word. Great as your powers are, they are not great enough to persuade or force us into a breach of promise. You understand.'

Had she not by now smelt the fox? Suspected what this was all about? Very probably. For the moment, though, he was sure, she would go on playing the game, if only to see where it led. Indeed, she had little choice. Her eyes, now showing no confusion, glittered watchfully as he nodded, plucked at his lip, uttered the light exclamation which indicated an idea. '"My powers," yes, madam. There we have, I think the answer.' Before Cornelia could interrupt or interfere, he reached out, pulled one girl toward him and pushed the other away from him. Then he raised his arms and began a counter-enchantation. It was not a long one.

'Henceforth,' he said, concluding the spell, 'she who was known as Laura shall be known as Phyllis. She who was heretofore called Phyllis shall be called Laura. I adjure you to speak nothing but the truth. *You*' – he pointed to the 'servent maid' – 'who are you?'

'Laura,' she said, confused and a bit frightened.

'So. Laura. Not Phyllis. Then if you are Laura, *she* must be Phyllis. So. Hmm. Curious, is it not, madam, that all the while you and I and all of us were so engaged in fashioning a major speculum to locate Laura, Laura was *here*? It is *most* curious. Indeed, I know not how to account for it at all … unless someone – I know not who for sure

214

– had persuaded the true Laura to play a perjured part and had caused the true Phyllis to be so bewitched as to deceive both herself and others or had perhaps bewitched both.'

Cornelia stood as still and silent as one of the ancestral statues around about the room. Indeed, no one moved as Vergil spoke on. 'Suppose this to be true,' he said. 'In that case we must construct a hypothesis to account for it ... and in order to do this it will be necessary to look back over the past. Forgive me – madam – and maidens – if I seem to look too closely for complete comfort.' Silent and still she watched him – watched past him.

Cornelia was the daughter of Amadeo, the late Doge of Naples, He'd had no sons, to his sorrow, on either side of the blanket. But it was known that he'd had another daughter, by a woman of the servants' quarters, and she – Cornelia's half sister – had gone off with the legitimate daughter in the entourage to Carsus. Where she had, inevitably, unfortunately attracted the attentions of that comely, weak, and amorous man, King Vindelician. To whom, nine months later, she bore a daughter of her own, named Phyllis.

Cornelia did not move.

The child Phyllis was therefore half sister to the child Laura, daughter of the same father; more, she was the daughter of Laura's mother's half sister, granddaughter of the same grandfathers, double cousins. It was no wonder that the girls so closely resembled one another, and more and more closely as they grew older. It was no wonder that, although Phyllis was supposed to be Laura's servant, they had grown up as close friends, traded clothes and jewels ... though of course Laura had so much more of each ... perhaps this was why that one copper fibula in the form of a brooch came to be traded back and forth between the two on alternate days, like a game.

Neither child knew anything of any secret compact made before their own births. It was said that such had been made between a woman and a phoenix – in part for love; in part for passion; and in part in return for the promise of a throne. This compact was for long a source of hope and strength and joy – and then the note fell due before it was expected to, and it had to be paid. Or – did it?

'Suppose the woman who was the promised bride of the Phoenix was a woman of extraordinary powers. She would thus be able to set up wards and guards ... but even so, always, always, there was the fear and terror that they might slip down. More, this woman would be in constant agony for her daughter, lest the Phoenix claim the child in place of the parent. Do you see?

'What should she do? What *could* she do? Let us hypothesize, assuming that this woman be you, madam. What could she do? Why, she could have her daughter, Laura, come with her from Carsus, disguised as Phyllis, the servant, leaving Phyllis, enchanted into believing that *she* was Laura, to come along later. This might be done in hopes of the Phoenix' doing what he did in fact do – have the wrong girl kidnapped. In this way both the loved-hated lover and the hated-loved servant would be gotten rid of together on that far-off pyre, where no mystic union would occur at all, perhaps, but only a painful death by fire. There was no way of knowing that the Troglodytes would waylay the Phoenix' hired kidnappers or that Old Cyclops would rescue Phyllis or that the Phoenix would fear to face him and take her.

'But when the Phoenix, guised as a mere Phoenician, appeared in Naples, it was obvious that something had gone wrong. He came, he went, the uncertainty must have been agonizing. If my hypothesis be correct, madam, then your anxiety, your intense desire to fashion the major speculum, was not for fear that the false Laura had come to harm, but that she had *not* ... That is my hypothesis.'

Cornelia said only, 'It is false.'

Vergil shook his head. 'I fear me, it is true. I myself first observed the true Laura my first day here at the villa, posing as a servant. It was the fact that she was holding unfinished embroidery copying the design on your ring which caught in my mind. The design, as I later observed, was mate to the Red Man's ring – a phoenix sejant upon a pyre. And on a subsequent visit here Clemens had seen her too, and recognized her from the miniature in Doge Tauro's possession.'

For a moment her head drooped, face went gaunt and utterly without hope. Then her head went up once more, and now hope was in her face. 'And if I do admit it,' she asked, 'will you protect me?'

He felt in the muscles of neck and shoulders the weight of heavy burdens, 'You have admitted it,' he said. 'And I have protected you.'

Even now her eagerness and relief were mixed with fear. 'But will you continue to protect me?' she demanded. 'It's not my life alone I fear to lose, for what is the pleasure of this life here compared to that of life hereafter in the Islands of the Blest? I would do anything for him, anything but lose myself inside himself, anything but vanish behind his own overpowering person. For that – don't you see? – that is the real source, I didn't know it before but now I do, that is the real source of the Phoenix's immortality and strength: he assumes his woman, he consumes his woman, he becomes *He* plus *She*, but the *She* vanishes utterly as soul and person, and only the *He*-soul and -person is reborn. The *She* has given ... and then she is quite gone.'

'I know.'

Fear diminished but did not vanish. If he knew this, then he knew what it was she feared, what the deadly danger really was. And she repeated, 'Will you protect me? Will you? Forever? Forever?' Her eyes sought his. A look came over her face, which became tender and almost haunting in its affection. 'You will, then. I know.' Her voice sank, she gestured him near. 'And I know why, And I know what reward you really want. You shall have it. Forever.'

She reached for his hand. 'Come, then,' she said.

But the hand he took was not hers. 'I have gone with you once, my Lady,' he said. 'And we both know to what result.'

Affection was replaced by stupefaction. 'But then ... unless ... I could never be sure ... how could I believe ... You prefer her to me? To *me*? Protect me? *You?*'

Her face became like that of another person, twisted into a horrible mask; her hands like talons clawed the air. She cursed. She cursed in the formal, liturgical imprecations of Latin, Etruscan, and Greek. She shrieked things which (by Laura's wincing) could only be maledeictions in the tongue of Carsus. And then, like a veteran fishwife, she flung at him the foulest phrases in the Neapolitan dialect, cursing him with her words, her spittle, her very gestures: her finger made horns, she showed him the fig – the girl, she screamed, was a bastard and a bastard's child-ill-hap and nothing else were the two of them to Cornelia and to Cornelia's mother – mirror images, the one of the other.

'Why did I spare her life? I should have drowned her like a mongrel pup at birth! I saved her for this – for this – only for this! Why should she live and I die? I was promised at least five hundred years of life. Should I not even live out my normal span, and this whore's daughter survive me? *No! No! No!*'

Her rage grew more and more uncontrollable and un-thinking, surpassing anything that Vergil had ever seen. 'But I will destroy her yet!' she shrieked, foam forming on the corners of her lips, her hair torn by furious hands from its careful folds and now seeming to writhe like a gorgon's, the ointments and paints so carefully applied to her face running and smearing from the tears and sweats

218

of rage, her voice thin and high and trembling. All was ugliness and desperation. 'I will destroy her yet! And you! And you! Wizard! Conjurer! Necromant! Mountebank! Bawd and punk and pimp! I will destroy you, too!'

Vile, vile, violent and vivid were the threats which now poured from her pale and cracked lips, she paused to draw a shuddering breath. He said, 'My quest is won. At every level, you have disdained me … despised me … repulsed me … I leave you now forever. Phyllis, come.' He turned and, holding the shaking girl by the arm, strode quickly away.

He had not stepped a score of steps when a fearful scream behind spun him around. Cornelia stood where he had left her, but now the Red Man stood beside her, and then the Red Man wrapped his arms around her, and next the flames enwrapped them both. So unthinking was her rage that she had let slip all her watches, wards, and barriers; so that with this, and Vergil's equally unwitting removal of the ban pronounced before the Libyan pyre, the Phoenix, from across the leagues and leagues of land and sea, had claimed his bride at last.

It had been useless for Vergil to try to counter those furious flames. He might as well have attempted to quench Vesuvio, or to prevent the blaze which follows the conjunction of the terebolim, those male and female fire-stones. Yet, strange, it seemed the Phoenix had been right: likely that single scream was one of fear alone, for Cornelia had seemed to feel no pain; indeed, while the fire endured and made its great, deep sighing sound, her face grew calm, her body relaxed almost contentedly into her lover's fiery embrace, her eyes closed upon the world: wrapped and rapt in flames, the both, she all submission, he all triumph. For a while their individual lineaments could be traced within the ashes, then these fused in a way which no merely human eye could fathom, then – very quickly – something lay there which for lack of better or more descriptive word might have been thought of as a great and glowing egg; this cracked in fiery heaps and something stirred and writhed as might a worm ...

Then the heap of ashes fell in upon itself.

Those who remained still stood there, aghast, eyes dazzled and benumbed. A sudden breeze dispelled the last of the heat and stirred the heap of ashes. Vergil's voice said something which was not a word. A stripling stood among the ashes before him, and even as they looked, struck with awe, he brushed the ashes from his red and naked skin and took a fumbling step ... then two ... then walked with utter certainty and absolute indifference to-ward those who gazed and stared amazed at him. It might (was Vergil's thought) have been An-Thon in the first days of his youngest manhood ... but ... somehow ... not quite. One slight and almost involuntary movement of his head did the new Phoenix make as he passed Vergil and Phyllis. Something nashed at them out of the corner of his pale blue-green eyes which was almost Cornelia – and then was quite gone.

As was he.

The screaming servants had fled, to spread who knows what story abroad. Laura lay upon the couch, her face buried in her arms. Vergil trembled, sighed, and shook his head and Phyllis leaned against him.

But Tullio half-knelt, half-lay upon the floor and sobbed and wept.

Finally he said, broken-voiced, as though to himself. 'We wanted a kingdom and we wanted an empire. It wasn't worth it. It wasn't worth it ...'

(Later, to Clemens, Vergil said, 'What she really wanted was immortality.' 'Vain quest ... for her,' Clemens answered. 'Only alchemy can hope to provide it. You know that.' 'I don't know that I do ... What was it which

220

first brought me to her? It wasn't jewels that I was seeking among the manticores that day. The child they stole – everyone knows the story – and kept a captive for so long – it was a hundred years ago, but he is still alive and looks much less than half his years ... She had great gifts, Cornelia. We might have done things together. It is too bad, too bad....')

Yes, they might have, helped one another, Vergil and the Lady Cornelia, if things had been far different. They might have loved each other well, instead of ill. But, and meanwhile, there were other things to see to. For example, Laura.

And Laura, free now forever from her scheming, dominating mother, what did she want for herself? Neither the bull-like Doge nor the chronically philandering Emperor. She wanted, first of all, her home in hill-girt, craggy Carsus, confident that there, among her brother's lairds, she'd find a husband to her taste.

'It's so flat and bland here,' she summed it up. 'Won't you be glad to get back, Phyllis? It will be quite different now. Brother can have you legitimized – I'll *make* him! – and we can fix up the old summer palace and live there together. I'm sorry about all this, but it wasn't my fault. I didn't know about all this wicked magic and all that. Besides, well *you* know *mother*. What could *I do?* But now we can have all kinds of fun and change clothes as we used to and pretend ... well, maybe not. But, anyway, Phyllis ...'

There was no doubt that Phyllis made her royal sister-cousin seem rather flat and bland herself. Vergil ganced at her while Laura chatted on, and he knew as he read the glance with which she answered his that Phyllis was not going. Not to Carsus, anyway.

Scorpio, sign of regeneration ... of eagle, serpent, phoenix ... serpent which casts off its skin as the ore casts off its dross, serpent at the point of death, dull, dazed, struggling; serpent, finally, alive and quick; renewed ... Fire consuming phoenix ... out of the fire, the phoenix ... must be destroyed in order for it to be created ... burned in the fire which utterly annuls all manner of form and life, in order for it to be given new form and new life ... my lady's for the fire ...

The Fair White Matron had at last wedded the Ruddy Man.

In Vergil's mind he could see a certain rustic farm he knew well of old; the beehives, the hound-eared sheep, the furrows yielding to the plowman's pressing tools; in the oak and beechy woods beyond, the tusky boar besought by hunters. Too, he could see a certain village in the Calabrian hills, known to him in later times, the spare lean houses perching like eagles upon their crag, the rushing streams – incredibly cool, wonderously clear – the quiet pools where lurked the cautious fish, the sweet-smelling woods and flowery glades. How much he should love to visit either place, sink gratefully into the quiet, and float there forever ... or at least until his weariness was all laved and washed away. To be sure, all the great questions remained unanswered, their problems unresolved, though that of the Phoenix and the Mirror had been. He had, so to speak, been forced to look into the sun; though the image of a great, dark disc no longer hung over and obscured his vision, had this vision been made quite, quite clear? His complete psyche had been restored to him, but in what way was he any more than he had been before?

A slight breath, a slight movement lifted him from revery. She stood by his side, slightly smiling at him.

Phyllis was more.

His soul had been captured again, it seemed. But this time without pain. Clemens might growl and grumble at the presence of a young woman in the strange, high house on the Street of the Horse-Jewelers. But the gift of the two old books of Eastern music he had always coveted would quiet even Clemens' grumbles.

Milford, Pennsylvania
Amecameca, Mexico
Belize, British Honduras

Avram Davidson was born in New York in 1923 and was active in SF fandom from his teens. He is remembered as a writer of fantasy fiction, science fiction and crime fiction, as well as many stories that defy easy categorisation. Among his SF and Fantasy awards are two Hugos, two World Fantasy Awards and a World Fantasy Life Achievement award; he also won a Queen's Award and an Edgar Award in the mystery genre. Although best known for his writing, Davidson also edited *The Magazine of Fantasy and Science Fiction* from 1962 to 1964. He died in 1993.

A full list of Fantasy Masterworks can be found at
www.gollancz.co.uk